W9-BQX-840

Dear Reader,

Christmas is a time for love, and so it is with great
pleasure that we present to you three brand-new
romances set within the wonder of the season!

Sherryl Woods will delight you with "The Perfect
Holiday," a tale of a matchmaking aunt who brings
together two wounded hearts, just in time for the
season. The question is, will Aunt Mae succeed in
getting Savannah Holiday and Trace Franklin to
say "I do" to love?

For the brooding bodyguard in Beverly Barton's
"Faith, Hope and Love," Christmas is just another day
of the year. Until he finds himself face-to-face with
the woman who stole his heart during one forbidden
night of passion. Now Worth Cordell is about to get
another gift—when he learns this sweet beauty is
also the mother of his child!

Leanne Banks will tickle your funny bone and warm
your heart with this tale of the pretty schoolteacher
who finds herself sharing her home with a grumpy
cowboy for the holiday. You'll love watching as
Amy Winslow gets sexy scrooge Lucas Bennett to
open up his heart to the holiday—and to love—in
"A Rancher in Her Stocking."

We hope you enjoy this special collection. Happy
holidays to you and yours!

The Editors
Silhouette Books

SHERRYL WOODS

"Sherryl Woods...writes with a very special warmth, wit, charm and intelligence."
—*New York Times* bestselling author Heather Graham

Whether she's living in Florida or Virginia, Sherryl Woods always makes her home by the sea. A walk on the beach, the sound of waves and the smell of the salt air all provide inspiration for this author of over seventy-five romance and mystery novels. You can write to Sherryl January through March at P.O. Box 490326, Key Biscayne, FL 33149 or check out her Web site at www.sherrylwoods.com. From April through December, stop by and meet her at her bookstore: Potomac Sunrise, 114 Washington Avenue, Colonial Beach, VA 22443.

BEVERLY BARTON

"Beverly Barton writes with searing emotional intensity that tugs on every heart string."
—*New York Times* bestselling author Linda Howard

An avid reader since childhood, Beverly Barton wrote her first book at the age of nine. After marriage to her own "hero" and the births of her daughter and son, Beverly chose to be a full-time homemaker, aka wife, mother, friend and volunteer. The author of over thirty-five books, Beverly is a member of Romance Writers of America and helped found the Heart of Dixie chapter in Alabama. She has won numerous awards and has made the Waldenbooks and *USA TODAY* bestseller lists.

LEANNE BANKS

"When life gets tough, read a book by Leanne Banks."
—*New York Times* bestselling author Janet Evanovich

Leanne Banks, a bestselling author of romance, lives in her native Virginia with her husband, son and daughter. Recognized with two Career Achievement Awards from *Romantic Times,* Leanne likes creating a story with a few grins, a generous kick of sensuality and characters that hang around after the book is finished. Contact Leanne online at leannebbb@aol.com or write to her at P.O. Box 1442, Midlothian, VA 23113. A SASE for a reply would be greatly appreciated.

Sherryl Woods
Beverly Barton
Leanne Banks

So This Is
Christmas

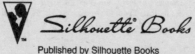

Silhouette Books

Published by Silhouette Books

America's Publisher of Contemporary Romance

SILHOUETTE BOOKS

ISBN 0-373-48479-8

SO THIS IS CHRISTMAS

Copyright © 2002 by Harlequin Books S.A.

The publisher acknowledges the copyright holders
of the individual works as follows:

THE PERFECT HOLIDAY
Copyright © 2002 by Sherryl Woods

FAITH, HOPE AND LOVE
Copyright © 2002 by Beverly Beaver

A RANCHER IN HER STOCKING
Copyright © 2002 by Leanne Banks

This edition published by arrangement with Harlequin Books S.A.

® and TM are trademarks of Harlequin Books S.A., used under
license. Trademarks indicated with ® are registered in the United States
Patent and Trademark Office, the Canadian Trade Marks Office and in
other countries.

Visit Silhouette at www.eHarlequin.com

Printed in U.S.A.

CONTENTS

THE PERFECT HOLIDAY   9
Sherryl Woods

FAITH, HOPE AND LOVE   149
Beverly Barton

A RANCHER IN HER STOCKING   279
Leanne Banks

THE PERFECT HOLIDAY
Sherryl Woods

Dear Friends,

The holiday season has always seemed to me to be a time for gathering those we love close to share old memories and create new ones. I've always found it especially sad when families are separated or when holiday memories hold only disappointment.

In "The Perfect Holiday," I've written about two people who've been disillusioned by most of the people in their lives. Yet both hold fond memories of one incredible woman who touched them in the past and whose death brings them back together. In the special atmosphere of Holiday Retreat, they're able to open their hearts to the possibility of love.

This story of hope and renewal is my holiday gift to you. May the joy of the season touch your life now and forever.

Sheryl Woods

Chapter 1

"**M**om, it's snowing," Hannah shouted from the living room.

Savannah heard the pounding of her daughter's footsteps on the wood floors, then the eight-year-old skidded to a stop in front of her, eyes shining.

"Can I go outside? *Please?*" Hannah begged. "This is so cool. I've never seen snow before."

"I know," Savannah told her, amused despite herself. "We don't get a lot of snow in Florida."

"Wait till my friends back home hear we're going to have a white Christmas. It is *so* awesome. I am *sooo* glad we moved to Vermont."

Though she could understand her daughter's excited reaction to her first snowfall, from Savannah's perspective the snow was anything but a blessing. Since her arrival a couple of days ago, she'd discov-

ered that the furnace at Holiday Retreat wasn't reli-
able. The wind had a nasty way of sneaking in
through all sorts of unexpected cracks in the insula-
tion, and the roof—well, the best she could say about
that was that it hadn't fallen in on their heads…yet.
With the weight of a foot of damp snow on it, who
knew what could happen?

It had been three weeks since the call had come
from the attorney informing her that she was a ben-
eficiary of her aunt Mae's estate. The bittersweet
news had come the day before Thanksgiving, and for
the first time since her divorce the year before, Savannah had thought she finally had something for
which to be thankful besides her feisty, incredible
daughter. Now that she'd seen the inn, she was beginning to wonder if this wasn't just another of Fate's
cruel jokes.

Holiday Retreat had been in the family for generations. Built in the early 1800s as a home for a
wealthy ancestor, the huge, gracious house in the
heart of Vermont ski country had become an inn
when the family had fallen on hard times. Savannah
could still remember coming here as a child and
thinking it was like a Christmas fantasy, with the
lights on the eaves and in the branches of the evergreens outside, a fire blazing in the living room and
the aroma of banana-nut bread and cookies drifting
from the kitchen. The tree, which they cut down
themselves and decorated on Christmas Eve, always
scraped the twelve-foot ceiling.

Aunt Mae—Savannah's great-aunt actually—had

been in her prime then. A hearty fifty-something, she came from sturdy New England stock. She had bustled through the house making everyone in the family feel welcome, fixing elaborate meals effortlessly and singing carols boisterously, if a bit tunelessly. It was the one time of the year when there were no paying guests at the inn—just aunts and uncles and cousins all gathered for holiday festivities. To an only child like Savannah, the atmosphere had seemed magical.

If the house had been in a state of disrepair then and if the furniture had been shabby, she hadn't noticed it. Now it promised to be one of the world's worst money pits.

"Mom, did you hear me?" Hannah said again. "I said it's snowing."

"I heard," Savannah said glumly.

Hannah's blue eyes were alight with excitement. "Isn't it great?"

Savannah tried to work up some enthusiasm to match her daughter's, but all she could think about was the probability that too much snow would make the sagging roof plummet down on top of their heads as they slept. Still, she forced a smile.

"There's nothing like a white Christmas," she agreed.

"Can we get a tree and make hot chocolate and sing carols like you used to do when you were a kid?" Hannah pleaded. "Then it won't matter if we don't have any presents."

Savannah cringed at the realistic assessment of their financial plight. The divorce had left her with

next to nothing. Her ex-husband hadn't yet been persuaded to send even the paltry child support payments
required by the court. As for alimony, she had a
hunch hell would freeze over before she saw a penny
of that. Since their divorce had hinged on her objections to his workaholic tendencies, Rob clearly saw
no reason she should benefit from the income derived
from those tendencies.

Last night, after Hannah had gone to bed, Savannah
had sat for hours with her checkbook, a pile of final
bills from Florida, and a list of the repairs needed
before the inn could be opened to paying guests in
the new year. Her conclusion had left her feeling
more despondent than ever. It was going to take more
than a glistening snowfall and a few carols to brighten
her spirits.

No matter how hard she tried telling herself that
they were better off than they had been, she still
wasn't totally convinced. Maybe if they'd stayed in
Florida, she would have found a better-paying job,
something that wouldn't have left them scraping by
after making house payments and buying groceries.
At least they wouldn't have had to worry about the
kind of exorbitant heating bill from last winter that
she'd found in a kitchen drawer here. Maybe selling
the heavily mortgaged house that had been her home
with Rob had been another error in judgment. It had
given her barely enough cash to make the trip and to
make a start on the repairs the inn needed.

"Mom, what's wrong?" Hannah asked. "Are you
afraid we made a mistake?"

Seeing the concern that filled her daughter's eyes and the worried crease in her forehead, Savannah shook off her fears. Hannah deserved better than the hand she'd been dealt up to now. For the first time since the divorce, she was acting like a kid again. Savannah refused to let her own worries steal that from her daughter.

"Absolutely not!" she said emphatically. "I think coming here was exactly the right thing to do. We're going to make it work. How many people get to live in a place that looks like a picture on a Christmas card?"

She gave her daughter a fierce hug. "How about some hot chocolate?"

"Then can we go out in the snow?" Hannah pleaded.

"Tell you what—why don't you bundle up in your new winter jacket and go outside for a few minutes so you can see what it feels like? I'll call you when the hot chocolate's ready."

Hannah shook her head. "No, Mom, I want you to come, too. Please."

Savannah thought of all she had to do, then dismissed it. It was only a few days till Christmas. Most of the contractors she'd spoken to said they couldn't come by till after the first of the year. Until she and Hannah made a trip into the small town at the foot of the mountain, she couldn't strip the old wallpaper or paint. Why not think of this as an unexpected gift of time?

"Okay, kiddo, let's do it," she said, grabbing her

coat off a hook by the door. "Only for a few minutes, though. We're going to need some heavy boots, wool scarves and thick gloves before we spend much time outside. We don't want to start the new year with frostbite."

"Whatever," Hannah said, tugging her out the door, seemingly oblivious to the blast of icy air that greeted them and froze their breath.

There was an inch of damp, heavy snow on the ground and clinging to the towering evergreens already, and it was still falling steadily. With no chains or snow tires on the car, they'd be lucky if they got out of the driveway for a couple of days, Savannah concluded, sinking back into gloominess.

Then she caught the awed expression on Hannah's face as she tilted her head up and caught snowflakes on her tongue. She remembered doing the exact same thing the first time she'd visited Aunt Mae and seen snow. She'd been even younger than Hannah, and for several years the Christmas trips to Vermont had been the highlight of her life. She couldn't recall why they'd stopped coming as a family.

She'd come on her own several times after she was grown, but those visits had dwindled off when she'd met, then married, Rob. He was a Florida boy through and through and flatly refused to visit anyplace where the temperature dropped below the midfifties.

Now that Aunt Mae was gone, Savannah deeply regretted not having done more than write an occasional letter enclosing pictures of Hannah. Her aunt had never once judged her, though, and she'd been totally supportive when Savannah had told her about the breakup of her marriage. She'd sent one check explained away as a birthday gift and offered more, but Savannah had turned her down. She'd lied and said they were getting along okay, but she knew now that her aunt had seen through her. She had done in death what Savannah hadn't permitted her to do while she was living.

If other members of her family resented the gesture, Savannah didn't know about it. She'd lost touch with most of them years ago. She'd been estranged from her parents ever since she'd divorced a man of whom they enthusiastically approved. Aunt Mae had tried to broker a peace agreement between Savannah and her father, but he'd remained stubbornly silent and unyielding. He'd been convinced Savannah was a fool for divorcing a man who brought home a steady paycheck.

"Mom, I love it here!" Hannah announced, throwing her arms around Savannah. She was shivering even in her heavy coat. "I want to build a snowman. Can we?"

"I think we'll need a little more snow than this," Savannah told her. "Besides, I'm freezing. How about that hot chocolate?"

"I want to stay out here. I'm not cold," Hannah insisted.

"Then why are your teeth chattering?" Savannah teased. "Come on, baby. Even if you won't admit to freezing, I will. There will be more snow once we've warmed up. I'll teach you how to make snow angels."

"What are snow angels?" Hannah asked, her interest immediately piqued.

"You'll see. Aunt Mae taught me when I was a little girl. Now come inside and get warm."

Far more agreeable lately than she had been for months, Hannah finally acquiesced, following Savannah into the kitchen. Savannah studied her daughter's sparkling eyes, pink cheeks and tousled hair and knew she'd done the right thing, no matter what struggles might lay ahead.

Despite the sad state of the inn, they were going to have the fresh beginning they both deserved, she decided with a surge of determination. And it was going to start with the very best Christmas Hannah had ever had, even if she was going to have to do it on a shoestring. Some of her very best holiday memories had cost nothing.

As for the practicalities—the repairs, the marketing plan she needed to devise—they would just have to wait for the new year.

Mae Holiday had been one of the most eccentric people Trace Franklin had ever known. He had met her when he'd been dragged to Vermont for an idyllic summer getaway by one of the women he'd dated. That had been eight or nine years ago. Twice that number of women had passed through his life since then. Of them all, the one he hadn't dated—Mae— had been the most memorable.

She'd been the grandmother he'd never had, the mentor who tried her best to bring some balance into his life. Until the day she'd died at seventy-eight, it had frustrated her no end that she hadn't managed to convince him that romance was just as important as money.

Trace knew better. His parents had been madly in love, but it hadn't brought either one of them a blasted thing except heartache. Love had kept his mother with a man who never had two nickels to rub together, a man whose big killing was always "just around the corner."

While John Franklin had spun his dreams, his wife had cleaned houses, worked in fast-food chains and, finally, when it was almost too late to matter, gotten a steady job selling toys to families that could afford to give their kids elaborate backyard swing sets and fancy computer games.

When Trace was fifteen, his mom had brought one of those games home to him, but by then he'd been way past playing childish games. He'd been working with single-minded focus on graduating from high school with honors and getting a scholarship to the best college in the state. He didn't want to play with toys. He wanted to own a whole blasted toy company.

And now he did. The irony, which Mae had seen right away, was that he still didn't have time to play. He wasn't even sure he knew how.

He was driving along the snow-covered roads of Vermont right now, because of Mae. On his last visit to see her at the end of October, she had made a final request. She had known she was dying, had known it for fully a year before the cancer had finally taken her, but she hadn't said a word to Trace until that last visit when she had detailed her losing battle, reciting the facts with a stoicism and acceptance that had awed him.

"I want you to promise me something," she had said as they'd sat in front of the fire on his last night there. Despite the heat of the blaze, she'd been wrapped in blankets, and still she had shivered.

"Anything," Trace had responded, and meant it. Not only was Mae one of the earliest investors and biggest stockholders in Franklin Toys, she was his friend.

"I want you to spend Christmas here at Holiday Retreat."

It was only a couple of months away and it would require some juggling of his schedule, but there was no question that he would do it. "Of course, I will," he said at once. "We'll have a wonderful time."

She had squeezed his hand. "I won't be here, Trace. You know that."

Even now, the memory of that moment brought the sharp sting of tears to his eyes. Her gaze had been unrelenting. From the beginning of her illness, she had refused to sugarcoat the truth to herself. Now that she was revealing it to others, she expected them to face it, as well. The cancer had spread too far and too fast before the doctors had had the first inkling there was anything wrong. She was dying and there was going to be no reprieve.

Trace had returned her unflinching gaze, heartbroken yet unable to face her death with less bravery than she was showing. ''Why, Mae? Why would you want me here after you're gone?''

''Just do it for me,'' she whispered, her voice fading. ''Promise.''

''I promise,'' he'd said just as her eyes drifted close. He'd been willing to do anything that would give her comfort. He owed her that much, and more.

Two weeks later Mae Holiday had died peacefully, a lifelong friend—a man she had loved deeply but never married—by her side. Now Trace was on his way to Vermont to pay his respects…and to keep his promise.

Chapter 2

There was smoke curling from the chimney at Holiday Retreat. Lights were blazing from the downstairs windows. Trace sat in his car and stared, trying to make sense of it. He'd expected to spend the Christmas holiday alone here, mourning Mae in private, reliving the happy times they'd spent together over the years they'd known each other.

And, he conceded with a rueful grimace, catching up on the mounds of paperwork he'd brought with him, along with his cell phone, laptop computer and fax machine.

What the dickens was going on? he wondered, thoroughly disgruntled by this turn of events. Mae had said nothing about anyone else being here. Nor had the attorney in the note that had accompanied a key to the inn. The note had merely advised that Mae had seen to having plenty of food and firewood on hand and that she hoped his visit would be a memorable one. If he had any problems, he was to contact Nate Daniels, the man Trace had heard of, but never met, the man who was the shadowy love of Mae's life.

Trace fingered the old-fashioned key in his pocket as he walked through the foot or so of recently accumulated snow. He was halfway to the door when he spotted indentations, a hectic swirl of footsteps and something else. He looked more closely and saw...not one but two snow angels, the sort made by flopping down in new-fallen snow and moving outstretched arms to create wings.

At first the sight brought a smile, reminding him of innocent, long-ago days as a kid before the unpredictability of the family's day-to-day existence had registered with him. Winters back home had been relatively mild, so that rare snowfalls had been regarded with sheer delight. He hadn't owned a sled, but he'd had his share of snowball fights and made more than a few snow angels.

Then the full implication of the snow angels sank in, and pleasant memories gave way to edginess. Judging from the smaller size of one snow angel, there was a kid on the premises and that generally meant noisy chaos, the last thing he'd anticipated when he'd made the commitment to Mae to spend the Christmas holidays here. For a man who made his living by providing expensive hobbies and toys to children, Trace was amazingly uneasy when confronted with an individual child. For him, toys were a multimillion-dollar business, not entertainment. Unless he could persuade himself to use whatever child was around to conduct market research, this whole situation had just gone from bad to worse.

He was about to turn tail and run, but then he heard Mae's voice in his head as she'd extracted that promise from him. He'd never gone back on his word to her, ever. He wasn't about to start now.

Filled with a sense of dread, he made his way to the front door. He stood on the slick porch debating whether to ring the bell, rather than walking in on whoever was here. Then, again, he had just as much right to be here as the unknown occupant did. More, perhaps. That remained to be seen.

He stuck the key in the lock, turned it and pushed open the heavy door, noting as he did that it was in serious need of paint. It had once been bright red, as had all the shutters on the house. Now it was faded to a shade only slightly deeper than pink. Maybe he'd take care of that while he was here. It would be a fitting homage to Mae to see the doors and shutters restored to their scarlet holiday brilliance.

He was about to close the door when a girl—just about the size of the snow angel outside, he noted— skidded to a stop in front of him on one of the scooters his company made. It had been the hottest gift of the holiday season two years ago. It was not meant to be used indoors, though he could understand the temptation given the wide expanse of hardwood floors. And it wasn't as if those floors were in partic-

ularly great shape. They could do with sanding and a
fresh coat of wax. Something else he could do while
he was here…in Mae's memory.

First, though, he had to figure out who was this
imp of a child regarding him with blatant curiosity,
her golden hair scooped through the opening of a
baseball cap, her T-shirt half in and half out of her
jeans.

"Who are you and what are you doing here?" he
demanded in the no-nonsense tone he used on exec-
utives who'd failed to deliver on their division's
projections.

The kid didn't even flinch. "I'm Hannah and I live
here. Who are you? And how come you have a key
to my house?"

Trace's head began to throb. What the devil was
Mae up to? "Are your parents here?"

"Just my mom. My dad divorced us. He lives in
Florida. My mom's baking Christmas cookies." She
cast an appealing smile at him. "Don't they smell
great?"

Trace automatically sniffed the air. They did smell
fantastic, just the way Mae's always had. He'd eaten
fancier food than what was served at Holiday Retreat,
but he'd never had any that tasted better or was prepared with more love. He wondered if Hannah's mom
shared Mae's talents in the kitchen, then sighed. That
was hardly the point.

"Want me to get my mom?" Hannah inquired.

"I'll find her," Trace said, heading determinedly
toward the kitchen. He'd taken only a step before he

turned back. "By the way, that scooter is not an indoor toy."

The kid's smile never faltered. "Maybe not, but it works great in here." And off she went, completely unimpressed by his admonishment.

Trace sighed and went in search of her mother.

He wasn't sure what he expected, but it certainly wasn't the frail wisp of a woman who was bent over in an incredibly provocative pose, her head stuck halfway into the huge, professional quality stainless steel oven that had been Mae's pride and joy.

This room was where Mae had splurged, spending her money to design a kitchen that was both welcoming and efficient. Everything in it, from the refrigerator to the granite countertops, was top of the line. When she had shown it to Trace a few years ago, she'd been as excited as a kid on Christmas morning. She told him it was how she'd spent her first dividends from her stock in Franklin Toys.

And now there was an interloper in here, he thought, feeling oddly possessive on Mae's behalf. Unless this woman could prove her right to be on the premises, Trace would have her packed up and out of here before nightfall, even if he had to call on local law enforcement to toss her out on her attractive backside.

Despite his impatience to accomplish that task, and rather than risk scaring her half to death while she was that close to incinerating herself, he waited, barely resisting the desire to haul her out of there immediately and demand an explanation for her presence.

Of course, he was also having some difficulty resisting the urge to smooth his hand over that narrow curve of her denim-clad bottom. That, he concluded, was a very dangerous temptation. He admonished himself to forget it the same way he'd scolded Hannah only moments earlier. He hoped he paid more attention to the warning than she had, since there was likely a lot more at stake than scarred floorboards.

The woman finally retreated, holding a tray almost as big as she was. As she turned to set it on the granite countertop, she spotted him and let go of the tray with a yelp of surprise. Trace caught it in midair, then let out a curse of his own as the hot metal seared his fingers. He dropped the tray with a clatter. Cookies went flying. And the woman regarded him as if he were a living, breathing embodiment of Scrooge and he'd deliberately set out to ruin her Christmas.

"Look what you've done," she said, scowling at him as she bent to pick up the broken remains of sugar cookies decorated with pretty red and green designs. She waved a hatless Santa with half a beard under Trace's nose. "Just look at this."

She didn't seem one bit concerned with the fact that he'd burned himself trying to save her blasted cookies. He stepped past her and stuck his hands under cold running water. That finally got her attention.

"Oh, fudge, you burned yourself, didn't you?" she said. "What was I thinking? I'm sorry. Here, let me see."

She nudged up against him and grabbed his hand. Her touch was anything but soothing. In fact, now Trace was suddenly burning on the inside, too.

"Sit," she ordered before he could unscramble his thoughts. "There's a first-aid kit around here somewhere."

"Cabinet next to the stove," Trace told her, blowing on his fingers.

She stopped and stared. "How do you know that?"

"Mae was always getting distracted and having little accidents in the kitchen. She said it paid to keep the bandages close at hand."

Rather than fetching the first-aid supplies, the woman sank down onto a chair, her eyes promptly filling with unshed tears. "She did say that, didn't she?" she whispered. "I must have heard her say it a hundred times. And even before she remodeled in here, she kept aloe and antiseptic spray and bandages right by the stove."

Trace was startled by the depth of emotion in this stranger's voice. Her love for Mae was written all over her face. That much raw pain was more than he knew how to deal with...his own emotions were shaky enough. He stepped carefully around her and got his own ointment and bandages, using the time to collect himself and try to fill with renewed resolve the tiny chink she'd created in his desire to be rid of her.

When he was finished repairing the damage to his hand, he finally risked another look at her. The color had returned to her cheeks, but there was no mistaking the signs of a woman on the edge. He'd seen that same stressed expression often enough on his mother's face, the same tightness around the mouth, the wariness in her eyes.

"You okay?" he asked at last.

She nodded, still blinking back tears. "Sometimes it just catches me off guard, the fact that she's gone. I hadn't seen her in several years, but I always had such wonderful memories of being here, especially around the holidays."

That must have been a long time ago, Trace thought with a surprising surge of anger on Mae's behalf. He'd been here with Mae every year since that trip when they'd first met. He'd never been entirely sure how she'd cajoled him into coming, but year after year he'd found himself driving north from New York City, looking forward to spending time with the closest thing he had to family now that his folks were both dead.

Oddly, on none of those trips had he ever caught a glimpse of the man in Mae's life. Only at the end had she explained why, that Nate had his own family responsibilities, duties that he had never once shirked through all the years they had loved each other. It had been an unconventional love—an impossible love— she had explained to Trace. The man's wife had suf- fered a nervous breakdown years before, when his children were little more than toddlers. Nate could never bring himself to divorce her during all the long lonely years when he'd struggled as a single dad, watching his wife's mind deteriorate degree by de-

gree. He had been the rock that held his family together…and the other half of Mae's soul. If she regretted anything about their long, secret affair, she
never once complained of it to Trace. And it had certainly never soured her on the possibilities of
romance.

It was little wonder, though, that Mae had sought
out Trace's company around the holidays, he had realized as she told him the story. The loneliness at a
season meant for sharing with family and friends must
have been unbearable. Trace wondered if this woman
even knew about that part of Mae's life.

"If you hadn't been here for years, why are you
here now?" Trace asked, unable to hide the note of
bitterness in his voice. "Did you come to pick over
her belongings?"

She seemed startled by the hostility in the question—or maybe by the fact that he thought he had the
right to ask it.

"I'm here because my aunt left Holiday Retreat to
me," she said eventually. "Not that it's any of your
business, but I'm Savannah Holiday. Mae was my
grandfather's sister. And you are? How did you get
in here, anyway?" She sighed. "Hannah, I suppose.
I've told her and told her about not opening the door
to strangers."

It didn't seem to occur to Savannah Holiday that it
had taken her a long time to get around to asking
about his identity. In New York, the police would
probably have been called the second he appeared in

the kitchen doorway and the answers to all those questions could have been sorted out later.

"I'm Trace Franklin," he said. "A friend of Mae's." He retrieved the key from his pocket and plunked it on the table where it glinted in the sunlight. "And I got in with this, though I did see your daughter as I came in."

She stared at the key. "Where did you get that?"

"From your aunt."

"Why would she give you a key to Holiday Retreat?"

"Because she'd invited me here for the holidays." He was only now beginning to grasp just how diabolical that invitation had been. His finding the alluring Savannah Holiday and her daughter underfoot was clearly no accident, but Mae's last-ditch effort at matchmaking. He wondered if Savannah Holiday had figured out what her aunt was up to.

He regarded his unexpected housemate with a wry expression. "Merry Christmas!"

Chapter 3

Compared to the man sitting across from her with his cool, flinty gaze and designer wardrobe, Savannah felt like a dowdy waif. She was pretty sure there was flour in her hair and, more than likely, red and green sprinkles on her nose. When it came to baking, she did it with more enthusiasm than tidiness or expertise. The results were equally unpredictable, though she'd been particularly proud of the batch of golden cookies that were currently lying in crumbles around her feet.

She regarded this interloper with caution, in part at least because his presence rattled her. She'd felt a little flicker of awareness the instant he'd entered the kitchen. At first she'd attributed it to surprise, but then she'd realized it was a whole lot more like the sensation she'd experienced the first time she'd met Rob. It was the caught-off-guard, heart-stopping reaction of a woman to a virile, attractive male...or a doe when confronted by a rifle-toting hunter. She was stunned to discover that she was even remotely susceptible to a man after the bitterness of her divorce, especially to a man wearing the clothes of a business executive to a country inn. It was something her uptight ex-husband would have done.

Because her reaction made her uneasy, she focused on the one topic guaranteed to take her mind off of it. "You said Mae invited you here. You do know that my aunt died, right?" she asked.

"Yes."

His expression was almost as bleak as the one Savannah saw in the mirror every morning. "But you came anyway," she said, impressed despite the instinct that told her this man was anything but sentimental.

"It's what she wanted," he said simply. "I promised I would."

"And you always keep your promises?"

"I try," he said. "I don't make that many, and the ones I do make mean something."

"What about your family? Won't they miss you over the holidays?"

"In recent years Mae was the closest thing I had to family. What about *your* family?"

"Hannah's here. For all intents and purposes, she's all I have. My husband and I divorced a year ago." She hesitated, then added, "My parents and I aren't on speaking terms at the moment."

"I see."

She was grateful that he didn't bombard her with a lot of questions about that. "How did you know Mae? Forgive me, but you don't look as if you spend a lot of time in the country."

He laughed at that, and it transformed his face. The tight lines around his mouth eased. His dark eyes sparkled. "What gave me away?"

"The clothes, for starters. I'm amazed you stayed upright walking from the car to the house in those shoes. I don't think snow is kind to Italian leather. And I can't imagine that you'd be able to spend more than a few minutes outdoors before freezing in that shirt. Men around here tend toward flannel."

"But I think the real secret is what they wear under it," he said, barely containing what promised to be a wicked grin.

Savannah's thoughts automatically veered off in a very dangerous direction. She had the oddest desire to strip off his clothes to see if there were practical long johns underneath. She'd never thought that sort of men's underwear to be particularly sexy, but she imagined Trace Franklin could do amazing things for the look.

"You're blushing," he said, regarding her with amusement.

"Well, of course I am! I hardly know you, and here we are discussing underwear."

"It can be a fascinating topic, especially if we move from cotton to satin and lace."

She frowned at him. "You're deliberately trying to rattle me, aren't you?"

"Why would I do that?" he asked, trying for a serious expression. The twinkle in his gray eyes betrayed him.

"I can't imagine, especially when all I was trying to find out was what drew a city man like you to spend time in a country retreat." She studied him thoughtfully, then said, "There must have been a woman involved."

"Bingo. The woman who brought me here years ago was envisioning a quiet, romantic getaway with long hikes through the woods." He shrugged and gave her a beguilingly sheepish look. "Instead I spent the weekend holed up in Mae's study with my computer and fax machine taking care of a business crisis."

Savannah immediately felt a surprising empathy for the woman. "Now, *that* I can imagine. Your friend must have been disappointed."

"Dreadfully."

"What sort of business?"

"I own a company in New York," he said in such a dismissive way that it sparked her curiosity.

"Franklin," Savannah recalled thoughtfully. "Not Franklin Toys, by any chance?"

He seemed startled that she'd grasped it so quickly. "That's the one. How on earth did you figure that out?"

"There were some articles about that company on Mae's desk. Obviously she kept up with it."

"I imagine so," he said, his expression noncommittal.

"Because she knew you from your visits here?" Savannah persisted, sensing there was more.

He shrugged. "That was the start of her interest, I suppose."

She frowned at his evasiveness. "What aren't you saying?"

"What makes you think I'm leaving something out?"

"Instinct."

"Okay, then, here's the whole story in a nutshell. I suppose I owe you that, since I've shown up on your doorstep out of the blue," he said. "Your aunt was the one who encouraged me to start the company. I'd been with another toy manufacturer for a few years. I'd learned all I could, and I had a lot of ideas for ways to do it better. Mae was an early investor in Franklin Toys. Over the years she and I made a lot of money together, but I owe every bit of that success to her initial encouragement."

"I see," Savannah said slowly. "So that first trip here wasn't a waste of your time after all. Did your relationship with the woman last?"

"Only for as long as it took me to get her back to her apartment in New York that Sunday night," he said with no hint of regret. "My friendship with Mae lasted much longer."

"Then you came back here often?" she asked, feeling a vague sense of regret and guilt that he'd spent these last years with her aunt, when she should have been the one spending time here.

"As frequently as I could," he said. "Your aunt

was a remarkable woman. I enjoyed my visits with her.''

"Even if she did live essentially in the middle of nowhere," Savannah said, needing to remind herself that this man bore way too many resemblances to her ex-husband.

"Funny thing about that," he said, picking up one of the few sugar cookies they'd managed to salvage and breaking off a bite. "I got used to the peace and quiet. And the phone lines, fax and Internet connections work just fine."

"So even though you're here for the holidays, I suppose you brought all of your equipment along," she guessed.

"Of course."

Savannah shook her head. "I hope you watch your cholesterol. Anybody's who's as much of a workaholic as you appear to be is clearly a heart attack waiting to happen."

"I'll try not to have one while I'm here," he promised solemnly.

"Thank you for that. I'm afraid I don't have the kind of insurance it would take to cover your medical expenses if you collapse and fall down the stairs."

He grinned. "I do."

"Well, then, I suppose you can stay," she said grudgingly, thinking of the extra work involved in having a guest in a house that was all but falling down around them.

He regarded her with a wry expression. "I had no intention of doing anything else."

"You'll have to pitch in and help," she said, deliberately ignoring his remark. "I'm afraid the inn isn't officially ready for guests again."

"I'm not a guest—not the way you mean, anyway. And I came expecting to take care of myself. The attorney said the refrigerator would be stocked, and I brought along plenty of food from the city."

"Caviar, I imagine," she said, feeling strangely testy at the thought of sharing the house with a man whose tastes, like Rob's, probably ran to the expensive and exotic. "Maybe some imported Stilton cheese? Smoked salmon? The finer things you absolutely couldn't live without?"

His grin spread. "Junk food, if you must know."

Once again, Savannah felt the full effects of that devastating smile. She hoped he wouldn't do it too often. It might make her forget that he was completely unsuitable for a woman who'd already been burned by a man who put his work before his family.

"What exactly do you consider junk food?" she asked.

"Potato chips. Popcorn." He leaned closer and lowered his voice to confide, "I also have a cooler filled with chocolate mocha almond ice cream. I'm addicted to the stuff."

Her eyes widened. Chocolate mocha almond was an indulgence she rarely allowed herself. Aside from the calories, the brand she loved was outrageously expensive. She'd developed a taste for it during her marriage, but had had to forego it since the divorce. The store brands simply didn't live up to the gourmet ice cream. She had a hunch that cooler of Trace's was stocked with the best.

"Exactly how much ice cream did you bring?" she asked, hoping it sounded like a purely casual inquiry.

"Enough for you and Hannah…if you're good," he teased.

"When it comes to chocolate mocha almond, I can eat a lot," she warned him.

He surveyed her slowly, appreciatively, then shook his head. "Not as much as I can," he said. "And I brought enough for a week. I'll make you a deal. If you let me share in whatever you're fixing for Christmas dinner, I'll provide dessert."

"But that's three days away," Savannah protested.

He winked. "I know. Patience is a virtue."

"Another of Mae's favorite sayings," Savannah recalled as again a wave of nostalgia hit. "Are you sure I can't talk you into sharing sooner?"

He glanced at the piles of cookies on the table and the obvious remnants of hot chocolate in two mugs. "Are you absolutely certain you won't go into some sort of sugar overload crisis?"

"Absolutely."

"Then I'll bring it in," he said.

"I'll help," Savannah said eagerly, grabbing a jacket off a hook by the door and following him outside.

The instant she spotted his fancy new four-wheel-drive sports utility vehicle out front, she was momentarily distracted from thoughts of ice cream. It could turn out that Trace Franklin was the answer to her prayers.

"I don't suppose you'd be willing to let me borrow your car?" she asked.

"First you want my ice cream, and now you're after my car," he said, shaking his head. "You ask a lot for someone I've barely met."

"I need to get to town to pick up paint and things to start on the work that's needed around here." She glanced toward her own car, a faded six-year-old sedan with questionable tires. "I doubt my car will make it down the mountain, much less back up on these icy roads."

His expression grew thoughtful. "Okay, here's my best offer. I'll trade you breakfast tomorrow for a trip into town."

Apparently the man's obsession with business never quit. "You really do like to negotiate, don't you?"

He shrugged. "Force of habit. I like creating win-win situations. Is it a deal?"

Savannah held out her hand. "Deal." She hesitated. "You could have dinner with Hannah and me this evening, if you like. It won't be fancy. I'm fixing spaghetti."

He seemed startled by the invitation. "It just so happens that I love spaghetti." His gaze narrowed suspiciously. "What do you want in return for that?"

"Ice cream for dessert?" she asked hopefully.

Rather than answering, he reached in the car, then turned back with something in hand and tossed it to her. Savannah caught it instinctively. It was a pint of ice cream. And she'd been right—it was the best.

"It's all yours," he said. "Consider it a gesture of good faith."

He retrieved a huge cooler, which obviously contained the rest. Savannah eyed it enviously. "Is that thing really filled with more of this?"

"Packed solid," he told her. He studied her warily. "Am I going to have to put a lock on the freezer?"

"I would never steal your ice cream," she said with a hint of indignation, then grinned. "That doesn't mean I won't try to talk you out of it."

His gaze locked with hers and anticipation slid over her once again, making her senses come alive.

"This is really, really good ice cream," he said quietly. "It could take more than talk."

Savannah barely resisted the urge to fan herself. She was surprised steam wasn't rising around her. Oh, this man was dangerous, all right. She was obviously going to have to watch her step the whole time he was underfoot. Any man who prided himself on being a shark when it came to business was likely to be equally determined when it came to anything else he wanted.

Well, she'd just have to make sure he didn't decide he wanted her. One glance comparing her flour-streaked jeans to his tailored wool slacks put that notion to rest. They weren't in the same league at all.

She lifted her gaze to his, caught the desire darkening those gray eyes. Uh-oh, she thought. Apparently clothes didn't matter to Trace, because the look in his eyes was anything but neutral.

More worrisome, though, than that discovery was the realization that she wasn't nearly as upset by it as she probably ought to be. In fact, a little *zing* of anticipation had her blood heating up quite nicely. She could probably strip off her sheepskin-lined jacket and be quite comfortable in the twenty-degree temperature out here.

"You'll want to get all your stuff inside," she said, her tone suddenly brisk. "Who knows how many deals you might have missed while we've been talking?"

"The ones worth making can always wait," he said.

"Still, I'd hate to feel responsible for you missing out on something important. Besides, I promised Hannah that she and I would go cut down a Christmas tree this afternoon."

He regarded her as if she'd just mentioned a plan to cut down the entire forest.

"There's a perfectly good tree lot in town. I passed it on my way out here," he said. "Those trees are already cut. Less work. Less waste."

"Is that an expression of environmental concern?" she inquired. "Because the trees I'm talking about are grown specifically for the holidays. It's how some people make their living."

He looked skeptical. "Still seems like a lot of work."

"But this is a tradition," she countered.

He looked as if she'd used a foreign term.

"Didn't you have any holiday traditions when you were growing up?" she asked.

"Sure," he said at once. "Staying out from underfoot while Mom and Dad argued over how much money was being wasted on presents."

Savannah couldn't imagine a home in which the

holidays had meant anything other than a joyful celebration. For all of the problems she and her parents were having now, they had given her years of memories of idyllic Christmases. Very little of that had had anything at all to do with the materialistic things. It had been about family togetherness, laughter…traditions. For some reason, she suddenly wanted to share just a little of that with this man to whom tradition meant so little. She'd never been able to get through to Rob, but maybe Trace Franklin wasn't a lost cause.

"Would you like to help us?" she asked impulsively.

He looked even more disconcerted by that invitation than he had been by her request that he join them for dinner. "I had planned to get some work done this afternoon," he said predictably.

"Surely the company founder can take a break for a couple of hours," she coaxed. "Most people do relax around the holidays. I doubt anyone will be too upset if they don't get a fax today or even tomorrow. Some people might actually be hoping to leave work early to finish their holiday shopping."

A vaguely guilty expression passed across his face, as if he'd already forgotten that Christmas was only a few days away.

"You're right," he said eventually. "The work can wait. In fact, maybe I'll call my secretary and tell her to let everyone leave early."

Savannah grinned at the unexpected evidence that Scrooge had a heart. "That's the spirit," she said. "I'll get my coat and hurry Hannah along. You'd better change into something warmer, too. My hunch is that this could take a long time. Hannah rushes through most things, but she's never made a quick decision about a Christmas tree in her life.''

As Savannah left Trace to finish putting his groceries away, she was all too aware that his gaze followed her as she exited from the kitchen. And that she unconsciously put a little extra sway in her hips because of it.

Oh, so what? she thought as a guilty blush crept into her cheeks. If she could grant Hannah's not-so-secret Christmas fantasy of a pair of skis, then surely Fate wouldn't mind granting her the chance to flirt with a handsome man for a couple of days. After the holidays, what were the chances she'd ever see Trace again? Slim to none, more than likely. He was the perfect guy on which to practice a little harmless flirting. She had to get back into the dating game one of these days. Here was her chance relearn the rules with a man who absolutely, positively was not her type, and better yet, a man who wouldn't be around long enough to break her heart.

Then she recalled that desire she'd read in Trace's eyes only moments before. Harmless was not the first word that came to mind. Okay, she concluded, wicked would be nice, too.

Chapter 4

Trace hauled all of his business equipment into Mae's den, but before he could plug any of it in he was so overcome with emotion that he sank into the chair behind her antique desk and drew in a deep breath. As he did, he was almost certain he could still smell the soft, old-fashioned floral scent she had worn.

The room looked as if she'd just left it moments earlier. A jar of her favorite gourmet jelly beans sat on the desk. He noted with amusement that most of the grape-flavored ones were gone. They had been her favorites, though she had claimed that she continued to buy assorted flavors precisely so she wouldn't get in a rut. She'd never realized that Trace had added a half-pound or so of the grape-flavored jelly beans each and every time he came to visit, secretly stirring them into the mix.

The inn's guest book was still beside the phone with reservations carefully noted. He turned to to-day's date and saw his own name written in her grace-ful, flowing script. He saw that Savannah's arrival had been noted for a date only a few days earlier in a script that seemed less steady.

Had she made those final arrangements for her niece's inheritance when she'd known the end was near? Had she cleverly schemed to bring him together with Savannah even as her health was failing? It would have been just like her to plot something for those she loved, something to make them less lonely once she was gone.

Ironically he didn't think Savannah had picked up on the scheme yet. He'd been the subject of so much matchmaking in recent years that he'd seen what Mae was up to the instant he'd realized he wasn't going to be alone at Holiday Retreat over the holidays. It was no accident that he and Savannah were here at the same time. Mae had wanted some of the seasonal magic to rub off on her heart-weary niece and a man she thought was missing out on romance.

So, why hadn't he run? He could have apologized for the intrusion and headed back to New York and the safety of his workaholic routine. It wasn't entirely duty to Mae that had kept him here but—mostly, he had to admit—the sweetly vulnerable Savannah her-self. Though she wasn't complaining, it was obvious that her life hadn't been easy lately. Still, she'd maintained an air of determination and her sense of humor. She was too unsophisticated to be his type, but there was something about her—a fragility encased in steel—that drew him just the same. It reminded him of a young man who'd fled Tennessee years ago with little more than a dream and the determination to make it come true. And in many ways it reminded him of his mother, who'd had the strength to endure poverty and hardship. Only in recent years—after spending most of his youth condemning her for the choices she had made—had he come to realize just how strong she had been.

"Trace, are you ready yet?" Savannah asked quietly, startling him. "My goodness, you're not even changed. Is everything okay?"

He met her concerned gaze. "Sorry. I got distracted."

Savannah came closer and perched on the edge of the desk. She regarded him with sympathy. "You feel her presence in here, don't you? I feel it most in the kitchen. It's like she's watching over my shoulder." A grin tugged at the corners of her mouth. "Making sure I don't burn the place down, more than likely."

"She wouldn't have left the inn to you if she didn't trust you to take care of it," he told her, knowing with everything in him that it was true. Mae had been sentimental, but she had also had a practical streak. Her New England heritage, no doubt. "This place meant everything to her. When Franklin Toys started doing really well, I suggested she retire. She had plenty of money to live comfortably for the rest of her life. Know what she told me?''

''That retirement was for people waiting to die,'' Savannah said. ''She told me the same thing. She loved having her company, as she referred to the guests who came here year after year. She said they kept her young. What she missed was having family underfoot for the holidays.''

''You and Hannah and I are here this year,'' Trace said, unable to keep a note of sorrow from his voice.

''Too late,'' Savannah said, a tear sliding down her cheek.

Trace thought of his suspicions about Mae's reason for bringing them together. Not that he intended to get too carried away trying to see that *all* of her wish came true, but celebrating this Christmas with her niece was the least he could do for the woman who'd believed in him.

''You said yourself that you think she's watching over you,'' he reminded Savannah. ''What makes you think she's not here right this second, gloating over having gotten us up here to celebrate the holiday and her memory at the same time?''

Savannah's expression brightened. ''You're absolutely right! Let's not disappoint her. We'll make this the most memorable holiday ever. We'll do everything just the way she used to do it, from the greens in the front hall to the candles on the mantel and in the windows.''

''Perfect,'' he said enthusiastically. ''Give me a minute to call my office and change, and I'll meet you and Hannah out front. We'll find the best tree on the tree farm.''

"It has to be huge," Savannah warned.

He hesitated, phone receiver in hand. "How huge?"

"Really, really big." She held her arms wide. "And very, very tall."

"How were you and Hannah going to get such a huge tree back here by yourselves?"

"I was counting on help."

"Are you sure you didn't know I was coming?"

"Nope. Mr. Johnson has a truck. He also has a fondness for Mae's sugar cookies."

Trace winced. "The ones on the kitchen floor?"

"Those are the ones."

"Think he'll accept any other sort of bribe?" he asked, knowing that he was going to hate the alternative if Mr. Johnson declined to haul that tree.

"Nope. I think this tree is riding in your pristine, shiny SUV, shedding needles all the way," she said happily.

Trace groaned. "I was afraid of that."

She patted his hand, sending a jolt of awareness through him.

"I'll go get a blanket to lay in the back," she said soothingly. "Now, hurry, or you'll have Hannah to deal with. Trust me, she's worse than a nagging splinter when she's anxious to get someplace. Right now she's making a family of snow angels on the front lawn, but her enthusiasm for that will wear off shortly."

"I'll hurry," Trace promised, unable to tear his gaze away as she left the room. He sighed, then dialed his office.

Two minutes later, he'd told his stunned secretary to shut the company down until after the new year, changed into warmer clothes and was heading out the front door, only to be greeted by squeals of delight as Hannah upended her mother into a snowbank. Savannah was sputtering and scraping snow out of her mouth. There was a dangerous glint in her eyes as she regarded her traitorous daughter.

Oblivious to her mother's reaction, Hannah spotted Trace. Emboldened by her success with her mother, she raced in his direction. Trace braced for the hit. "Oh, no, you don't," he said, scooping her up when she would have tried to knock him on his backside. He held out a hand and helped Savannah up, even as Hannah tried to squirm free of his grip.

He looked into Savannah's dancing eyes. "What do you think? Should I drop her in that snowdrift over there?"

"No!" Hannah squealed. "Put me down. I'll be good. I promise."

Trace kept his gaze on Savannah's. "Your call."

"Hannah does keep her promises," she began thoughtfully. "Then again, that snow was really, really cold. She needs to know that."

"I know it. I know it," Hannah said. "Really, Mom. I swear."

Before he realized what she intended, Savannah scooped up a handful of snow and rubbed her daughter's face with it, dribbling a fair amount inside the collar of his coat while she was at it. Accident? he wondered. Probably not.

"Mom!" Hannah squealed, laughing.

Savannah clapped her gloved hands together to get rid of the excess snow and regarded Trace with a pleased expression. "I think it's okay to put her down now."

He lowered Hannah to her feet and caught her grin. "I hope you learned a lesson," he said, fighting to keep his own expression somber.

"Oh, yes," she retorted just as seriously. "I learned that my mom is very, very sneaky."

Trace nodded, shivering as the snow melted against his suddenly overheated skin. "I caught that, too. What do you think we should do about it?"

"Hey," Savannah protested, backing up a step. "Don't you two even *think* about ganging up on me."

"Never dream of it," Trace said, winking at Hannah.

She winked back, then giggled. "Never," she agreed.

Savannah looked from one to the other. "I'm going to regret this eventually, aren't I?"

"Could be," Trace said. He took a step closer, reached out and tucked a flyaway strand of hair back behind her ear. "But you'll never see it coming."

Her gaze locked with his, and suddenly the tables were turned. The desire to kiss her, to taste her, slammed through him with enough force to rock him on his heels. He hadn't seen that coming, either.

* * *

"We are never in a million years going to get this tree into the house," Trace said, eyeing the giant-size pine that Hannah had picked out. "What about that one over there?" He pointed to a nice, round, five-foot-tall tree. It was cute. It was manageable. Hannah was already shaking her head.

"No," daughter and mother replied in an emphatic chorus.

"I suppose it's also a tradition that the tree has to be too big to fit inside," he grumbled as he began to saw through the trunk. He'd worked for a lawn service one summer and had some skill at sawing down trees and branches, but nothing this size. He should have brought along a chain saw.

"Exactly," Savannah said, grinning and apparently thoroughly enjoying his struggle with the tree.

"I think my mother had the right idea after all," he said. "A ceramic tree that lit up when she plugged it in."

"Oh, yuck," Hannah said. "That's so sad."

As he breathed in the scent of pine and fresh, crisp air, Trace was forced to agree with her. Despite his grumbling about the endless search for the perfect tree and his protests over the size of their choice, he hadn't felt this alive in years. Something that might have been the faint stirrings of holiday spirit spread through him. He couldn't remember the last time he'd felt like this.

"Stand back, you two. When this thing falls, you don't want to be in the way," he warned as he heard the crack of the wood and felt the tree begin to wobble. One hard shove and it would hit the ground. Before he could touch it, the tree began to topple…straight at him. It knocked him on his back in the deep snow. He found himself staring straight toward the sky through a tangle of fragrant branches.

"Uh-oh," he heard Hannah whisper.

Her mother choked back a giggle and peered through the branches. "Are you okay?"

"What the devil happened?" he asked, frowning up at her.

"I gave the tree a teeny little push to help it along. I guess I pushed the wrong way. You aren't hurt, are you?" The twinkle in her eyes suggested she wasn't all that worried.

Trace bit back his own laughter and scrambled out from beneath the tree. "You are in such trouble," he warned even as she began backing away, her nervous scramble hampered by the deep snow.

"You wouldn't," she said, regarding him warily.

"Oh, but I would," he responded quietly. "Nobody pulls off a sneak attack on me twice in one afternoon and gets away with it."

She tried to escape, but she was no match for his long legs. He caught up with her in a few steps, scooped her up and dropped her into the cushion of snow.

Hannah's laughter mingled with theirs. He whirled on her. "Okay, young lady, you're next. Don't you know better than to injure a man's pride?"

Hannah was quicker to scamper away, but Trace

still caught up with her, grabbed a handful of snow and rubbed her face with it. Just then he felt himself being pelted with snowballs from behind. In seconds all three of them were engaged in a full-fledged snowball fight.

"Oh, my," Savannah said a few minutes later, collapsing into the snow. "I haven't laughed that hard in ages."

"Me, either," Trace said, his gaze clashing with hers. In fact, he could barely recall ever laughing that hard.

Or wanting a woman as much as he wanted the virtual stranger lying beside him in the icy snow right this minute. With all the heat crackling between them, he was surprised they hadn't melted the snow right out from under them.

He started to reach out to touch her cheek, but recalling Hannah's presence, he drew back. "Do you know what I'd like to do right now?" he asked, his gaze locked with Savannah's.

She swallowed hard at the question and shook her head.

Trace realized that her thoughts had drifted down the same dangerous path as his own. "Not *that*," he protested, deliberately teasing her.

Her cheeks, already pink from the chill in the air, turned an even brighter shade. Another woman might have called his bluff, but she merely kept her gaze on him, apparently waiting to see just how deep a hole he intended to dig for himself.

"What *I'd* like to do," he said, "is go back to the

house, build a nice warm fire in the fireplace, and…"
He deliberately let the suspense build. He saw the
pulse beating a little more rapidly in her neck. He
permitted himself a hint of a smile, then said softly,
"Take a nap."

She was still blinking in confusion when Hannah
plopped down between them and said, "Grown-ups
don't take naps."

"Sure we do," Trace told her. His gaze went back
to Savannah. "In fact, sometimes when adults take
naps, we have the very best dreams ever."

Savannah shot him a knowing look, then rose
gracefully to her feet. "Well, by all means, let's get
home so you can get some sleep," she said testily.

She muttered something more, something obviously meant for Trace's ears, not Hannah's. He
caught her hand and held her back until they were
well out of Hannah's hearing.

"What was that?" he inquired.

She leveled a look straight at him. "I said, I hope
you have nightmares."

"No dream with you in it could ever be a nightmare," he said, locking gazes with her once more.
"Then, again, you could take a nap with me."

"In your dreams," she retorted.

He winked at her. "Exactly."

She stopped in her tracks and scowled up at him.
"Is this some sort of game with you?"

There was a hint of anger behind the question that
threw Trace completely. "Game? I'm not sure what
you mean."

"When you found me at the inn, did you decide I was Aunt Mae's gift to you or something? Because I am here to tell you that hell will freeze over before I fall into bed with you just because it's convenient."

With that, she whirled away and stalked off as gracefully as the deep snow permitted, leaving him to deal with the tree. He considered running after her, trying to explain, but maybe it was better to give her time to cool down.

So he struggled with the monster tree, finally getting a firm grip on the trunk, then dragging it through the snow. The trek took forever. By the time he reached the car, Savannah and Hannah were nowhere to be seen. Since the inn was less than a mile down the road, they'd probably decided to walk.

Trace wrestled with the tree and finally got it half in and half out of the SUV, cursing at the mess it was making of the car's interior. He tied it securely, then climbed into the vehicle and turned the heater up full blast.

He was still stinging from Savannah's tongue-lashing as he drove back to the inn. Granted, he'd only been teasing her, but she didn't know him well enough to understand that. He'd deserved every bit of scorn she'd heaped on him.

As he pulled up in front of the house, he noted that the lights were blazing and that smoke was curling from the chimney. Dusk was falling rapidly, and along with it, the temperature was dropping.

He lugged the tree onto the porch, then left it there to be dealt with after he warmed up with a cup of coffee or maybe some of that hot chocolate Savannah and her daughter were so fond of.

Inside, he stomped the snow off his boots and tossed his jacket over a chair, then headed for the kitchen where he could hear the low murmur of voices. He found Savannah at the stove stirring a pot of spaghetti sauce. The weathered older man to whom she was talking caught sight of Trace and gave him a wink.

"You must be Trace. Savannah here's been giving me an earful about you," he said. "'Course, it's not exactly the same high praise I was used to hearing from Mae."

Trace saw Savannah's back stiffen, but she didn't turn around. Obviously, the walk had done nothing to cool her temper. She was still royally ticked at him. The apology he owed her would have to wait, though. The man regarding him with such amusement had to be Mae's longtime lover.

"You must be Nate Daniels," Trace guessed at once. "I heard a lot about you over the years, as well, all of it good."

"Only because Mae never had a sharp word to say about anyone," Nate said. "Maybe that's because she brought out the best in people."

"I know she did in me," Trace said solemnly, his gaze on Savannah.

Nate looked from him to Savannah, then stood up and began pulling on his jacket. "Think I'll be going along now."

Savannah whirled around at that. "I thought you might like to stay for dinner."

"Not tonight," Nate said, shooting a commiserating look toward Trace. "I'll be around next time you're interested in having company. Meantime, you two need anything, you give me a call. I'll be happy to do what I can. You both meant a lot to Mae. I know she'd be happy that you're here together for the holidays."

Savannah regarded him with a disappointed expression. "Come by anytime," she said, her voice husky, her eyes shimmering with unshed tears. "I want to hear everything you can tell me about my aunt."

Nate clasped her hand in his. "Come on, now, girl. Don't you be crying for your aunt. She's at peace."

"I know. I just wish I'd been here for her."

"She understood why you couldn't be here," Nate assured her. "And I was here. She wasn't alone."

"Thank you for that," Savannah said.

"No need to thank me. My place was by her side," he said simply. "I only wish I'd been able to give her more. Now let me get out from underfoot, so you folks can have your dinner." He regarded Trace with a stern expression. "And a nice long talk."

Trace accepted the admonishment without comment. "I'll walk you out," he offered.

Nate shook his head. "No need. I know the way. Seems to me like you have better things to do," he said, casting a pointed look at Savannah, who'd deliberately turned her back again.

"Yes," Trace agreed.

He waited until he heard the front door close before attempting his apology. "Savannah?"

"What?"

"I'm sorry if I offended you earlier."

"If?" she asked with a hint of disdain. She faced him, eyes flashing heatedly. "You all but propositioned me in front of my daughter!"

"I made sure that Hannah was out of earshot before I said a word," he reminded her, but she didn't seem the least bit pacified. She turned away and began stirring the spaghetti sauce with a vengeance. "Okay, I'm just plain sorry. I never meant to give the impression that I seriously thought you and I ought to be back here tumbling around in bed together."

"Oh, really?" she asked skeptically. "Then exactly what *did* you mean?"

"I was just teasing. Your cheeks get all flushed and your eyes sparkle when you get indignant. That was the only reaction I was going for. I was out of line."

She turned slowly and studied him. "Apology accepted. I probably overreacted anyway. It's been a long time since I've flirted with a man."

"You'll get the hang of it again." He reached for her hand and tugged lightly until she was standing directly in front of him. "I only think it's fair to warn you, though."

"Warn me? About what?"

"Next time I might not be teasing."

She gulped visibly, then nodded. "I'll keep that in mind."

"Is it all right if I stay here, or would you rather I go?"

She seemed startled—perhaps even dismayed—by his offer to leave. "Aunt Mae invited you here. I'm certainly not going to kick you out."

"I know what Mae wanted," Trace said. "What do you want?"

She drew in a deep, shuddering breath, then stiffened her shoulders as she looked straight into his eyes. "I want you to stay."

The satisfaction that swept through Trace felt a lot like the exhilaration he felt when a difficult business negotiation ended well. "Then that's what I'll do," he told her solemnly.

She muttered something that he couldn't quite make out.

"What was that?" he asked.

A flush crept up the back of her neck. "I said, like I really had a choice."

"Of course you have a choice."

"Not if I want that tree to get put up tonight," she said, facing him with a renewed sparkle in her eyes.

Trace laughed despite himself. "I do love a woman who's always working an angle."

"Of course you do," Savannah said. "Makes you feel more at home, doesn't it? I'll bet you spend most of your time with female boardroom piranha types."

Trace chuckled at the all-too-accurate assessment. "True enough," he admitted. "But something tells me that's about to change."

Chapter 5

Savannah sent Trace in search of Hannah, while she got dinner on the table. She also needed the time to compose herself. She knew precisely why she had overreacted to Trace's teasing. It was because she had actually been tempted to take him up on his offer to slip away for a so-called *nap*. Even if they'd actually done no more than crawl into bed together and snuggle, it would have satisfied the yearning that had been building in her ever since he'd arrived earlier in the day.

Of course, she doubted a man like Trace would have settled for simply holding her in his arms. He would have wanted much more, and while she was tempted by that, she didn't want to wind up with her heart broken when he left in a few days. It was better that she'd made her position perfectly clear. If she was lucky, there would be no more temptations.

Next time I might not be teasing.

Trace's words suddenly came back to haunt her. How convenient that she had forgotten the warning.

At the sound of his laughter as he and Hannah came toward the kitchen, Savannah's pulse raced a little faster. The same wicked yearning that had gripped her earlier teased her senses now. She sighed. Resisting him was going to be a whole lot harder than she'd ever imagined. She'd just have to keep reminding herself that he was cut from the same cloth as her workaholic ex-husband.

"Mom, can we put the Christmas tree up tonight?" Hannah pleaded as they finished up bowls of ice cream after the best spaghetti Trace had eaten in years.

"According to tradition, we never put it up till Christmas Eve," Savannah told her, but she sounded regretful, as if this were one tradition she could be persuaded to change.

"Maybe it's time to start your own tradition," Trace suggested, earning a high-five from Hannah. "Besides, the sooner the tree is in its stand and has some water, the better it will be, right? It'll last much longer, and it will fill the house with the scent of pine. Why not start enjoying it now?"

Hannah studied her mother, clearly trying to gauge her mood. "Please," she begged finally. "I'll go up in the attic and bring down all the decorations you said are up there. Trace will put it up and string up the lights. You won't have to do anything."

"Except keep the carols going on the CD player and the hot chocolate flowing," Trace corrected. "What do you say, Savannah?"

"I say that you two are a formidable team," she said, feigning an air of resignation that was belied by the spark of excitement in her eyes. "Go on. Bring in the tree."

"Do you know where you want it?" Trace asked. "Once it's up, I don't want to be hauling it all over the house."

She frowned at him. "It goes in front of the window in the living room. That's where it's always been."

"And you're happy with that?" he persisted.

"Why wouldn't I be?"

"Since you're starting new traditions and all, I just thought you might want to go for broke and pick a new location."

"I think the old one is just fine," she said. "That way, anyone driving up to the house will be able to see the lights on the tree."

Trace resigned himself to moving the sofa that normally sat in front of that window. "Where should I move the sofa?"

Savannah regarded him blankly. "The sofa?"

"The one in front of that window."

Her eyes suddenly lit with understanding. "So that's why you were so eager to have me put the tree somewhere else. You're going to be stuck moving furniture."

"Hey, I'm not complaining." He glanced at Hannah. "Did you hear me complain?"

"No," she said at once.

"I'll put that sofa just about anywhere you want it except the attic," he insisted.

Savannah regarded him with a wry expression. "I think on the wall facing the fireplace will do."

"Got it. Tree in front of the window. Sofa in front of the fireplace. And the easy chairs currently on that wall? Where should they go?"

A chuckle erupted from deep inside her, lighting up her face. "Maybe Hannah and I can rearrange the furniture while you get the tree in its stand."

"No way," Trace protested. "I'm providing the brawn here. Just give me instructions."

By the time Savannah finished with the instructions, he was pretty sure that not one single piece of furniture in the living room would be where it had started out. He figured he could live with that, as long as she didn't change her mind a million times.

"That's it?" he questioned. "You're sure?"

"As sure as I can be before I see what it looks like," she said.

Trace sighed. "I'll get started. You might want to hunt for some painkillers and a heating pad in the meantime."

"Very funny."

He leveled a look at her. "Who's joking?" he

asked as he headed for the living room to rearrange the furniture.

By the time everything was in its newly designated place, including the tree, the room did have a cozier, more festive air about it. A fire crackled in the fireplace, and the fresh scent of pine filled the air.

Hannah had brought down stacks of boxes of decorations from the attic. They were now scattered over every surface, as she took each one from its tissue and examined it with wide-eyed delight.

"These must be really, really old, huh?" she asked him.

"They certainly look as if they're antiques," Trace said, noting the loving care with which she handled them. It must be nice to have family heirlooms to be brought out year after year, each with its own story. But now with Mae gone, who would share those stores with Hannah?

Savannah came in just then carrying a tray of steaming mugs filled with hot chocolate. Her eyes widened as she saw the decorations.

"Oh, my," she whispered. "I remember these. Mae used to tell us kids about them when she'd take them out of the boxes. We were never allowed to touch them because they were so old and fragile, but we each had our favorites."

She immediately picked up a blown-glass rocking horse, its paint beginning to wear away. "This was mine. This and the angel that goes on the top of the tree. Is that still here?"

"Over here," Hannah said excitedly, picking it up gingerly. "She's beautiful."

Dressed in white satin with red velvet trim, the angel had flaxen hair and golden wings. The delicate porcelain face had been rendered with a serene look totally appropriate for gazing down on the holiday festivities year after year. Even Trace, with his jaded, unsentimental view of the season, could see the beauty of it.

"We always drew straws to see who would get to put it on the top after all the other decorations were on the tree," Savannah said as she held the angel. "My dad or one of my uncles would lift up whoever won so we could reach the very top."

"Can I put it on this year?" Hannah asked. "Trace could lift me high enough."

"Maybe this year your mom ought to do it," Trace suggested, seeing the nostalgia in Savannah's eyes.

"No," Savannah said at once. "It was always one of the kids. Of course Hannah should do it—that's the tradition."

"Well, it'll be morning before we get to it unless we get started," Trace said. "There are a lot of lights here, and there must be hundreds of decorations. You two sit back and relax while I get the lights on. You can tell me when they're in the right place."

"Ah, my favorite job," Savannah teased, settling onto the sofa with Hannah beside her. "Supervisor."

Trace had a devil of a time untangling all the lights, making sure they worked and then getting them on the tree. It was the first time such a task had fallen to him, and he was beginning to see why his father had always grumbled about it. Trace would have settled for three or four strands strategically placed, but Savannah was having none of that.

"At least four more strands," she insisted. "I like a lot of lights."

"I'm not hearing any carols while I work," Trace chided. "What happened to the music? Isn't that your job?"

"Oops. I forgot. What will it be?" She shuffled through a stack of CDs. "Bing Crosby? Nat King Cole? Kenny G? The Mormon Tabernacle Choir? Vince Gill? The Vienna Boys Choir?"

"Your aunt certainly had eclectic taste," Trace commented.

"She loved Christmas music. She used to buy at least one new album every year. Obviously she kept up that tradition. So, what's your pleasure?"

"Surprise me," Trace said.

Despite the suggestion, Savannah didn't surprise him at all when she chose the old standards of Nat King Cole. As the singer's voice filled the room, Trace recalled the way his father had scoffed at the sentimentality of the holiday music. Trace had inadvertently carried that same disdain with him into adulthood. Now, though, with Savannah and Hannah singing along with the music, he began to enjoy the songs.

"Come on," Savannah encouraged. "Sing with us."

"No, thanks, I'd rather listen to you," he said as he wrapped the final strand of lights around the tree.

"But singing helps to get you into the holiday spirit. It doesn't matter if you're off-key," she told him.

"Sorry," he said, his voice a little tight. "I don't know the words."

She stared at him with obvious astonishment. "You never learned the words to all the old standard Christmas carols?"

"They weren't played much at our house. My father objected. He said it was just more crass commercialism. We were lucky he let us put up a tree. After a few years, he carried on so about that, that my mother settled for the little ceramic tree I told you about earlier."

"But you must have heard the carols when you were at your friends' houses," she persisted. "Or on the radio."

"I didn't pay much attention," he said defensively.

"How awful," she said, studying him with sympathy.

"Savannah, I got along okay without knowing the words to a bunch of songs that get played once a year."

She studied him seriously. "Can I ask you something?"

"Sure," he said, despite the wariness creeping over him.

"As a man who doesn't seem to have many happy

memories of the holidays, how did you end up running a toy company?''

"Long story," he said.

"It's still early. We have time."

"I don't want to bore Hannah with all this. Besides, we've got a tree to decorate." He deliberately turned to Hannah. "Sweetie, are you ready to start hanging those decorations?" he asked, shutting down the topic of his career.

"Sure," Hannah said eagerly. "Mom, you've got to help."

Savannah cast one last curious look at him, before smiling and picking up several decorations.

By the time they were finally finished and all the boxes were empty, there wasn't a bare spot on the tree's branches.

"Ready for the lights?" Trace asked.

"Wait. Let me turn off the overhead lights," Savannah said. "It's better in the dark."

As soon as the main lights were off, Trace plugged in the tree's. The hundreds of lights shimmered, reflecting off the ornaments and filling the room with dazzling color. Even he was a bit in awe as he stared at it.

"It's beautiful," Hannah whispered.

"The very best tree ever," Savannah agreed.

Suddenly she was slipping her hand into Trace's. "Thank you," she said.

"Just following directions," he said.

"No. It's more than that. I think we all need a

touch of magic in our lives this year, and you've made sure we have it."

"All I did—"

She cut off his protest. *"Thank you,"* she repeated emphatically, gazing up at him.

Trace thought he'd never seen anything so lovely in his life as he gazed into her sparkling eyes, which put the lights on the tree to shame. "You're welcome," he said softly, resisting the need to kiss her only because Hannah was in the room.

"I think I'll go to bed," Hannah announced with rare impeccable timing.

"Night, baby," Savannah said, sounding just a little breathless.

"Good night, Trace. Thanks for helping with the tree." Hannah stood on tiptoe to give him a peck on the cheek.

"Good night, angel."

"I'm glad you're here," she murmured sleepily as she headed for the stairs.

Trace looked into Savannah's eyes, aware suddenly that he was caught up in something he couldn't explain with his usual rational practicality. "I'm glad I'm here, too."

The most amazing sense of contentment stole through Savannah as she settled onto the sofa with Trace beside her. He was careful not to sit too close, but she could still feel the heat radiating from him, and she was drawn to it more than ever.

It had been an incredible evening. Even listening

to Trace and Hannah bickering over where to place the ornaments on the tree had been wonderful. Hannah wouldn't have risked such a debate with her father. Things were always done Rob's way. It was a lesson Hannah had learned early, to keep peace in the family.

It was more than that, though. Maybe it was the cozy fire. Maybe it was the hot chocolate and salvaged chunks of sugar cookies.

Or maybe it was simply that for the first time in years, there was no real dissension as the holidays got under way. It had always been a battle to get her husband home from the office in time to help with the preparations. And unlike the bantering between Hannah and Trace, there had been a superior edge to her ex's tone that had always sent Hannah to her room in tears.

"Can I ask you something?" Savannah said, studying Trace intently.

He kept his guarded gaze directed toward the fire, but he nodded.

"Christmas is still a couple of days away. Why did you come up here early?"

"I told you."

"I know. You promised my aunt. But she's been gone for several weeks now. You could have waited till the last second and still fulfilled your promise."

He glanced at her, then looked back at the fire. "You'll think I'm crazy."

Savannah laughed. "I doubt that. Even in the brief

time I've known you, I can tell you definitely have all your wits about you.''

"Okay, then, here it is. I was planning to wait till Christmas Eve, rush up here, spend the night and rush right back to the city on Christmas Day.''

"But you changed your mind. Why?''

"I woke up this morning with this weird feeling that I needed to be up here today.'' He met her gaze. "Normally I would have dismissed it and kept to my original plan....'' His voice trailed off.

"But?'' Savannah prodded, intrigued by the distinctly uncomfortable expression on his face. For a man who exuded confidence, it was a rare display of vulnerability.

"You know that cooler of chocolate mocha almond ice cream?''

"Very well. What does that have to do with anything?''

"It was delivered to my apartment this morning with a note that said I should get it up here before it melted.''

Savannah stared at him. "Someone sent you that ice cream as a gift?''

His gaze held hers. "Not just *someone*. It was your aunt's handwriting.''

"Oh, my,'' Savannah whispered. "How could that be?''

"I called the store and the delivery service. The arrangements had been made weeks ago.'' He shrugged ruefully. "I guess Mae was afraid I might not keep my promise without a little nudge from beyond the grave. Needless to say, I packed my bags and hit the road.''

She studied him closely. "Are you teasing me?"

"Absolutely not," he said. "I have no sense of humor. Ask the people who work for me. Heck, it's even in most of the articles about Franklin Toys."

"That's absurd," Savannah said, dismissing the suggestion out of hand. "You've been joking and laughing with Hannah and me since you got here."

"I know," he said, his expression serious. "What do you make of that?"

"We're good for you," she said, her voice suddenly a little breathless. Could it really be that she had something to offer this man who had everything money could buy?

"Which, I suspect, is exactly what your aunt had in mind when she plotted this meeting."

Suddenly it all made sense to Savannah. The inheritance of Holiday Retreat at a time when she desperately needed a change in her life. The unexpected arrival of a handsome stranger on the inn's doorstep. Yes, indeed, Aunt Mae had been scheming, all right. The realization horrified her.

"I am so sorry," she told Trace with total sincerity. "She shouldn't have dragged you up here with an ulterior motive. If you want to get back to the city and your friends for Christmas, I will certainly understand."

Her declaration seemed to amuse Trace for some reason. His eyes were glinting humorously, when he reached out to caress her cheek. "Are you kicking me out, Savannah?"

"No, of course not. I just wanted you to understand that you're free to go if there's someplace you'd rather be, people you'd rather be spending the holiday with."

As an answer he leaned forward and touched his lips to hers in the lightest, tenderest of kisses. There was a whisper of heat, the promise of fire...and then he was on his feet.

"I'll see you in the morning," he said as he headed for the stairs.

"You're staying?" she asked.

"Of course I'm staying."

"Because it was what Mae wanted?" she asked, determined to clarify the reason.

"No, darlin'. Because it's what *I* want." He winked at her. "Besides, I promised to take you into town tomorrow."

With that he was gone, leaving Savannah staring after him. She touched a finger to her lips, where she could still feel his mouth against hers. "And you always keep your promises," she whispered to herself. It was such a little thing, but it meant more than Trace could possibly imagine.

She lifted her gaze to seek out a picture of Aunt Mae that sat on the mantel. "Thank you."

Just knowing that there was one man left who kept his promises restored her faith that the future would turn out all right.

Chapter 6

The scent of fresh-brewed coffee drifted upstairs, pulling Trace out of a perfectly fascinating dream. For once it had nothing to do with mergers and acquisitions, but with a woman—Savannah, to be precise.

How could a woman with so little guile, so little sophistication, get under his skin the way she had? That kiss the night before—little more than a friendly peck by most standards—had packed more punch than any kiss he'd experienced in years. He'd left the room, not because he believed in hasty, uncomplicated exits, but because he wanted so much more. If he'd gone after what he'd wanted, more than likely he would have scared her to death. Then she would have kicked him out and he would have spent another lonely holiday season back in New York.

"I hope to hell you knew what you were doing, Mae," he muttered.

When the scent of sizzling bacon joined that of the coffee, Trace quickly showered and dressed in a pair of old jeans, a dress shirt and a heavy pullover sweater. That was about as casual as his attire ever got these days. He reminded himself if he was going to paint the front door and trim and sand the floors, he needed to buy something else to wear.

When he walked into the kitchen, Savannah regarded him with flushed cheeks and wisps of curls teasing her face. "Is that your idea of work clothes?" she asked. "Or do you intend to supervise today, the way I did last night?"

Trace noted that she, too, was wearing jeans, but her University of Florida sweatshirt had seen better days, as had her sneakers. She still looked fabulous. He still wanted her. A part of him had been hoping that last night's desire had been an aberration.

"Did I say I was working?" he inquired as he poured himself a cup of coffee, breathed in its rich scent, then took his first sip. "Good coffee, by the way."

She grinned. "Glad you like it, since it's yours. I figured you wouldn't approve of the instant I had on hand."

Trace shuddered. "Good guess." He met her gaze. "Exactly what sort of work are you planning to do today?"

"I want to pick up paint for the guest rooms, a tarp for the roof and..."

"Whoa! Why a tarp for the roof?"

"Because it's leaking."

"Why not get it fixed?"

"I would if I could get the contractor over here," she explained with exaggerated patience. "He said he can't come till after the first of the year."

"Then call another contractor."

She frowned at him. "Don't you think I thought of that?"

"I'll handle it," he said at once.

"What do you mean, you'll 'handle it'?"

"I'll get someone over here to repair the roof."

"Even if you are a business mogul, I doubt you'll be any more successful than I've been," she said. "Besides, there's at least a foot of snow up there. They won't even be able to look at it, much less start the repairs."

"Okay, you have a point," he conceded. "Though that would also seem to make the tarp a waste of time, too, unless you're planning to put it over the snow."

She frowned at him. "Okay, then, no tarp."

"What else do you want from the hardware store?"

"The paint and tools to scrape the wallpaper will do it. I don't want to spend any more till I know what the rest of the repairs are going to cost. And I have to set some money aside for new brochures and advertising. I need to start getting paying guests back in here as soon as possible. I've already missed the start of the ski season."

Trace thought he heard a hint of desperation in her voice that she was trying hard to hide. "Savannah, do you have the money to get this place up and running again?''

"I have enough," she said tightly.

"What about a loan? I could—"

"Absolutely not. I won't take money from you."

"Then let me talk to the bank."

"No, I am not going to start off my new life with a pile of debts. Things will get done when I can afford to do them."

Trace admired her pride and her independent streak, but as a practical matter he knew it was better for a business to present its best face from the outset so that word-of-mouth would spread. She might not take money from him, but she wasn't in a position to turn down a little practical assistance in the form of labor. She could hardly tell him not to pick up his own supplies. He'd just have to be a little sneaky about it. That meant getting in and out of the hardware store without her catching sight of his purchases.

"Fine," he said. "Holiday Retreat is yours."

There was one more thing he could do, too. It would require a few phone calls, routing his attorney away from his new girlfriend for a couple of hours, but he could pull it off by Christmas.

"Is Hannah coming into town with us?" he asked as he ate the scrambled eggs Savannah put in front of him.

"Of course. She's dying to take a look around. We stopped at the grocery store on our way up here, but that's all she's seen. I'll go get her. We can be ready to leave whenever you're finished with breakfast."

"Did you eat?"

"I had a piece of toast," she said.

Trace frowned at her. "I have enough eggs here for three people." He stood up, grabbed a plate from the cupboard, then divided up his eggs, added two slices of bacon and set it on the table. "Sit. You need the protein."

Savannah opened her mouth to protest, but his scowl achieved what his directive had not. She sat down and picked up her fork.

"You know, I have to get used to serving the guests around here without sitting down to eat with each and every one of them," she told him.

"I'm not a guest."

She nibbled thoughtfully on a piece of bacon. "Which means I probably shouldn't have cooked this for you," she said.

"Right. I told you I'd look out for myself."

"I'll remember that tomorrow morning."

He regarded her slyly. "Of course, it wouldn't hurt to get in a little practice in the kitchen. You wouldn't want the first real guests to starve, would you?"

She laughed. "I don't think there's any chance of that. I may not have had a lot of practice at cooking for a crowd, but Aunt Mae has a whole box filled with recipes she perfected over the years. I can read directions with the best of them."

"I seem to recall some sort of baked French toast Mae used to make," Trace said, his gaze on Savannah. "I don't suppose…"

To his surprise, Savannah's eyes lit up. "I remember that. She always made it Christmas morning."

"Then it's a tradition?" Trace asked hopefully.

"Yes, it's a tradition. And, yes, I'll make it. And, yes, you can have breakfast with Hannah and me on Christmas morning."

"Before or after we open presents?" Trace asked, only to see her shoulders stiffen slightly.

Hannah arrived in the kitchen just in time to hear the question. "We're not having presents this year, 'cause we're poor," she said with absolutely no hint of self-pity.

"We are *not* poor," Savannah said, obviously embarrassed by her daughter's comment. "It's just that the divorce and the renovations needed on this place have left us temporarily strapped for cash, so we're keeping Christmas simple."

"I see," Trace said slowly.

Simple might be good enough for Savannah, maybe even for Hannah, who seemed resigned to it, but not for him. For the first time in years, he had the desire to splurge on the holidays.

Oh, he always sent truckloads of toys to various homeless shelters in the city, but his personal gift list was small and mostly confined to business associates. He couldn't recall the last time he'd had anyone in his life to whom he'd wanted to offer even a small token of affection.

He made a mental note to make a few more calls the second he had some privacy.

"Why don't you guys grab your coats, while I

clean up in here?" he suggested. "I'll meet you at the car in a few minutes."

Savannah regarded him curiously, almost as if she suspected something was up because he'd let her description of their financial plight pass without comment.

"Go on. Warm up the car," he encouraged, tossing her the keys. "You cooked. I'll clean up. That's *my* tradition."

"I thought you didn't have any traditions," she replied.

"I'm starting a new one."

To his relief, she seemed to accept that.

"We'll be outside," she said. "Try not to break any dishes."

"Hey," he protested, "I know what I'm doing."

He loaded the dishwasher, turned it on, then grabbed his cell phone. It took less than ten minutes to set things in motion. That was one of the benefits of being rich. Trace rarely threw his weight or his money around. When he did, people were eager enough to do as he asked. He'd always been satisfied in a distant sort of way when he thought of the delight his toys would bring to kids on Christmas morning, but he'd never actually experienced that sense of awe and wonder that was pictured in his commercials. Maybe this year things would be different.

Satisfied that Christmas was under control, he grabbed his coat and joined Savannah and Hannah, who'd already retreated to the slowly warming interior of the car. Hannah shivered dramatically when he opened the door.

"I hate cold weather," she declared.

Trace regarded her in the rearview mirror. "You're living in the wrong place, then, kiddo. Weren't you the one who was out here half-buried in snowdrifts yesterday?"

"It's colder today," she insisted. "And now I've seen snow. Yesterday I hadn't."

"Does that mean you want to move back to Florida?" Savannah asked.

There was no mistaking the note of trepidation in her voice, Trace thought. He glanced over and saw the tight lines around her mouth.

"No," Hannah said at once. "Even if it is cold, I want to stay here."

Savannah's relief was almost palpable. "Why?" she asked.

"Because since we got here, you've started laughing again," Hannah said quietly. "You never laughed in Florida."

Savannah turned her head away, but not before Trace saw a tear sliding down her cheek. He wanted to reach for her, to hold her...to make her laugh.

Instead he glanced toward Hannah. "How about you and me making a pact?" he said. "The one who makes your mom laugh the most today wins."

Hannah's eyes lit up. "Okay. What's the prize?"

"Hmm," Trace began thoughtfully. "If you win, I make us all hot fudge sundaes for dessert tonight."

"Good prize," Hannah said enthusiastically. "What if *you* win?"

"Then you make me the biggest, mushiest Christmas card ever, something I can hang on my office wall."

"Deal," Hannah said, slapping his hand in a high five.

He glanced toward Savannah and saw that her lips were twitching. It wasn't a real laugh, but it was at least the beginning of a smile. He pointed it out to Hannah.

"I get the first point," he said.

"That's not a real laugh," Hannah scoffed. She leaned over, slipped her hand down her mother's back and tickled Savannah until she giggled aloud. "*That's* a real laugh," Hannah said triumphantly.

Savannah wriggled away, then scowled at both of them. "What do *I* get, if I maintain a totally stoic facade all day long?"

"Never happen," Trace said.

"No way," Hannah agreed.

"Bet I can," Savannah retorted, her eyes twinkling.

"Okay, that does make it more interesting," Trace agreed. "If you win—and that's a really big *if*—you get Hannah's mushy card."

"What about you? What will you give me?"

Trace met her gaze evenly and felt his heart take a leap into overdrive. "Same as last night," he said softly.

He noted the flush that crept into her cheeks as she remembered that fleeting kiss they'd shared.

"You'll have to do better than that," she challenged.

His gazed remained steady. "Oh, I promise you, darlin', it will take your breath away."

The blasted heater in the car must have shot the temperature into the nineties, Savannah thought, barely resisting the urge to fan herself as Trace's words hung in the air.

Unlike the day before, when his seductive teasing had merely irritated her, today she was immediately all hot and bothered and wishing for more...maybe because she knew for a fact exactly what Trace's kiss could do to her. Worse, she wanted another of those kisses so badly, she was going to have to try really, really hard not to laugh for the remainder of the day. Given Hannah's determination to win that bet she'd made with Trace, Savannah was going to have a real struggle on her hands.

She could do it, though. She just had to remember her resolve...and keep a whole lot of distance between herself and those two co-conspirators.

The second they reached the hardware store, Hannah begged to take a walk through town.

"Back here in thirty minutes," Savannah instructed, relieved to be rid of one of them. She looked at Trace. "I'll meet you back here in a half hour, too."

"You sure you don't need my help?" he asked, regarding her with a knowing grin.

"Nope. I'm sure someone will help me carry whatever I buy."

"Here's the spare key, then, in case you finish before I get back. You don't mind if I come in and pick up a few things myself, do you?" he asked.

"What sort of things?" she asked suspiciously. Trace didn't strike her as the type who had a lot of fix-it projects back home. Then again, didn't most men get a little giddy around wrenches and screwdrivers and power tools? Maybe he just wanted to soak up the atmosphere.

"This and that," he said vaguely. "I'll know when I see it."

"Fine. It's a big store. I'm sure you won't be in my way," she said.

They parted at the front door. Savannah headed straight for the paint supplies. She'd already thought about the colors she wanted for each of the guest rooms—rich, deep tones, accented by white trim. In no time at all, she'd picked out the appropriate paint chips and had the colors being mixed, while she chose brushes, rollers, an edger for trimming, and a paint pan.

Just as she headed through the store toward wallpaper-removal materials, she thought she spotted Trace coming around the end of the paint aisle, but then he vanished from sight. She didn't see him again until she was unloading her purchases into the back of his SUV.

"Find everything you were looking for?" he asked, tucking his own mysterious packages beside hers.

"Yes. What about you?" she asked as he lifted something heavy into the car. "What on earth is that? It looks as if it weighs a ton."

"Just a tool," he said, immediately turning his attention to the street. "Any sign of Hannah yet? Maybe we should go meet her. We could grab some lunch while we're in town. There's a little restaurant on Main Street that Mae used to like."

"The Burger Shack," Savannah said at once. "Is it still in business?"

"It was last time I was here. I took Mae a burger, fries and a chocolate shake from there."

"I can almost taste their shakes," Savannah said. "They made 'em the old-fashioned way with milk and ice cream. They were so thick, a straw would stand straight up in them."

When she looked at Trace, his lips were curving into a grin.

"Sounds like that's a yes," he said.

"Absolutely," she said eagerly. "And here comes Hannah."

She noticed that her daughter was carrying a shopping bag and that her eyes were sparkling with excitement. "What did you buy?" Savannah asked.

"Mom, I can't tell. It's almost Christmas, remember?"

Savannah started to question where Hannah had gotten the money to buy a gift, then stopped herself. Rob had probably slipped her a little money before they'd left Florida. Knowing him, that had been his gift to her, and she was turning right around and spending it on Savannah. On Trace, too, more than likely. Her daughter had the most generous heart of anyone Savannah knew, something she clearly hadn't inherited from her father.

"And that's all you need to tell us," Trace said, making room in the back of the car for Hannah's purchases. "Your mom and I were just talking about lunch. You interested?"

"Only if you're talking about that burger place on Main Street. The smell coming out of there is awesome. And I saw lots of kids my age going in. It must be the cool place to go."

Trace grinned. "Then it sounds like it's unanimous."

"Guess what?" Hannah asked excitedly. She went on without waiting for a response. "I met this girl at the store. Her name's Jolie. Isn't that a great name? And she's my age. We'll be in the same class at school. She says the teacher is really great. Her name's Mrs. Peterson. She's been here like forever, but everyone loves her, because she's so nice."

"Really?" Savannah said, since Hannah didn't seem to expect much of a response. She was already rushing on.

"And guess what else?" she said. "Jolie says there's going to be caroling in town tonight and that everyone will be there, so we should come, too." She regarded Savannah hopefully. "Can we, please?"

Savannah instinctively thought of how uncomfortable Trace had been when she'd asked him to sing carols at the house the night before. She glanced at him.

"I think it sounds like a wonderful idea," he said with apparent sincerity.

Hannah grinned at him. "Jolie says they give out song sheets, so you'll know all the words."

"Then I definitely say we do it," Trace said. "Savannah?"

Being out on a cold, snowy evening two days before Christmas singing carols with her daughter and Trace? Savannah couldn't imagine anything more romantic. That probably meant she ought to say no, but of course she wouldn't. Not if it meant disappointing Hannah.

Sure, as if that were the real reason, she mentally scolded herself. She was going to do it because there was no place on earth she'd rather be tomorrow night.

"Yes," she said, noting the smile that spread across Hannah's face. It was almost as bright as the warmth stealing through her.

Chapter 7

Savannah had the radio blasting as she got into a rhythm of applying paint to the walls of the first guest room. The beautiful deep shade of green brought the color of the evergreens in the surrounding forest inside. When the white trim was added, it would be reminiscent of the way the scenery looked right now with snow clinging to the trees' branches. She envisioned a thick, warm comforter in shades of green and burgundy on the queen-size bed, with aromatic candles to match on the dresser.

Glancing out the window, she caught a glimpse of Hannah building her first snowman and chattering happily, no doubt to Trace, though Savannah couldn't figure out exactly where he was. He'd been up to something, though for the life of her she couldn't figure out what it was. The instant they'd arrived home after lunch, he'd disappeared into Mae's den. She hadn't seen him since.

Despite her declaration that she intended to handle the painting task on her own, a part of her had been counting on his defiance of that. She'd expected him to show up by now, if only to critique her work, maybe try to coax a laugh out of her in his ongoing attempt to win that bet with Hannah. Instead, much as her ex-husband would have done, Trace had retreated to whatever work he considered more important.

Oh, well, this was her job, not his, she thought with a sigh. And a man she barely knew was hardly in a position to disappoint her.

Besides, the painting was going very well, she decided, as she stood back and surveyed the room. There was an elegance and warmth to the result. Once the finishing touches were in place—probably after she could hit the January white sales at the Boston department stores—it would be perfect.

Satisfied, she snapped the lid back on the can of paint and prepared to move on to another room, the one she thought of as the blue room, though at the moment it had faded wallpaper that needed to be stripped. It was already late afternoon, so she probably wouldn't get much of the stripping completed before they left for the caroling in town, but any progress on the messy task was better than none.

She was about to peel off her first chunk of paper when something that sounded a lot like a big-time power tool kicked on downstairs, followed by a muttered curse, then giggles and deep, booming laughter. Savannah went to the top of the stairs and looked down just in time to see Hannah and Trace cast a furtive look in her direction.

"Uh-oh, we're busted," Trace said.

"If she heard you cussing, she'll probably send us to our rooms," Hannah said, looking downcast.

Hands on hips, Savannah scowled at them. "What are you two doing?"

"Nothing bad, Mom. Honest." Hannah's expression was filled with sincerity.

"Trace?"

"She's right. It's just a little surprise," he said.

Savannah remained skeptical. "A surprise, or a shock?"

Hannah giggled. "Mom's not real good with surprises."

"Maybe because I've had so many bad ones," Savannah said. "By the way, I'm not hearing any reassuring explanations. Do I need to come down there?"

"No," they both said at once.

The quick chorus only roused her suspicions further. She started down the steps, only to have Trace take the bottom steps two at a time and meet her when she was less than halfway down. Putting both hands on her shoulders, he gazed into her eyes.

"Do you trust me?" he asked.

Now there was a sixty-four-thousand-dollar question. "I suppose," she said, hedging. Only Mae's faith in him was giving him her current benefit of the doubt.

"Well, you can," he said, clearly disappointed by the less than wholehearted response. "You need to go back to whatever you were doing and let Hannah and me finish up what we're doing."

She returned his gaze without blinking. "I was thinking of quitting for the day, maybe coming downstairs for a snack."

"I'll bring you a snack," he said at once. "Anything you want."

"An entire pint of your ice cream?"

"If that's what you want," he said at once.

"Okay, that's it. Something bad is going on down there, isn't it?" she said, trying to brush past him.

"Mom, please," Hannah wailed. "You'll spoil everything. It's not bad. I promise."

Savannah told herself that it was her daughter's plea, not the pleading expression in Trace's eyes that won her over. "You can't keep me up here forever, you know."

"Just another couple of hours," he said, looking relieved. "Still want that ice cream?"

"No, that was just a test."

He grinned. "I figured as much."

Savannah sighed. "I'm going back to strip wallpaper."

"Maybe you ought to take a break," he suggested. "Maybe take a long, leisurely bubble bath or something."

"Who has time for that?" Savannah grumbled. "This place isn't going to get fixed up by itself."

He tucked a finger under her chin. "When you start saying things like that, it's exactly the time when you need a break the most."

"This from a workaholic like you?" she scoffed.

"Actually that's something your aunt used to say to me every time I protested that I couldn't get away from the office to come visit. It got me up here every time," he said, an unmistakable hint of nostalgia in his voice. "And she was always right. I always felt better after a few days with her. I even got so I barely cracked open my briefcase the whole time I was here."

"Did she talk you into taking a bubble bath, too?" Savannah teased.

"Nope, but you probably could," he retorted, then added in an undertone, "especially if you were joining me."

Heat and desire shot through Savannah like a bolt of lightning. "Any bubble bath I take, I'll be taking alone," she told him, keeping her own voice muted.

"Too bad."

Before she made the fatal mistake of agreeing with him, she whirled around and went back upstairs. She started toward the room where she'd been about to work, then changed her mind and headed another floor up to her bathroom, where she poured some lavender-scented bubble bath into the tub and turned on the water, knowing that the sound would be enough to keep Trace's imagination stirred up. He wasn't the only one under this roof who had a wicked streak, she thought with satisfaction as she sank into the warm water. Hers had just been on hold for a while.

Unfortunately the memory of his suggestion that he join her and the sensual feel of the water against her skin combined to make the bath far less relaxing than she'd envisioned. In fact, she concluded as she stepped from the tub and wrapped herself in a thick terry cloth towel, it really was too bad that she wouldn't find Trace waiting for her in her bed. Thank goodness they were going caroling in a couple of hours. It was definitely going to take a blast of icy air to cool off her wayward thoughts.

"Quiet," Trace admonished Hannah when they heard Savannah moving around upstairs. Since they were due to leave for the caroling in less than a half hour, he figured they had five minutes, maybe less, before she started down from the private quarters on the third floor. He squeezed Hannah's hand. "Not a word till she gets all the way down and sees what we've done."

They'd only made a dent in the work that was needed to put Holiday Retreat back into shape for guests, but the outside of the front door and the exterior trim were now a bright red, the brass fixtures glistened and the foyer and living room floors were polished to a mellow sheen. Hannah had even fashioned some greens and ribbon into a decoration that had been hung from the brass knocker. In his opinion, with just a little effort, they had made a vast difference in the appearance of the inn. It looked as it had on his first few visits, before Mae had let some of the maintenance slip.

Beside him, Hannah was practically bursting with excitement as they waited for her mother.

"I should open the door," she whispered. "Otherwise, how will she know about the paint and the decoration?"

Trace grinned at her. "Good point. Why don't you sneak out the back door, run around to the front and open it when I give the word that she's almost down the steps? I'll make sure it's unlocked."

Hannah took off, thundering across the floor in her eagerness.

"Don't forget your coat," Trace called after her just as he heard Savannah's footsteps descending from the third floor to the second.

Since he didn't want Savannah to miss Hannah's grand entrance, he stepped into view as she started down the last flight and blocked her way. She paused halfway down, regarding him warily.

"I am not going back up," she told him.

"Never said you should."

"Then why are you standing in my way?"

"Am I in your way?" he asked, still not budging.

Savannah sighed heavily, just as Trace heard Hannah hit the porch running.

"You look lovely," he said in a voice meant to carry outside.

Her gazed narrowed. "Announcing it to the world?"

"Why not?" he said. "It's worth announcing."

At that instant he heard Hannah turn the doorknob. He stepped aside as the door burst open.

Clearly startled, Savannah looked straight at her daughter, then caught sight of the freshly painted door. Her eyes lit up.

"Oh, my," she said softly. "It's beautiful." She looked from Hannah to Trace. "Is that what you two were up to?"

"Only part of it, Mom," Hannah said. "Come down the rest of the way and look around some more."

As soon as Savannah stepped off the bottom stair, she glanced around, her expression puzzled.

"Down," Hannah said impatiently.

Savannah's gaze shifted to the floor with its brand-new shine. "What on earth?" There were tears in her eyes when she turned to Trace. "You did this? That's what I heard down here? I couldn't imagine the wood ever looking like this again. It's beautiful."

Hannah beamed at her. "I helped, Mom. Trace and I did it together."

"It's just a start," Trace said. "We only had time to do the foyer and the living room. We'll do the dining room tomorrow."

The tears in Savannah's eyes spilled down her cheeks. "I don't know how to thank you."

"You could start by not crying," Trace said mildly, stepping closer to brush the dampness from her cheeks. "We wanted to do something to help. Hannah made the decoration for the door. She's got a real knack for that sort of thing."

Savannah's gaze shifted to the greens. "Trace is right, sweetie. It's absolutely beautiful. Aunt Mae would be so pleased with all of this."

She turned to Trace. "I know you did it for her, but thank you."

It had started as something he wanted to do for Mae, but that wasn't how it had ended up. Trace realized he had done it to put that sparkle into Savannah's eyes, the sparkle that shimmered even through her tears.

"It was the least I could do," he said. "Now, do you want to admire our work some more, or shall we head into town for the caroling?"

"Let's go," Hannah said at once. "Mom can look at this forever when we come home."

Savannah laughed. "So much for savoring the moment."

"I made you laugh," Hannah gloated. "That's a whole bunch of points for me and hardly any for Trace. Those sundaes are mine!"

"Ah, well," Trace said with an exaggerated air of resignation. "I suppose the art already on my office wall will have to do."

Savannah was quiet on the ride into town. Too quiet, in Trace's opinion. When they'd finally found a parking place a few blocks from the town square and Savannah was exiting the car, he pulled her aside. "Everything okay?"

"Of course," she said brightly, though her smile was as phony as that too-chipper tone.

"Tell me," he persisted.

She sighed. "I was just thinking about all the Christmases I missed with Aunt Mae, years when I could have had this, instead of...well, instead of what we had."

"You can't go back and change things," Trace reminded her. "You can only learn from your mistakes and look ahead."

She regarded him intently. "Are there things about your life that you'd change, mistakes you regret?"

He hesitated over the answer. "I wish things had been easier for my mother," he said slowly. "But I was a boy. I had no control over that. She made her own choice to stay married to a dreamer who was very good at criticizing everything *she* did, but did nothing himself."

A half smile touched Savannah's lips. "You say that, but you sound as if you still believe that you should have fixed it somehow."

"I suppose I do believe that," he admitted. "But by the time I had the money to make a difference in her life, it was too late. She'd already died of pneumonia. She'd let a flu go untreated too long, because my father thought she was making too much out of a little cold. Once she got to the hospital, there was nothing they could do. That was the beginning of the end for my dad. He was devastated. I finally saw that in his own way, he had felt my mother was everything to him. He died less than six months later."

"Oh, Trace, I'm so sorry," Savannah said.

He forced aside the guilt that the memory always brought. "Time to take my own advice. I can't change the past. I have to let it go. We all do." He managed a smile. "I think I hear a band warming up. It must be about time for the caroling to begin."

As if on cue, Hannah, who'd been hurrying ahead of them, bolted back. "Hurry up, you guys. The carols are starting. And I see Jolie. Can I go say hi to her?"

"Of course," Savannah said. "But then you come back to join us. Got it?"

"Got it," Hannah said, racing away from them.

Left alone with Savannah, Trace reached for her hand and tucked it through his arm. "This is nice," he said, looking into her shining eyes. "The stars are out. The air is crisp. I can smell the bonfire up ahead. It definitely feels as if Christmas is in the air. And there's a beautiful woman on my arm."

In the glow of the gas lamps on the street, Trace could see Savannah blush. If a simple compliment rattled her so, it must have been years since she'd heard any. Which made her ex-husband even more of a fool than Trace had imagined.

"You know, as much as I loved growing up in Florida," Savannah said, "this is the only place it's ever really felt like Christmas to me. Just look around. All the stores are decorated along Main Street. There's a tree in the center of the green that's all lit up, and snow underfoot. It's like a Currier and Ives Christmas card. What could be more perfect?"

She looked up into Trace's eyes, and he felt his heart slam to a stop.

"You," he said softly.

"What?"

"You're the only thing I can think of that's more perfect than all of this."

For the second time that evening, she was blinking back tears.

"Hey," he protested. "I didn't mean to make you cry again."

She gave him a watery smile. "It's just that no one's ever said anything so sweet to me before."

"Then you've been spending time with the wrong people," he said emphatically.

Suddenly she stood on tiptoe, and before he realized what she intended, she was pressing a kiss to his cheek. "Thank you. I'm really glad you're spending Christmas with us."

Trace could have let it go at that. It was a tender gesture, not an invitation, but the night was cold and that kiss promised heat. He captured her chin and gazed into her eyes, then slowly lowered his head until his mouth covered hers.

She tasted of mint and felt like satin. Then the anticipated heat began to work its way through his system, hinting of a simmering passion just waiting to be unleashed. He unzipped her jacket and slid his arms inside, pulling her close until their body heat mingled. She melted against him. They were a perfect fit, her curves soft and yielding, his body hard and demanding.

Trace could have been content to stay right here, doing nothing more than learning the shape and texture and taste of Savannah's mouth for hours on end, but sanity finally prevailed. This was a small town. Savannah was a newcomer. The last thing she needed was him stirring up gossip. Whatever happened between them—and there was little doubt that something would—he didn't want there to be regrets. Not of any kind.

With a sigh, he slowly released her. His gaze clung to hers as he slid the zipper of her jacket up, then tucked her scarf more securely around her neck.

"Trace, what…?" She swallowed hard. "What was that about?"

"New beginnings," he suggested. He drew in a deep breath of the cold air, then added, "And speaking of that, I had an idea I thought I'd run by you."

"If it's anything like that last one, the answer's yes," she replied, amusement threading through her voice.

"Don't agree until you've heard it," he said. "What about holding an open house at the inn tomorrow before midnight church services? The downstairs rooms can be ready by then, and it would get people talking about the place."

She was staring at him, her expression dazed. "Are you crazy? I can't be ready for an open house tomorrow night! Even if we could finish up with the downstairs rooms, what about food? We'd need wine and eggnog. All of the good dishes would have to be washed, the table decorated. I can think of a million reasons why it would never work."

He waited through the tirade, then asked, "Is that it? Any other objections?"

"I think those are quite enough."

"Okay, your turn to listen to me. I can have a caterer here first thing in the morning. He's already on standby. He'll bring all the food, the drinks, the table decorations, linens, crystal and china. All you need to do is say yes and stay out of his way." He pulled his cell phone out of his pocket. "What's it going to be?"

She regarded him with obvious astonishment. "You've already done all that?"

"I put it into motion, checked to make sure the caterer I use for our big marketing events was available. I haven't given the go-ahead. That's up to you. I thought it might be the perfect way for you and Hannah to get to know your neighbors, a way to let them know that the inn is back in business."

She looked torn. "It's a wonderful idea, but I can't let you do it."

"Why?"

"Because..." Her voice faltered. She frowned at him. "I don't know why exactly. It's just too much. Besides, how would we let people know?"

He sensed that she was weakening and pressed his advantage. "I think we can count on Hannah and her friend to take care of that. Say the word, and we can send the two of them through this crowd. It'll be faster than an instant-message e-mail."

"What if no one comes?" she asked worriedly. "It is Christmas Eve, after all. People have plans. Then you would've gone to all that expense for nothing."

"I'm not worried about that. I'm sure people are curious. Some are probably anxious to know if you intend to reopen the inn. It's been an historic landmark in the town for years. I think they'll be more than eager to take a little side trip on their way to church." He waited while the wheels turned in her head. He could practically see the pros and cons warring in her brain, as her expression shifted from dismay to hope and back again.

"You're absolutely certain we can pull this off?" she said at last. "It won't be the biggest mistake either of us has ever made?"

"Darlin', when it comes to business, I try really hard never to make mistakes."

"Okay, then," she said decisively. "Make that call. Then let's find Hannah and Jolie and put them to work."

Trace confirmed the plans with the caterer, who was eager to do anything for the bonus Trace had promised him. After that, finding the girls wasn't all that difficult. They were right in front, singing at the top of their lungs. Trace pulled Hannah aside and told her the plan.

"That is so awesome!" she said. "Jolie will help."

She pulled her friend over, introduced her to Trace and Savannah, then told her the plan.

"Sure," Jolie said at once. "I'll tell my mom and dad to spread the word, too. They know everybody.

And this will be way better than sitting around at home while my relatives say the same old things they say every year.''

"Tell them I'll appreciate whatever they can do to let people know," Savannah told her.

The two girls were about to race off when Jolie turned back. "I was supposed to ask you if it would be okay for Hannah to spend the night at my house tonight. A couple of my other friends are coming over, and my mom said it would be okay. She's right over there, if you want to meet her."

Trace saw the indecision on Savannah's face, but he also saw the anticipation on Hannah's. "Let's go over and say hello," he suggested. "You can discuss it with Jolie's mother."

Five minutes later, Savannah had given her approval for Hannah to spend the night at Jolie's. Donna Jones had been reassuring about the slumber party and enthusiastic about the open house at Holiday Retreat.

"I can't wait to see it," she said. "And I know all my friends are dying to meet you. Mae Holiday was loved and respected, and everyone wants to let you know that. You'll have a huge crowd. An open house on Christmas Eve is a lovely thing to do for the community."

Savannah looked relieved by her genuine excitement. "I'll see you then. What time should I pick Hannah up tomorrow morning?"

"Oh, don't worry about that," Donna said.

"You'll have enough to do. I'll bring her by around noon, unless you'd like her there earlier to help out."

"Noon will be perfect," Savannah said, just as the band began to play "Silent Night." She slipped her hand into Trace's and began to sing.

A sensation that felt a whole lot like contentment stole through Trace. Not that he was familiar with the concept. For all of his success, for all of the people who filled his life day in and day out, he'd never experienced a moment quite like this. Maybe there was something magical about the holidays after all.

Or maybe Mae had been even wiser than he'd realized. Maybe she'd known exactly how to grant wishes before they'd even been made.

Chapter 8

The bright-red front door closed softly behind Savannah, and she suddenly realized that she was all alone in the house with Trace. Her heart thundered in her chest as she met his gaze and saw the familiar heat slowly begin to stir.

As he had earlier, he reached for the toggle on her jacket zipper and slowly slid it down, his intense gaze never once straying from her face. His knuckles skimmed along the front of her sweater, barely touching it, yet provocative enough to have her breasts swelling, the peaks instantly sensitive.

"Tell me to stop now, if that's what you want," he said quietly.

"I…" Her voice quavered. She swallowed hard and kept her gaze level. "I don't want you to stop."

"Thank God," he murmured, his mouth covering hers.

Savannah hadn't expected the whirlwind of sensations that tore through her at his touch. Trace had kissed her before, each time more amazing than the last, but this was different somehow. Probably because of where it was destined to lead.

It had been so long since any man had wanted her, since she'd been open to feeling this reckless surge of desire. From the moment of her divorce, she had resolved never to let another man take away even one tiny bit of her control over her life or her body. In little more than a couple of days, Trace had made that resolve crumble. She'd wanted him almost from the moment he'd stepped into the kitchen on that first day.

The reaction then had been purely physical. Now it was so much more. She knew the kind of man he was, had seen for herself that the workaholic traits she despised covered a vulnerability spawned years ago. She knew he was kind and generous. Best of all, he'd had Aunt Mae's apparently unwavering faith. That stamp of approval alone would have been enough to convince Savannah that Trace was someone to be respected and admired...maybe even loved.

In one corner of her brain, she wanted to apply reason to all of the feelings he stirred in her, wanted to dissect them with logic, but the rest of her mind was clamoring for something else entirely. Majority wins, she thought, barely containing a giddy desire to laugh with sheer exhilaration.

And then Trace's tongue was teasing her lips, tasting her, and the last rational thought in her head fled. From that instant on, it was all about sensation, about dark, swirling heat and a racing heartbeat, about the brush of his hand over flesh, about the clean male scent of him and the way his eyes seemed to devour her as he gauged the effect of each lingering, provocative caress.

She felt a connection with this near-stranger that she hadn't felt in years with her ex-husband. It was as if Trace could read her mind, as if he knew exactly which part of her was screaming for his touch. Savannah knew he believed that Mae had brought them together with something exactly like this in mind. And maybe that was how it had happened. It hardly mattered, because it felt right. It felt as if she was exactly where she belonged with exactly the right man. Fate or Aunt Mae—it hardly mattered which— had brought them to this moment.

She was breathing hard and barely able to stand when he finally paused to take a breath. "Come upstairs with me," she said, then hesitated, suddenly uncertain. "That is what you want, isn't it?"

"Darlin', I've never wanted any woman more than I want you right this second," he said with flattering sincerity. "Are *you* sure, though? I don't ever want you to regret this."

"I've made mistakes and I have my share of regrets, but this won't be one of them," she said with total conviction.

She held out her hand and Trace took it. Together

they walked up the stairs, past the floor of guest rooms and on to the private quarters on the third floor. In recent years Mae had kept a small room for herself on the ground floor, but Savannah had opted for the privacy upstairs for herself and Hannah. She led Trace to her room, which had a panoramic view of the mountains lit by moonlight glistening on the snow.

She walked to the window and stood looking out. "Every time I look at this view, I feel this amazing sense of peace come over me. It's so incredibly beautiful."

She felt Trace come up behind her, his arms circling her waist.

"I think you're more beautiful," he said softly, his breath whispering against her cheek.

His hands slid up to her breasts, cupping them. As if the exquisite sensation weren't enough, the reflection in the window of his hands exploring her so intimately doubled the sweet tug deep inside her.

She was already shivering when his fingers slid beneath her sweater to caress bare skin. Eyes closed, she leaned back against his chest as he made her body come alive. Her breasts were heavy and aching before he undid the zipper on her jeans and repeated the delicious torment between her legs. She shuddered at the deliberate touches, each more intimate than the last, each coming closer to sending her over the edge.

She could feel the press of his arousal against her backside, could feel the heat radiating from him in waves. When she risked another look into the glass, she saw the tension in his shoulders, the hooded look in his eyes as he pleasured her. She'd never known a man could give so much without demanding anything in return.

The complete lack of selfishness inflamed her even beyond the effect of Trace's touch. Savannah turned in his arms, then slipped from his embrace. Her gaze locked with his, she stripped her sweater over her head, then let her already-unhooked bra fall to the floor. She knew the precise instant when he saw the reflection of her actions in the window, when that image merged with the one before him and deepened his desire.

She shimmied out of her jeans and panties, then reached for the hem of his sweater. She slid her hands over his chest, which felt like a furnace in the chilly room.

"One of us has way too many clothes on," he said in a husky growl as he tried to push her hands aside to relieve her of the task of ridding him of his sweater.

"Oh, no, you don't. I get to do this my way," she challenged.

A smile curved his lips. "By all means," he said. "Just hurry it up, will you?"

"Some things should never be rushed."

"And some things can't be stopped," he said, drawing her to him, bending down to circle each throbbing nipple with his tongue in a way that had her gasping.

The gesture pretty much destroyed her intent to torment him. Instead, she began to rush the task that only moments before she'd planned to draw out until he felt the same urgency she felt. Within seconds, they were both naked and moving toward the bed, knees weakened by exploring hands, desire ratcheted up to a height Savannah had never before experienced.

When Trace finally entered her, she was already crying out with the first explosive climax. He stilled while the pulsing sensations slowly died away. Then he began to move deep inside her, stirring her all over again, turning restless need into a demanding urgency that stretched every muscle taut with anticipation, until at last, with one sure, deep stroke, he took them both tumbling into a whirlpool of shuddering sensation.

Finally, still cradled in his arms, she fell into the first dreamless sleep she'd had in months.

Trace's heartbeat was easing, his pulse slowly quieting as he gazed down at Savannah. Such a sweet, innocent face to pack so much heat. If he hadn't been enthralled before, the last few hours would have been a revelation. She had a wicked, wanton streak that could lure a man into the fires of hell. Who would have thought it?

The strength and resilience he'd seen in her from the beginning took on new meaning when it came to making love. She'd all but exhausted him, yet he couldn't seem to stop looking at her—touching her— long enough to fall into desperately needed sleep.

Her porcelain-fine skin was still flushed, her hair tousled. Her chest rose and fell with each breath she took, drawing attention to breasts so perfect they took his breath away. Amazingly he wanted her again. In fact, he suspected that after tonight there would never come a day when he didn't want her.

Forever? The word he'd always avoided like the plague popped into his head and wouldn't go away. Forever meant commitment. It meant compromising, joining his life with someone else's, putting her needs above his own. Was he capable of such a thing? Or was he his father's son in that regard? His father had certainly never considered for a second what his irresponsible choices meant for the rest of the family. Trace had always made sure that there would be no one in his life to be affected by the choices he made.

Oh, really? This time when he heard the voice in his head, it was Mae's. More than once she'd scolded him for such self-deprecating comments. She'd pointed out that he had hundreds of employees who counted on him for their livelihoods, that he'd never once let them down, that he'd never let *her* down.

He let his gaze linger on Savannah. Was it possible that he could give her everything she needed? Everything she deserved?

And what about Hannah? Being a stepparent wasn't easy. Oh, they got along well enough now, but what if the rules changed? What if he were here all the time? Would she balk at any attempt by him to take the place of her father…in her life or in her mother's?

He chided himself for getting way ahead of himself. Just because he and Savannah were compatible in bed, just because they'd spent a couple of incredible days that felt magical, didn't mean there was a future for the two of them. She might not even want that. Hell, *he* might not want it. If ever there was a time for clear, rational thought, for not looking beyond the moment, this was it.

Just then, Savannah sighed deeply and snuggled more tightly against him. Heat shot through him. Heat and need. The need went beyond sex, he realized. He needed what she represented—steadiness, love, family—things he'd never imagined himself wanting.

It was his turn to sigh then, his turn to tuck his arms more tightly around her. Maybe morning was soon enough for answers. Maybe tonight was simply meant for feeling fresh, new, enticing emotions.

He breathed in her scent—flowers with a hint of musk—then pressed a kiss to her shoulder. In minutes, he was asleep.

Savannah lay perfectly still, her eyes closed against the brilliance of the sun and against whatever she might discover in Trace's expression. It had been so many years since she'd experienced a "morning after" that she had no idea what to expect. Awkwardness topped the list of possibilities, though.

"You're playing possum," Trace teased, his voice low and husky and warm as it whispered against her cheek.

"Am not," she denied, feeling a smile tug the corners of her mouth.

"Come on, Sleeping Beauty, wake up. We have a million things to do today."

"I don't suppose any of them include staying right here in bed?" she asked wistfully.

"Afraid not."

To her relief, he sounded as disappointed about that as she felt. "And once Hannah's back under this roof, I suppose any more nights like this are out of the question, too."

"Your call, but I'd say that's the sensible way to go."

She opened her eyes then and met his gaze. Fighting against the uncertainty spilling over her, she asked, "Then this was a one-night thing?"

His gaze never wavered. "Not if I can help it," he said emphatically. "I think that's something we need to discuss in detail, don't you?"

Actions seemed vastly preferable to words in Savannah's current frame of mind, but he was right. Talking was definitely indicated, someplace and at a time when temptation wasn't inches away.

"I suppose there's enough time for me to do this," he murmured after a quick glance at the clock on the bedside table. "And this."

Kiss followed kiss until Savannah was writhing and crying out for him to slide inside her. The sweet urgency, the rush for one more taste, one more touch, made their joining even better than any they'd shared during the night before.

"Now we really do have to get up," Trace said with obvious regret. "The caterer will be here in an hour, and I've got to polish the dining room floor and be out from underfoot when he gets here."

"I'll fix breakfast," Savannah said. "And clean up the kitchen."

Trace's heated gaze roamed over her. "Or we could take a leisurely shower together, and to heck with breakfast and polishing the floor."

She grinned. "I think breakfast is highly overrated anyway."

"Not a sentiment you should be sharing with prospective guests," Trace advised as he scooped her up and carried her to the shower.

They were still damp and barely dressed when the doorbell rang.

"Nick of time," he said with a wink. "I'll get it. You might want to see if you can tone down that blush before you meet Henri. He's French and considers himself an expert on the nuances of romance. One glimpse of you, and he'll be offering more unsolicited advice than you ever dreamed of."

"Heaven help me," Savannah said wholeheartedly. "I'll be down in a minute...or an hour. However long it takes."

When Trace had gone, she sat down at her dressing table and studied her face in the mirror. He was right. She was flushed in a way that was entirely too revealing. Even so, she couldn't seem to stop the grin that spread across her face.

"Get a grip," she told herself firmly. "Tonight's too important for you to be frittering away time up here."

But no matter how important tonight was, she had

a very strong hunch it wouldn't hold a candle to last night, especially if Trace refused to share her bed again.

By eight-thirty, Savannah knew that the open house was going to be a roaring success. Neighbors were crowded into every room, sharing holiday toasts, commenting on the delicious food as Henri basked in their compliments. Again and again, they had paused to welcome her and Hannah and tell them how delighted they were that Holiday Retreat would be reopened.

"My parents honeymooned here," Donna Jones confided when she caught up with Savannah during a quiet moment in the dining room. "My mother claims I was conceived here, since I was born almost nine months to the day after their wedding night."

Savannah grinned. "I'll bet I know which room," she said. "Aunt Mae always referred to it as her honeymoon suite, because it's the largest room here. Want to take a peek? The decorating isn't finished, but I painted it yesterday."

"Oh, I'd love to," Donna said, following her upstairs.

At the door of the freshly painted green room with its white antique iron bed, she turned to Savannah with a gleam in her eyes. "It's going to be beautiful." She moved to the window that faced the mountains. "And the view is fabulous. I wonder if I could convince my husband to sneak off here for a weekend sometime."

Savannah heard the wistfulness in her voice and

considered it thoughtfully. "You know, it might not be a bad idea to offer an introductory weekend getaway special for locals. People get so used to living in a place like this, they forget that the tourists who come here see it entirely differently."

"And it seems silly to spend money to stay just a few miles from home," Donna said enthusiastically. "But if it were a special promotion, I'll bet you'd be jammed with reservations. There's no better way to build word-of-mouth. People would start sending all their out-of-town guests here. It could fill in the slack once ski season dies down."

"I'm going to do it," Savannah said, delighted by the whole idea. "And for giving me the idea, your stay will be free."

"Absolutely not," Donna protested. "That's no way to start a business."

"Sure it is. You'll tell everyone you know how fabulous it is, so when I offer the promotion, it will be sold out in minutes."

As they walked back downstairs, Donna regarded Savannah with open curiosity. "So, what's the story with you and Trace Franklin? I'm sorry if I'm being nosy, but everybody in town remembers his coming to visit Mae. A handsome, single man who owns his own company is bound to stir up comment. Have you known him long?"

Savannah felt a now-familiar flush creep into her cheeks. "Only a few days," she admitted.

"My, my," Donna teased, "you work fast! I know a lot of women who tried to get to know him on his prior visits, and he never gave any of them a second glance. Last night he couldn't take his eyes off of you, and, if anything, he's watching you even more intently tonight.''

''We're just—''

''If you say you're just friends, I'll lose all respect for you,'' Donna teased. ''Any woman who doesn't grab a man like that ought to have her head examined.''

''Talking about me, by any chance?'' Trace inquired, stepping up beside Savannah and slipping an arm around her waist.

Savannah felt her face heat another ten degrees. ''We were talking about—'' she frantically searched her brain for a suitably attractive, sexy bachelor ''—Kevin Costner.''

Trace regarded her with amusement. ''Oh? Is he in town?''

''No, but we do like to dream,'' she said, as Donna coughed to cover her laughter.

Trace leaned down to whisper in her ear. ''Liar,'' he said softly.

''I think I'll go chat with my husband and tell him about your offer,'' Donna said. She grinned at Trace. ''Nice to see you again. Merry Christmas.''

''You, too,'' he said.

When Donna had gone in search of her husband, Savannah lifted her gaze to meet Trace's. ''I think the party's a success. Thank you for talking me into it.''

''It's been fun,'' he said, as if that surprised him just a little. ''Mae's introduced me around before, but this is the first chance I've had to really talk to some of the locals. They're good people, and they really are delighted that you're reopening the inn. Not only has this place been a boon to the economy, its history and charm provide something that the chain hotels can't. I didn't realize that in its heyday, Holiday Retreat employed several full-time people on staff and that the dining room was open to the public for dinner. Is that part of your plan, as well?''

"Eventually," Savannah said. "I'm going to have to take things slowly, so that I don't get overextended financially. Once all the rooms are ready for paying guests, then I can start thinking about whether to offer more than breakfast. I can cope with making eggs or French toast—I'm not so sure I could handle gourmet dinners. And I know I can't afford any help yet."

"Your spaghetti was pretty good," he said.

She frowned at him. "Somehow I doubt that's up to the standard the guests would expect. Remind me and I'll show you some of the old menus. Mae stopped doing the dinners about ten years ago, when it got to be too much for her, but she saved all the records. Since she left the file right where she knew I'd find it first thing, I'm sure she was hoping that I'd open the dining room again in the evenings."

The rest of the party passed in a blur. Soon guests were putting on coats, thanking Savannah for having them over and leaving for the Christmas Eve services planned by the local churches. When the last guest had departed, Hannah found Savannah and Trace standing on the front porch.

"Mom, this was the best. I must have met everybody in my class at school. I can't wait to start after New Year's. And there's going to be an ice skating party in a couple of days and I'm invited. Isn't that totally awesome?"

"Totally," Savannah agreed.

Trace grinned. "Then you're back to being happy about living in Vermont?"

"Absolutely," Hannah said. "Can we go to church now?"

Trace glanced at Savannah. "What about it? Are you too tired?"

"I'm tired, but exhilarated. Besides, going to Christmas Eve services was always part of the tradition. I'll grab my coat."

Trace drove into town, which was teeming with many of the same families who had just left Holiday Retreat. They were all walking toward the various churches within blocks of the town square. Bells were ringing in the clear, crisp air.

As they entered the same little white chapel Savannah had attended with her family so many years ago, the scent of burning candles, the banks of red poinsettias by the altar, the swell of organ music, all combined to carry her back to another time. A wave of nostalgia washed over her.

How had she let moments like this slip away? As a child, she'd had no choice, but she could have insisted on coming back as an adult, even if she'd had to leave Rob behind to sulk in Florida. His mood had always been sullen around the holidays anyway. What would it have mattered if it got a little worse because she was sharing an experience like this with their daughter?

Ah, well, those days were behind her. She glanced at Hannah and saw the wonder in her eyes as the choir began to sing "O, Holy Night." Trace slipped his hand around hers as the familiar notes soared through the tiny, crowded church.

Savannah's eyes filled with tears at the beauty of the moment. Trace regarded her with such a concerned expression that she forced a watery smile. "Merry Christmas," she murmured.

"Merry Christmas, angel."

Hannah heard the murmured exchange and beamed at both of them. "Merry Christmas, Mom. Merry Christmas, Trace. I don't care if we don't have presents, this is the best holiday ever."

Gazing into Trace's eyes, Savannah couldn't help but agree with her daughter. It was definitely the best one ever.

Chapter 9

Savannah was hearing bells. Convinced it was a dream, she rolled over and burrowed farther under the covers.

"Mom! Mom! You've got to see this! Hurry!" Hannah shouted, shaking Savannah.

Groaning, Savannah cracked one eye to stare at her daughter. "This had better be good." She and Trace had sat up talking until well past midnight, and if she wasn't mistaken, the clock on her bedside table said it was barely seven. Even if it was Christmas morning, she had counted on at least another hour's sleep, especially since Hannah wasn't expecting Santa's arrival.

"It's not just good," Hannah said, clearly undaunted by her testy tone, "it's fantastic. Come on, Mom. Hurry. I'm going to wake up Trace."

"Wait!" Savannah shouted, but it was too late. Hannah was already racing down the stairs screaming for Trace. Savannah heard his groggy reply, which amazingly was far less irritated than her own had been. In fact, he sounded downright cheerful.

Even with all that commotion right downstairs, Savannah could still hear those bells, louder and more distinct now. She tugged on her robe and went to the window, then stood there, mouth gaping at the sight that greeted her.

There was a huge, horse-drawn sleigh coming through the snow toward the house, the bells on its reins jingling merrily. The back was piled high with sacks and wrapped packages. And the driver was... She blinked in disbelief and looked again. Nope, no mistake. The driver was Santa himself.

Savannah whirled around and headed for the stairs, pausing only long enough to run a brush through her hair and take a swipe at scrubbing her face and teeth. She met Trace at the second-floor landing. Hannah was already downstairs with the front door thrown open to allow in a blast of icy air.

Savannah studied Trace's expression, looking for evidence of guilt. "What do you know about this?"

"Me? I have no idea what you mean."

"Santa? The sleigh piled with gifts? It has your name written all over it."

"Actually I don't think you'll find that's true," he said, giving her a quick kiss. "Stop fussing and go down there. Santa's a busy fellow. I doubt he has all day to hang around here."

"Trace!"

"Go," he said, waiting until she led the way before following along behind.

They arrived downstairs just as Santa trudged up the steps toting two huge sacks. Still filled with suspicion, Savannah stopped him in his tracks. "Are you sure you have the right place?"

"Holiday Retreat?" he said, edging past her. "You're Savannah Holiday, right? And that young lady out there by the sleigh is Hannah?"

"Yes."

"Then this is definitely the place. Even after such a long and busy night, I try not to make mistakes. Sorry about not squeezing down the chimney the traditional way, but if I go home with this suit all covered with cinders, Mrs. Claus will have my hide."

Savannah barely managed to suppress a chuckle. "I had no idea Mrs. Claus was so tough on you."

The jolly old man with a weathered face and white beard, who looked suspiciously like Nate Daniels, rolled his eyes. "You have no idea. Now, where would you like these gifts?"

"Under the tree, I suppose."

"And that would be?"

"Inside, in the living room on the right."

Santa carried two loads of packages inside, declined Savannah's offer of hot chocolate, then left with a cheery wave and a hearty "ho-ho-ho" that echoed across the still air. Hannah stared after him, still wide-eyed.

"Mom, do you think that was really Santa?" she asked.

Savannah exchanged a look with Trace, trying to gauge from his reaction whether her guess about Nate Daniels was correct. Before she could respond, Trace spoke up.

"Looked exactly like Santa to me," he said. "And you said you weren't going to have presents this Christmas, so who else but Santa would bring them?"

"Oh, I have some theories about that," Savannah muttered under her breath, but she kept her opinion to herself. She might have a few words for Trace later in private, but she was not going to strip that excitement from her daughter's eyes. "How about breakfast before we open gifts?"

"No way!" Hannah protested. "I want to see what's in the boxes, especially that great big one. Santa could hardly get it up the steps."

"You know that Christmas is about more than presents," Savannah felt duty-bound to remind her.

"I know, Mom, but these are here and some of them are for me. I checked the tags."

"Only some? Who are the others for?"

"You, silly. And Trace."

"Me?" Trace said, looking more shocked than he had at any time since this incredible morning had begun.

Savannah studied him intently. His surprise seemed genuine. Was it possible he wasn't behind this? Or at least not all of it? Curious to find out for sure, she acquiesced to Hannah's pleas and followed her into the living room.

"Big box first," Hannah said, rushing over to it. "Okay?"

"Your call," Savannah agreed.

The big box turned out to contain skis and ski boots. Hannah immediately had to try them on. "These are so totally awesome," she said, then wailed, "but I don't know how to ski."

"Maybe Santa thought of that," Trace suggested, his expression innocent.

Hannah's expression brightened at once. She began ripping open her remaining presents in a frenzy, *oohing* and *aahing* over each toy, over a new ski jacket and finally over the certificate for ski lessons that came in a deceptively large box.

Though a part of Savannah wanted to protest the degree of excess, she couldn't bring herself to spoil the moment.

"Your turn now, Mom," Hannah said, bringing her a comparatively small box that seemed to weigh a ton.

"What on earth?" Savannah said, when she tried to lift it. She began carefully removing the wrapping paper until Hannah impatiently ripped the rest away, then tugged at the tape on the box. Inside, nestled in packing chips and tissue paper, was a tool kit, painted a ladylike pink but filled with every conceivable practical tool she could ever possibly need.

Her gaze shot to Trace. How had he guessed that she would prefer a gift like this to something totally impractical?

"It's perfect," she said, her gaze locked with his.

"Santa must know you pretty well," he agreed.

"Mom, there's a huge box here for you, too," Hannah said, shoving it across the floor.

This time she discovered a floor polisher, precisely the kind she would need if she was to keep the inn's floors gleaming. For most women, an appliance on Christmas morning would have been cause for weeping, but Savannah's heart swelled with gratitude.

"Wait, Mom. There's something little tucked inside with a note," Hannah said, her expression puzzled as she handed it to Savannah.

At the sight of the jewelry-size package, Savannah's breath caught in her throat. Her gaze shot to Trace, but he looked as puzzled as Hannah had. Then she caught sight of the handwriting on the envelope. It was Aunt Mae's.

Tears stung Savannah's eyes as she opened the note.

My darling girl,

I hope you are happily settled in by now and that you will love your new home as much as I have over the years. I've done what I could to be sure you find joy here.

Here's something else I hope will bring you happiness. It belonged to your great-great-grandmother.

With all my love to you and Hannah. I wish I could be there with you this morning, but

please know that wherever I am, I will always
be looking out for you.
Mae

Savannah sighed and blinked back tears. Finding
Mae's present tucked amid all the others made her
question everything. She'd been so sure that Trace
had sent them, but now? Recalling Santa's resemblance to Nate made her wonder if Mae hadn't been
behind this whole magical morning.

"Aren't you going to open it?" Hannah asked,
leaning against her and regarding the box with evident
fascination.

Savannah slipped off the wrapping paper, then
lifted the lid of the velvet box. Inside, on a delicate
gold chain, was an antique gold cross. The workman-
ship was exquisite. The gold seemed to glow with a
soft light of its own. She could remember Mae wearing this cross every day of her life. She had always
said it symbolized faith itself—so fragile yet
enduring.

She opened the delicate clasp, slipped on the neck-
lace, then fastened it. The gold felt warm against her
skin, as if it still held some of Aunt's Mae's body
heat. Once more, her eyes turned misty. She felt Trace
take her hand and give it a squeeze.

"Merry Christmas," he said quietly.

"Wait!" Hannah said. "There's another box. It's
for you, Trace."

Once more, he looked completely disconcerted.
Hannah gave him the present. He handled it gingerly,
studying the large, flat box with suspicion.

"What does it say on the tag?" Savannah asked, curious herself.

"Just Trace," he said. "No other name."

"Must be from Santa, then," she teased.

He slipped open the paper, then pulled out the box and lifted the lid. The grin that broke over his face was like that of a boy who'd just unexpectedly received his heart's desire.

"What is it?" Savannah asked, trying to peer over his shoulder.

"It's the biggest, mushiest card I could make," Hannah said, grinning. "And Mrs. Jones took me to get it framed so Trace could hang it on his office wall."

Trace stared at her, looking completely mystified. "But I lost the bet."

"I know," Hannah said delightedly. "But I could tell you really, really wanted the card, so I made it anyway." She threw her arms around his neck. "Merry Christmas!"

To Savannah's shock, there was a distinct sheen of tears in Trace's eyes as he hugged her daughter.

"It's the very best present I ever received," he told her with such sincerity that Hannah's whole face lit up.

If this didn't stop, Savannah was going to spend Christmas morning bawling like a baby. She was about to head for the kitchen to start on breakfast, when Trace grabbed her hand and halted her.

"Wait. I think there's one more present for you, Savannah," he said, pointing Hannah toward a flat box beside the chair where he'd been sitting earlier. "Bring that one to your mom."

The box weighed next to nothing, but when Savannah tore off the paper and looked inside, her mouth dropped open. "Stock certificates?" she asked, turning to Trace. "In Franklin Toys? I can't possibly accept such a gift from you."

"It's not from me," he said firmly. "Not directly, anyway. These were Mae's shares of the company. She gave me power of attorney to vote them for her during the last weeks of her illness, but she told me I'd know what to do with the shares after her death." He looked straight into Savannah's eyes. "I think she would want you to have them."

"But she left me the inn," Savannah protested. "And Franklin Toys is your company."

He grinned. "I hope you'll remember that when you vote, but in many ways the company was as much Mae's as it was mine. She'd want you to have the financial independence those shares can give you."

"But I don't know anything about running a corporation."

"You can learn," he said. "Or you can sell the shares back to me, if you'd prefer to have the cash. The choice is yours."

Savannah sat back, still filled with a sense of overwhelming shock and gratitude. And yet… She studied Trace carefully. "Is this really what you want to do? She gave you her power of attorney, not me. I think she wanted you to control these shares."

"She wanted me to do the right thing with them," he corrected. "And I think that's turning them over to you. They're yours, Savannah. My attorney took care of the transfer yesterday."

Once again, Savannah looked at the certificates. She had no idea what each share was worth in today's market, but it had to be a considerable amount. The thought that she would never again have to worry about money was staggering.

This truly was a season of miracles.

Christmas morning had been incredible. It was everything Trace had imagined, from the awe and wonder on Hannah's face to the amazement on Savannah's when she'd realized that her financial future was secure. Trace had given the two of them everything he knew how to give. He'd been deeply touched by their gratitude.

Somehow, though, it wasn't enough. He wanted more, but he had no idea how to ask for it, or even if he had the right to, especially after knowing the two of them for such a short time.

Struggling with too many questions and too few answers, he wandered into the kitchen where Savannah was just putting the turkey into the oven.

She turned at his approach, studied him for a minute, then gave him a hesitant smile. "Everything okay?"

"Sure. Why wouldn't it be?" he asked, feeling defensive.

"I'm not sure. You seem as if you're suddenly a million miles away."

"I've got a lot on my mind. In fact, if you don't need my help right now, I was thinking of taking a walk to try to clear my head."

"Sure," she said at once. "It'll be hours before the turkey's done, and everything else is set to go in the oven once the turkey comes out." She continued to regard him worriedly. "Want some company?"

Trace shook his head. "Not this time. I won't be gone long," he said, turning away before the quick flash of hurt in her eyes made him change his mind. How could he possibly think about what to do about Savannah if she was right by his side tempting him?

He heard her soft sigh as he strode off, but he refused to look back.

Outside the snow was a glistening blanket of white. The temperature was warmer than it had been, though still below freezing if the bite of wind on his face was anything to go by. He almost regretted the decision to take a lonely walk, when he could have been inside in front of a warm fire with Savannah beside him.

He headed for the road, then turned toward town. He'd only gone a hundred yards or so when Nate Daniels appeared at the end of his driveway. He was bundled up warmly, an unlit pipe clamped between his teeth. He paused to light the tobacco, then regarded Trace with a steady, thoughtful look.

"Mind some company?" he asked, already falling into step beside him.

"Did Savannah call you?" Trace asked.

"Nope. Why would she do that?"

"I think she was worried when I took off."

"She called earlier to wish me a merry Christmas, but that was hours ago," Nate said. He regarded Traced curiously. "Funny thing, she seemed to have the idea that I was over there this morning playing Santa. Where would she get a notion like that?"

"Santa did bear a striking resemblance to you," Trace said.

"You didn't tell her, though, did you? You let her go on thinking that Mae was behind all the gifts and that she was the one who conspired with me to bring them."

"Oh, she suspects I had something to do with it, but there were enough surprises to throw her off." He glanced at Nate. "So, if Savannah didn't call, what brings you out into the bitter cold?"

"The truth is, I was all settled down with a new book my son gave me for Christmas when I felt this sudden urge to go for a stroll."

"Really? A sudden urge?" Trace said skeptically.

Nate nodded. "Finding you out here, I'm guessing Mae put the thought in my mind."

Trace kept his opinion about that to himself. Maybe Mae did have her ways even from beyond the grave.

"Something on your mind?" Nate inquired after they'd walked awhile in companionable silence.

Okay, Trace thought, here was his chance to ask someone older and wiser whether there was such a thing as love at first sight, whether a marriage based on such a thing could possibly last.

"Do you think there's such a thing as destiny?" Trace asked.

Nate's lips didn't even twitch at the question. "'Course I do. Only a fool doesn't believe there's a reason we're all put on this earth."

"And that applies to love, too?"

"I imagine you're asking about you and Savannah," Nate said. "Now, granted I've only seen the two of you together once or twice, but looked to me as if there was something special between you. It's not important what I think, though. What do *you* think?"

"I don't know if I even believe in love," Trace said dejectedly.

"Well now, there's a topic with which I'm familiar," Nate said. "You know about Mae and me, I imagine."

Trace nodded.

"You probably don't know so much about me and Janie, my wife. Janie and I met when we were kids barely out of diapers," he said, a nostalgic expression on his face. "By first grade I'd already declared that I wanted to marry her, though at that age I didn't really understand exactly what that meant. Not once in all our years of growing up did I change my mind. Janie was the girl for me. We married as soon as I graduated from college, settled down right here and began raising a family."

He glanced at Trace. "Now that should have been a storybook ending, two people in love their whole lives, married and blessed with kids. But Janie's nerves started giving her problems. The kids upset her. Anytime I was away from the house for more than a few hours, she'd get so distraught, I'd find her in tears when I came home. The doctors checked for a chemical imbalance. They tried her on medicine after medicine, but slowly but surely she slipped away from me.''

Tears glistened in his eyes. "The day I had to take her to Country Haven was the worst day of my life. I told her she'd be home again, but I think we both knew that day wouldn't come. She's happy at Country Haven. She feels safe there. But there's not a day that goes by that I don't miss the carefree girl I fell in love with.''

"It sounds as though you still love her deeply," Trace said.

"I do," Nate said simply.

"Then what about Mae?"

"After Janie went into the treatment facility, Mae helped out with the kids from time to time. They adored her. They stopped by the inn every day after school, and she always had cookies and milk waiting for them. Soon enough, I took to stopping by, too. Mae was a godsend for all of us during that first year.''

He met Trace's gaze. "It's important that you know that nothing improper went on between us. I considered myself a married man and I loved my wife. But I loved Mae, too. Since you're not even sure if love exists, I don't know if you can understand that it's possible for a man to love two women, but I did. If I had thought for a single second that my friendship with Mae would hurt Janie, I would have ended it. But the truth was, there were times when Janie didn't even seem to know who I was, didn't seem to care that I was there to visit. That never kept me from going, but it did make me see that I didn't need to lock my heart away in that place with her. I gave Mae every bit of love I felt free to give her. I also gave her the freedom to choose whether to love me. I admired her too much to do anything less.''

He sighed. "Given the way of the world now, a lot of men would have divorced a wife like Janie and moved on. That wasn't my way. I'd made a commitment, and I honored it in the only way I knew how. And whether you believe it or not, I honored my commitment to Mae the same way.''

"I'm sorry you were in such a difficult position,'' Trace said. "It must have been heartbreaking.''

"Having Mae in my life was one of the best things that ever happened to me. I can't possibly regret that it couldn't have been more, except for her sake. She deserved better.''

"I think you made her very happy,'' Trace told him.

"I hope so,'' Nate said, then paused and looked directly into Trace's eyes. "There's a reason I'm telling you this. I always believed that one day Mae and I would be able to be together openly, that we'd marry and spend our remaining years together. Maybe even do a little traveling. We never had that chance.''

Trace understood what he was saying. "This is

your way or reminding me that life is short and unpredictable.''

"Exactly. If you love Savannah, don't waste time counting the days until it seems appropriate to tell her. Don't fritter away precious hours planning for the future. Start living every moment. I've lived a good long life, but I'm here to tell you that it's still a whole lot shorter than I'd like.''

They'd circled around and were back at Nate's driveway. "Think about what I said," he told Trace.

"I will," Trace promised. "Would you like to join us for Christmas dinner?"

"I would, but I'll be going out to see Janie in a while. She seems to like it when I come by to read to her.''

"Thank you for sharing your story with me," Trace said, genuinely touched that Nate had told him.

"Don't thank me. Take my advice." He grinned. "Otherwise, I have a feeling Mae will find some way to give me grief for failing her. That woman always did know how to nag.''

Nate was still chuckling as he walked slowly toward his house. Trace watched to make sure he didn't slip on the icy patches, then walked back to Holiday Retreat, his heart somehow lighter and more certain.

Chapter 10

For the life of her, Savannah couldn't read Trace's expression when he got back from his walk. She thought he looked more at peace with himself, but had no idea what that meant.

She was also still puzzling over his magnanimous decision to give her Aunt Mae's stock. Had that been his way of making her financially independent to ease his own conscience and rid himself of some crazy sense of obligation to look after her? Was that going to make it easier for him to pack his bags in a day or two and walk away? When he left, would he go with no intention of ever looking back on her or Holiday Retreat as anything more than a pleasant memory? If that happened, it would break Hannah's heart.

It would break Savannah's heart, too.

"How's the turkey coming?" Trace inquired, peering over her shoulder to look into the oven. "It certainly smells fantastic."

"Another hour or so," she told him, wishing he would stay right behind her, his body close to hers.

She stood up and turned slowly to face him, relieved that he didn't back away. She reached up and cupped his cheeks. "You're cold. How about some hot chocolate? Or some tea?"

"I'm fine," he said, slipping his arms around her waist. "I'd rather have a kiss. I'm sure it would do a much better job of warming me up."

Savannah tilted her face up for his kiss. His mouth covered hers and brought her blood to a slow simmer. She couldn't be sure if it was working on Trace, but her body temperature had certainly shot up by several degrees. She sighed when he released her.

"Warmer now?" she inquired with forced cheer.

"Definitely," he said, his eyes blazing with desire. "Too bad we can't send Hannah for a ski lesson right this second."

"Are you sure we can't?" Savannah inquired hopefully.

"Nope. They're all booked up at the lodge."

She stared at him, biting back a chuckle. "You actually checked?"

"Of course. I always like to know my options."

"Do we have any?"

"Afraid not."

"Oh, well, once we've eaten, I have it on good authority that the turkey will put us straight to sleep.

Maybe when we wake up, we'll have forgotten all about sneaking upstairs to be alone.''

"I doubt it," Trace said, his expression wry. "Besides, I promised Hannah we'd all go for a walk after dinner.''

"Why on earth would you do that? You just got back from a walk.''

"Which taught me the distracting power of exercise," he said. "Besides, maybe we can have another snowball fight, and I can tackle you in the snow.''

Savannah laughed. "Now there's something to look forward to.''

"Sweetheart, a frustrated man is willing to take any contact he can get.''

"Interesting. I would think the chill of the snow would be counterproductive.''

"I think I'd have to spend a month outdoors in the Arctic before it would cool the effect you have on me," he said with flattering sincerity. He tipped her chin up to look directly into her eyes. "By the way, let's make a date.''

"A date?''

He grinned. "You know, a man and a woman, getting together. A date.''

"Out on the town?''

"Or alone in front of a cozy fire.''

"Okay," she said with a surge of anticipation. "When do you want to have this date?''

"Tomorrow night?" he suggested.

The level of relief Savannah felt when she realized he intended to stay another day was scary. She had a feeling she wanted way too much from this man. Asking for a date—even making love—was hardly a declaration of undying devotion. She really needed to keep things in perspective and not get ahead of herself.

"Tomorrow would be fine. Maybe I'll see if Hannah can spend the night with Jolie again."

Trace grinned. "Best idea I've heard all day."

Savannah's heart beat a little faster at the promise beneath his words. The memory of the last night they had spent alone in this house brought a flush to her cheeks.

"Then I will definitely make it happen," she vowed. Because she was desperate for another one of those sweet kisses despite the risk of Hannah walking in on them, she backed away from Trace and moved to the stove, opening lids and checking on things that were simmering just fine only moments ago.

"Trace," she said without turning around, "if I ask you something, will you tell me the truth?"

"If I can," he said at once.

"You did make all the arrangements for Santa and the presents, didn't you?"

"Do you really want to know?" he asked, sounding vaguely frustrated. "Wouldn't you prefer to think it was part of the Christmas magic?"

She turned to face him. "Sure," she said honestly. "But I also believe in giving credit where credit's due. I'm not an eight-year-old who still believes in Santa, at least when it suits her. I know the kind of effort and money it takes to make a morning like the one we had happen. The person responsible should be thanked.''

He shrugged, looking as if her persistence made him uncomfortable. "Look, it was nothing, okay?"

"It was more than that and you know it. You made Hannah's Christmas, and mine."

"I'm glad," he said. "Can we drop it now?"

"Why do you hate admitting that you did something nice?"

"Because I didn't do that much. I just made a few calls, ordered a few little things. Nate was more than willing to play Santa, especially since he had that gift from Mae for you."

"Which was wonderful of him to do, but you bought me a floor polisher and a professional quality tool kit, for heaven's sakes."

"A lot of people would say that gift explains why I'm still single," he said.

"And I say it explains why I find you so completely and utterly irresistible," she said.

"Irresistible, huh?" A grin tugged at the corners of his mouth. "Come over here."

"Oh, no, you don't. We agreed that any more fooling around with Hannah underfoot would be a bad idea."

"Did we agree to that?"

"We did," she said emphatically.

"Does one kiss qualify as fooling around?"

"Probably not with a lot of people, but in my experience with you, it has a tendency to make me want a whole lot more."

His grin spread. "Good to know. I'll have to remember that tomorrow night."

Savannah met his gaze, her own expression deliberately solemn. "I certainly hope you do."

Trace woke up in a dark mood on the morning after Christmas. Rather than inflict his foul temper on Savannah or Hannah, he made a cup of coffee, then shut himself away in Mae's den and turned on his computer.

Even though he'd given his staff the week between Christmas and New Year's off, he checked his e-mails, hoping for some lingering piece of business to distract him. Aside from some unsolicited junk mail, there was nothing. Apparently other people were still in holiday mode. He sighed and shut the thing off, then sat back, brooding.

He'd spent the whole night wondering if he hadn't made the biggest blunder of his life the day before by giving Savannah that stock. It wasn't that he thought it was the wrong thing to do or that Mae would have disapproved. In fact, he was certain she'd known all along what he would do with her shares. No, his concern was over whether he'd given Savannah the kind of financial independence that would make her flat-out reject the proposal he planned to make tonight.

He was still brooding over that when the door to the den cracked open and Savannah peeked in.

"Okay to interrupt?" she asked.

"Sure," he said, forcing the surly tone out of his voice. "Come on in."

To his shock, when she walked through the door, she was wearing some sort of feminine, slinky night-gown that promptly shot his heartbeat into overdrive.

"On second thought," he muttered, his throat suddenly dry, "maybe you should change first."

"Why would I do that?" She glanced down. "Don't you like it?"

"Oh, yeah," he said huskily. "I like it. Maybe just a little too much."

Apparently she didn't get the hint, because she kept right on toward him. The next thing he knew, she was in his lap and his body was so hard and aching, it was all he could do to squeeze out a few words.

"What are you up to?" he inquired, staying very still, hoping that his too-obvious response to that wicked gown of hers would magically vanish. "Where's Hannah?"

"Gone," she said, brushing her mouth across his.

"Gone?"

"For the day," she added, peppering kisses down his neck.

"The entire day?" he asked, suddenly feeling more hopeful and a whole lot less restrained.

"She won't be home till five at the very earliest," Savannah confirmed. "I have Donna's firm commitment on that. She couldn't keep her tonight, so we compromised."

"I see," he murmured, sliding his hand over the

slick fabric barely covering her breast. The nipple peaked at his touch.

"Sorry my present's a day late," she said as she proceeded to unbutton his shirt and slide it away.

Trace gasped as her mouth touched his chest. "Oh, darlin', something tells me it will be worth the wait."

Savannah had never felt so thoroughly cherished as she did lying on the sofa in Trace's arms, a blanket covering them, as a fire blazed across the room. In a few short days, she had discovered what it meant to be truly loved, even if Trace himself hadn't yet put a label on his feelings. She wondered if he ever would.

She turned slightly and found him studying her with a steady gaze.

"You're amazing, you know that, don't you?"

She shook her head. "I'm just a single mom doing the best I can."

"Maybe that's what I find so amazing," he said. "You remind me of my mother."

"Just what every woman wants to hear when she's naked in a man's arms," Savannah said lightly.

He gave her a chiding look. "Just hear me out. You're strong and resilient. You've had some tough times, but you haven't let them turn you bitter. You've just gotten on with the business of living and making a home for Hannah. When I was a kid, I don't think I gave my mother half enough credit for that. I spent too much time being angry because she didn't tell my dad to take a hike. I realize now that she didn't see him the same way I did. She loved him, flaws and all. It was as simple as that, so she did what she could to make the best of his irresponsible ways.''

Trace caressed Savannah's cheek, brushing an errant curl away from her face. ''So, here's the bottom line. I meant to do this with a bit more fanfare, but since our date has turned out to be a little unorthodox, this part might as well be, too.''

He sounded so serious that Savannah went still. ''What's the bottom line?'' she asked worriedly.

''Will you marry me? I know we've just met and that you're still recovering from a divorce, but I've fallen in love with you. I talked it over with Nate—'' Savannah stared, sorting through the rush of words and seizing on those that made the least sense. ''You what?''

''Now don't go ballistic on me,'' Trace said, then rushed on. ''I ran into him yesterday. He saw that I had a lot on my mind, because I had all these feelings and I thought they were probably crazy, but he put it all in perspective for me. He said life is way too short to waste time looking for rational explanations for everything. I'm not all that experienced with falling in love, but apparently it doesn't follow some sort of precise timetable.''

Savannah's lips twitched at his vaguely disgruntled tone. ''No,'' she agreed. ''It certainly doesn't.''

''Then, again, I'm used to making quick decisions. And I do think it's exactly what Mae had in mind when she insisted I come here for Christmas.'' He met her gaze. ''And just so you know, with these quick decisions of mine, I rarely make mistakes.''

"Is that so?" Savannah said quietly. "Well, it's certainly true that Aunt Mae was an incredibly wise woman. She hasn't steered me wrong so far."

"Me, either," Trace said, regarding her warily. "So?"

"So what?"

"Bottom line? I've fallen in love with you. Something tells me that if I don't reach out for what I want with you now, it will be the biggest mistake of my life."

"Then reach," she said softly, her gaze locked with his.

Trace held out his hand. Savannah put hers in it, and for the first time in her life, Savannah felt as if she were truly part of a whole, something real and solid, with a future that was destined to last forever.

"There's something about this place," she said with a sense of wonder. "It must be Aunt Mae." She lowered her mouth to Trace's. "She always did get me the best gifts of all."

* * * * *

FAITH, HOPE AND LOVE
Beverly Barton

* * *

For my grandson, Mason Bryce Waldrep,
Grammy's precious little angel #2.

Dear Reader,

Writing a Christmas novella in THE PROTECTORS miniseries created a special challenge for me—how to incorporate the season of joy and peace into a romantic suspense love story. The idea for this story hit me as I was plotting my single title in THE PROTECTORS miniseries, *On Her Guard,* also available from Silhouette this month. In that book, two secondary characters began their own love story when Dundee agent Worth Cordell rescued shy, sweet Faith Sheridan, a nanny who had been abducted along with her charge, a billionaire's seven-year-old daughter. For Faith it was love at first sight, but hard-edged, tough guy Worth didn't believe in love or happily-ever-afters. However, Faith is certain that all he needs is time to realize his true feelings for her, so she arranges a date, time and place for them to meet—in six weeks, in the town square in her hometown, at eight o'clock on Christmas Eve. So that's how my novella, "Faith, Hope and Love" begins, with Faith, who has a happy secret to share, waiting in the Whitewood, South Carolina, town square for the man she loves.

This story combines several popular love story elements, including temporary amnesia, a secret baby and a heroine in jeopardy. Add to that the special ambience of the Christmas season in a small Southern town, a cast of special secondary characters and a deadly serial killer, and you have an emotionally charged, tension-filled holiday drama.

Enjoy!

Beverly Barton

Prologue

"I think that rain is going to change over to snow," Jody Crenson said as she gazed out the double windows in the living room of Faith Sheridan's duplex apartment. "You'd better not only take an umbrella, but wear a hat and gloves, too."

"I'm way ahead of you. I have my hat and gloves ready." Faith emerged from her bedroom carrying a brown knit hat and matching brown gloves. She laid both on top of her ankle-length camel tan wool coat hanging over the back of the sofa beside the closed umbrella. "I'll have to leave soon." She checked her watch again—for the tenth time in ten minutes. "We're supposed to meet at eight o'clock and it's nearly seven-thirty."

"The town square is only a ten-minute walk from here. You wouldn't be just a little overeager would you?'' As she turned from the windows, Jody grinned. ''Are you sure you don't want me to go with you? I'll disappear the minute he shows up.''

''I'll bring Worth back here and call you to come over and meet him. I promise. But once you meet him, I want you to make yourself scarce and go back to your apartment next door. Worth and I will have a lot of plans to make for our future.''

Jody forced a smile as she sauntered over to Faith and grasped her hands. ''Sweetie, nobody wants this to work out for you more than I do. But don't get your hopes up. I know what I'm talking about. I've had guys sweet-talk me into the sack, then forget my telephone number.''

''Worth didn't sweet-talk me. He's not like that.'' A sudden blush burned Faith's cheeks. ''I actually asked him to…well, you know.''

Jody shook her head. ''Ah, Faithie, I really hope the guy shows, but if he doesn't—''

''He'll be there,'' Faith said, with utter conviction. ''I know he loves me. And I'm sure by now he's figured out for himself just how much he loves me. We were meant to be together.''

''You're terribly in love with him, aren't you?'' Jody sighed. ''When you first told me about him— about the way you two met when he rescued you from those terrorist kidnappers over there in Subria—I thought you just had a major hero-worship crush on him. But it's more than that for you.''

''For him, too.'' Faith swung Jody's hands back

and forth, then released her and twirled around several times. "How do I look?"

"Lovely. I've never seen you looking prettier. You're absolutely glowing."

"That's because I'm in love and I'm happy and I'm—" Faith smiled broadly as she hugged herself. "Just think, less than two months ago I was a kidnap victim who could have been killed and now I'm home and safe and have a wonderful life ahead of me."

"If you and Worth decide not to come back here, you call me. Otherwise, I'll worry about you."

Faith picked up her hat and pulled it down over her long brown hair, the two almost identical in color, then she eased on her gloves and put on her coat. "If for any reason we don't come back here to my apartment, I'll let you know. But don't worry about me if I don't call until late. Worth may have made his own plans for us."

"If you aren't back by midnight and haven't called me, I'll send out the Highway Patrol."

Faith grabbed the umbrella and headed for the door. She glanced over her shoulder. "You're going to be my maid of honor, so you'd better start thinking about a fancy dress. Maybe something in velvet."

"Velvet will be kind of warm for a June wedding."

"We won't be waiting until June." Faith opened the door. "I'm sure when I tell Worth my news, he'll want us to get married right away."

"Your news?" Jody's eyes widened in a speculative stare. "What haven't you told me? And why haven't you told me?"

"Because I just took the test today."

"The test?"

"I've got to go. I want to be early, just in case Worth is."

Jody followed Faith out the door and onto the front porch that ran the length of the old house, which had been built in the thirties and later divided into two apartments.

"You're pregnant, aren't you?" Jody grabbed Faith's shoulder just as Faith opened the big tan umbrella.

Faith jerked away, went down the steps and out onto the sidewalk, then began skipping and humming "Singing In the Rain."

"Don't you dare leave here without telling me," Jody called after her.

"Yes, yes, yes," Faith sang out loud and clear. "I'm going to have Worth's baby and we're going to get married and live happily ever after."

Faith skipped away, the cold evening rain drizzling down all around her as she made her way up Somerset Avenue. She'd never been this happy in her entire life. Very soon she would have what she wanted most—a family of her own. She and Worth and their baby would be that family.

If anyone understood the way she felt, Jody did. They'd met when they were kids, both residents of the Whitewood Girls' Ranch for orphans outside of town. Faith had very little memory of her mother, who'd died in a car crash when Faith was three, but she had lots of wonderful memories of her father.

Alfred Sheridan had been a college professor. A shy, quiet man who'd been a gentle, loving parent. But her dad had been nearly fifty when she was born and suffered with heart problems that took his life when Faith was twelve. Without any close relatives, Faith had become an unwanted orphan. She wasn't particularly pretty and she'd always been shy. And not many people wanted to adopt a twelve-year-old.

Decked in holiday finery, with festive lights twined around roof lines, shrubbery and fences, the homes near downtown Whitewood proclaimed the season. When she passed the Dawsons' house, Horace barked at her from his dry perch on a footstool in front of the white wooden rockers on the front porch. Horace was a spoiled rotten, fourteen-year-old beagle. Lindsey Dawson opened the front door, lifted Horace off the stool, then threw up her hand to wave at Faith.

"Horace won't go out in the yard to do his business when it's raining like this." Lindsey shrugged. "What on earth are you doing out on a night like this? Don't you know it's suppose to start snowing any time now?"

Faith was in the church choir with Lindsey and they had become very friendly acquaintances since Faith's return to Whitewood a month ago. The Dawsons, Lindsey and George, were in their midfifties with three adult children who were spread out across the country; and none of them had given the couple grandchildren, much to Lindsey's consternation.

"I'm meeting Worth in the town square tonight," Faith said.

"Oh, dear me, I'd forgotten that your young man was coming to Whitewood on Christmas Eve. Such a romantic rendevous for the two of you."

Faith beamed with her happiness, feeling it through and through, as if this joyous feeling had taken over her body from the inside out. She wanted to shout from the rooftops that she was in love.

Within five minutes, she had made her way to Main Street. Last minute shoppers were scurrying about, rushing in and out of stores as they purchased Christmas presents. Whitewood, South Carolina—population 6,587—had seen its downtown area almost die out when a lot of businesses moved out near the four-lane highway back in the seventies. But in the late eighties, the townspeople had banded together to revitalize the buildings and the square between Main and Cherry Streets.

"Hey there, Faith." Margaret Tompkins stood in the doorway of her coffee and gift shop. "Off to meet Worth in the square?"

Faith stopped under the green awning over the doorway of Margaret's Goodies. "I thought you were closing up at seven tonight so you and Mr. Tippins could make it over to the Godfreys for their party."

"I had so many last-minute customers that I had to call Mr. Tippins to tell him I'd meet him there." Margaret frowned. "That Moselle Hutton had better not try to make time with my Mr. Tippins. The woman is nothing but a hussy."

"Well, if that's the case, you'd better hurry and lock up and get over to the Godfreys."

"You're absolutely right about that." Margaret's remarkably smooth face wrinkled slightly when she smiled. "Do bring Worth by to see me just as soon as you can."

"Yes, ma'am, I'll do just that."

Faith adored Margaret Tompkins, who'd given Faith her first after-school job when she'd been sixteen. And thanks to Margaret's kindness of keeping her employed at Margaret's Goodies, not only after school but in the summers, she'd been able to save enough money to buy an older model car when she was eighteen.

Margaret was what people had once referred to as an old maid; and sometimes Faith thought the sweet old woman—who was now seventy-four—saw a kindred spirit in Faith. But unlike Margaret, who had lost her fiancé during the Korean War, Faith was going to marry and have a family. And nobody was happier for her than Margaret.

The town square had been a part of Whitewood since the town's conception in the early 1800s. At Christmas the merchants decorated downtown Whitewood so perfectly that it looked like a winter wonderland, and the square was the pièce de résistance, the town's true showcase. The two gazebos were strung with white lights, green garland and huge frosty white bows. Inside one gazebo was a life-size Santa with a pack of presents on his back and Rudolph at his side. A group of five life-size carolers, song books in their hands, stood inside the second gazebo, and a taped selection of Christmas carols played twenty-four hours a day during the twelve days of Christmas. But the twenty-foot Christmas tree, decorated with thousands of sparkling white lights held the place of honor in the center of the square.

Faith scanned the square for any sign of Worth, thinking perhaps he'd been as eager as she for this night and had shown up early. But maybe Worth wasn't the type to be early or even on time for that matter. She knew so little about him, had so many things to learn. She didn't even know if he liked his coffee black or with cream and sugar. But they had the rest of their lives to become acquainted, to get to know each others' preferences.

Some people—like Jody—might think falling in love at first sight was a ridiculous notion, but Faith knew better. Well, maybe it hadn't been exactly at first sight, but within the first twenty-four hours. And once they had made love, she'd had no doubts that they were meant to be together forever.

Faith wandered around through the square, following the concrete sidewalk onto the brick walkway that led from one gazebo to the other. The recorded music blasted a cheery rendition of "Let It Snow." Peeking out beneath the umbrella, Faith saw no sign of snow. She held out her hand and several icy cold raindrops hit her knit glove. Suddenly a teenage couple came racing through the square, called out "Merry Christmas" to Faith, then ran across the street to the boy's parked Jeep. The kids jumped in, revved the motor and zoomed away.

Only two months ago she had been living on a Mediterranean island working as the nanny to billionaire tycoon Theo Constantine's seven-year-old daughter, Phila. She had loved her job and adored the Constantines and little Phila. Life had been pleasant and fulfilling. Faith truly believed that no job was as important as the care and nurturing of children. That's why she'd chosen a career as an au pair. But her idyllic life had ended abruptly when Phila and she had been kidnapped by a rebel terrorist group called the Al'alim, taken to the mountains in Subria and held for ransom.

In the end everything had turned out well, but Phila and she had endured a terrifying ordeal. Theo Constantine had hired his own small army to free them from their abductors and Worth Cordell had been Faith's personal rescuer. She would never forget his kindness the moment they first met. He had taken off his jacket and wrapped it around her because she'd been wearing nothing but a thin cotton gown. And when she'd cut her foot during their attempt to flee, Worth had swept her into his arms and carried her, keeping her safe.

Faith checked her watch. Five till eight. He'd be here soon. Then she'd take him back to her apartment, fix them cups of steaming hot cocoa and they'd cuddle on the sofa. The north wind picked up, whooshing fine pellets of sleet right into her face. Oh, dear, the rain had changed over to sleet.

But when Worth arrived, he'd take her into his arms and warm her immediately. Her mind recalled the night they'd spent together in the cave in Subria, the two of them, wet and cold. They'd stripped off naked, laid their clothes out to dry and cuddled together under a thin blanket in order to absorb each other's body heat. She'd been afraid that night might be her last night on earth, that by morning the Subrian rebels would find them and kill them. And one thing she'd known for sure was that she didn't want to die a virgin.

Suddenly the Methodist church bells rang out the hour. Eight o'clock. Faith listened, then smiled as memories washed over her. She'd never know where the courage had come from that night or how she'd been able to ask Worth to make love to her. Maybe it had been a courage born of fear. And Worth had been so sweet, so reluctant at first to take her. But in the end he had made sweet, passionate love to her and her life had changed forever.

Faith decided that she would stay warmer if she kept moving, so she walked around the square twice, then came back through it again. She checked her watch. Eight-twenty. Worth was late. Perhaps he'd run into bad weather on his trip from Atlanta. Or he could have gotten a late start, or taken a wrong turn.

Faith glanced across the street to see if Margaret had closed up shop. She had. All the stores on Main and on Cherry were closed. And there was no one on the streets. Occasionally a car passed, but there was no other sign of life. People were either home with their families, at holiday parties, or congregated in local churches for Christmas Eve services.

Her feet were cold, despite the thick socks she wore. And her hands were like ice under the knit gloves. *Where are you, Worth… Where are you?*

They had said goodbye in Subria six weeks ago, but they had agreed to meet here in the Whitewood town square at eight o'clock on Christmas Eve. If Worth loved her, he would be here. He'd promised. And she believed with all her heart and soul that Worth loved her as she did him. *He's just running a little late, that's all. He'll be here soon.*

For over a week she had suspected she might be pregnant. They hadn't used any protection when they'd made love. And Faith's monthly period was usually as regular as clockwork. This morning she had driven over to Greenville to a drugstore and bought a home pregnancy kit. She thought it best not to let the entire town of Whitewood find out about her condition—not until after she and Worth were married. She'd been excited at the thought of carrying Worth's child, but then she'd wondered how he'd feel about having a baby so soon. After all, even she had planned for them to actually date a few months before they got married. Originally she'd thought a June wedding was ideal, but now they'd have to push up the date. Maybe a New Year's wedding. Something simple at the church with only Jody and Margaret and perhaps the Dawsons.

The Methodist church bells chimed the hour. Nine o'clock. How was it possible that she'd been here for a whole hour? Of course, she was so cold that her hands and feet felt numb. What had happened to

Worth? Why was he an hour late? She knew that if he'd been detained, he would have contacted her. After all, it wouldn't be that much trouble to get her home phone number. She was the only Faith Sheridan living in Whitewood. Oh, God, what if he'd had a wreck? No, she refused to consider the possibility. Worth was on his way here and would show up any minute now.

Suddenly Faith looked through her moist eyes and noticed it was snowing. She sighed deeply and hugged herself, settling down on a bench to wait. When Worth arrived, their reunion would take place with snowflakes falling all around them. It would be like a scene from an old movie. Lovers reuniting in the town square on a snowy Christmas Eve.

Time passed, but Faith wasn't sure how much time. And when she heard Jody's voice calling her, she tried to open her eyes, but couldn't. Was she asleep? No, she couldn't be asleep. She was in the square waiting for Worth. He would be here any minute now.

Jody began shaking Faith as she repeated her name and said, "Wake up, Faithie, wake up. My God, how long have you been lying here on this bench, out in the snow? Come on, honey, let's get you up on your feet. I'm taking you to the hospital right now."

"The hospital?" Faith managed to speak, but even to her own ears her voice sounded weak. "Why do I need to go to the hospital?"

"Oh, honey, you've been sitting out here in the snow, waiting for that damn man for over four hours."

She felt Jody lifting her to her feet, then putting an arm around her and urging her to walk.

"What—what time is it?" Faith asked.

Before Jody could reply, the church bells rang out twelve times. Midnight. And Worth hadn't shown up yet.

"I can't leave," Faith said. "Worth might—"

"Damn it, Faithie, he's not coming. The guy's a no-show."

As Jody led Faith to her car, she heard her friend grumbling, "Men! They love you until they've had you, then it's on to the next woman. But don't you worry, honey, we'll be all right. You don't need him. You'll get by just fine without him."

"Worth," Faith whispered. "Worth, where are you?"

Worth Cordell woke from a drug-induced sleep in the ICU of an Atlanta hospital...or he assumed he was in Atlanta. He glanced around the meticulously sterile room. Pale-green walls. No windows. An array of tubes and wires hooking him to various machines. The quiet hum of nurses as they went about their duties within the intensive care facility.

What the hell am I doing here? he asked himself.

His brain was fuzzy. His body ached, but it was a medicated ache that told him his true pain was being masked by some high-powered medicine. Worth felt as if his right leg had been run over by an army tank.

His right leg! Now he remembered. He'd been shot. He tried to raise himself up enough to look at his leg, to make sure it was still there. During his time in the Rangers he'd seen guys get their legs blown off and later in the hospital say they could feel their missing limb.

A strong, feminine hand came down over Worth's chest and gently eased his head down on the pillow. "Lie still, Mr. Cordell. Don't try to move around. Not yet."

"Tell me something." Worth looked squarely at the brown-eyed, middle-aged nurse.

She glanced down at him and smiled. "What would you like to know?"

"Is my leg still there?" he asked.

"Your leg?" Her smiled widened. "Your leg is very much there and it's healing nicely. We should be able to transfer you to a private room by this time tomorrow."

"Thanks."

"You're welcome. Is there anything else I can do for you?"

"I'm not sure. I'm a bit crazy-headed right now."

"Your mind will clear up once we reduce your medication. Now take it easy and—" she pointed to a series of buttons attached to the railing on his hospital bed "—if you need anything, just punch right here and one of us will check on you."

Worth nodded.

The nurse paused at the doorway, glanced over her shoulder and said, "Merry Christmas, Mr. Cordell."

Merry Christmas?

"Is today Christmas Day?" he asked.

"Yes, it is."

"How long have I been in here?"

"You were brought into the E.R. three days ago, on the twenty-second, and Dr. Winthrop did emergency surgery. He saved your life and your leg."

"I am in Atlanta, aren't I?"

"You're in Piedmont Hospital and you've had visitors every day, but you probably don't remember."

"Visitors?"

"Your co-workers from the Dundee agency. A Mr. Sawyer, a Mr. Shea and a Ms. Evans."

"Oh, yeah, my co-workers."

Worth tried to remember exactly what had happened to him, but his memory was messed up. He'd been on an assignment, here in Atlanta, providing private security for some rock star in town for a Christmas concert. He could recall that much, but nothing about the particulars. When one of the guys from Dundee's came back to the hospital, he'd find out the details.

Lying there, his leg aching and his stomach rumbling—when had he eaten last?—he suddenly remembered that he'd had a very important date on Christmas Eve. Faith! He was supposed to have met her in Whitewood, South Carolina, at eight o'clock in the town square.

Well, by now, she realized he wasn't going to show up. She must have been really disappointed. Hell, he'd had every intention of meeting her. He'd owed her that much. After he had rescued her from kidnappers and gotten them back to safety, she'd developed a major crush on him. And he had developed a major case of the hots for her.

Maybe it was better for her—for both of them—that he hadn't been able to meet her. Being laid up in the hospital this way, he had saved them both from an unpleasant scene. He had planned to tell Faith that he wasn't the right man for her, that he wasn't the settling-down, one-woman-man she needed. He was a man with too many emotional battle scars for a sweet woman like Faith. Plain and simple—he was no damn good for her.

She might be crying today, but by this time next year, she'd probably barely remember what he looked like. Yeah, maybe fate had done them both a big favor. He could continue his life as it was and she could move on to that fairy tale happily-ever-after she wanted with some other guy.

Chapter 1

Faith Sheridan locked the door to Toddle Town Day Care, the business she had opened in February, only a few short weeks after her recovery from hypothermia and pneumonia nearly ten months ago. With a bank loan, cosigned by Margaret Tompkins, and seventy-five percent of her savings, Faith had purchased a downtown building that had once housed a dry goods store that had gone out of business a couple of years ago. Located on Hickory Avenue, a back street in Whitewood, the two-story building was ideal. Her office and nursery were upstairs, where the infants were kept away from the toddlers on the ground level. Out back Faith had cleared off the empty half lot and put in playground equipment.

Opening a day-care center had seemed the perfect choice for Faith since her background was in child care; plus she had the added bonus of being able to keep Hope with her all the time. But today, her baby daughter was running a fever and she couldn't risk exposing the other children to what the doctor had said was a twenty-four-hour virus. Luckily Lindsey Dawson had become like a grandmother to Hope, as had Margaret, and today Lindsey was looking after Hope.

Life wasn't perfect, but Faith was content. She had a new business that was thriving, good friends all around her in Whitewood and best of all, four-month-old Hope. Her baby was the absolute joy of her life. But despite everything being well with her, she hadn't forgotten Worth Cordell. How could she, when Hope was a living, breathing reminder of the man Faith still loved? She never talked about Worth anymore, not to Lindsey or Margaret—and certainly not to Jody, who was convinced Worth Cordell was a low-life scum.

As Faith headed toward her car, the November wind whipping chillingly all about her, she paused on the sidewalk and glanced around at both sides of the back street already decked out in holiday gear; not quite as elaborately decorated as Main Street, but shimmering with white lights. And each shop door on Hickory Avenue held a festive wreath. Every year, the decorations went up earlier and earlier. Here it was a few days before Thanksgiving and already the town was in Christmas mode.

The turn-of-the-century reproduction streetlights cast a mellow golden glow over the entire scene. Since she kept the day-care center open until six-thirty and all the other shops on Hickory closed at five-thirty, she was quite alone. But she never felt afraid, not here in Whitewood. Their crime rate was one of the lowest in the state.

Hitching her shoulder bag higher, she reached inside her coat pocket for her car keys, then headed straight for the used SUV she'd bought from one of Lindsey's sons who lived in Columbia. The back seat held Hope's infant seat and an array of toys scattered about, even in the floorboard. She couldn't wait to pick up Hope and head straight home. She was unaccustomed to being away from her child all day and she longed to hold her baby in her arms.

Faith unlocked the driver's door of the Chevy Blazer. Just as she stepped up to get inside, someone grabbed her from behind. She gasped, startled by the unexpected hand on her shoulder. When she tried to turn to face the person, she felt something hit her on the head. For a couple of seconds her vision blurred. What was happening? Was she being attacked? She opened her mouth to scream, but no sound came out. *Oh, God, help me!* Whoever had hit her was dragging her away from the car. She tried to struggle, tried to put up a fight, but she felt so weak. When she managed to squeak out a protest, something struck her head again.

Suddenly everything went black!

Worth Cordell finished the paperwork on his most recent assignment for Dundee's, pushed the print button on the computer and leaned back in his plush office chair as he waited for the information to print out. This job had lasted nearly a month and ended with the apprehension of a stalker who'd been obsessed with her college professor. The twenty-year-old coed had finally moved beyond threatening behavior to actually trying to kill the professor's wife. Worth had come damn close to taking the bullet meant for Marcia Hallmark.

After snatching the pages from the printer, he slipped them into a manilla file folder and laid it on his desk, then started to get up; but a sharp pain splintered through his bad leg. Hell! Leaning slightly to the left, he rubbed his thigh. The bullets he'd taken in that leg nearly a year ago had left him with a slight limp. For months after he'd been released from the hospital, he'd used a cane just to get around, but now, after endless therapy, he was about eight-five percent back to normal. He relied on the cane only when he'd been on his feet for too many hours and his limp grew decidedly worse. His life had pretty much returned to normal, but he'd have both the scars and the limp to always remind him of what had happened. He'd taken three bullets—two in the leg and one in the side—when a crazed fan had decided to become famous attempting to kill a rock star who had been in Atlanta for a concert.

"Worth Cordell," Dundee office manager, Daisy Holbrook, called as she knocked on the door, then stuck her head into Worth's office. "Mr. McNamara wants to see you right this minute. It's urgent."

Worth rose to his full six-four height, nodded to Daisy and said, "Tell him I'll be right there."

"Will do." Daisy beamed that thousand-watt smile of hers and scurried away.

The young woman ran the Dundee office in downtown Atlanta with unequaled efficiency and had for the past year, since she'd been hired to replace the retiring former office manager. Daisy had been the first employee that new Dundee CEO, Sawyer McNamara, had hired when Sam Dundee had asked Sawyer to take over the top job when Ellen Denby married and left the business. Sawyer was the right kind of guy to run Dundee's. He was smart, shrewd, and hard-nosed, as well as fair-minded. He was a no-nonsense type of man who instilled confidence and loyalty in his employees. Well, everyone except Lucie Evans. Worth had thought one of two things would happen when Sawyer took over the reins: either Lucie would resign or Sawyer would request her resignation. The two had been former FBI agents and the animosity between them apparently had deep roots. No one in the business knew the particulars; they only knew Lucie and Sawyer didn't like each other. But to everyone's surprise Lucie remained a Dundee agent and despite an occasional flare-up between the two, Sawyer and she somehow managed to coexist whenever they were both at the downtown office.

When Worth walked through Sawyer's open office door, he heard the voice of a newscaster coming from the television housed in a compact entertainment center in Sawyer's office suite.

"Come in. I thought you'd want to see this." Sawyer motioned for Worth to come over to his desk. "Wasn't Faith Sheridan the name of the Constantines' nanny?"

A shiver of apprehension raced up Worth's spine. He hadn't heard that name spoken in nearly a year, but he had thought about Faith more often than he liked to admit, even to himself.

"Yeah, that was her name. Why?" Worth made his way over to the side of Sawyer's desk.

"When the noon news first came on, they said something about a report coming up on a missing person named Faith Sheridan. I thought since you rescued Ms. Sheridan and took care of her after she and the Constantine child were kidnapped, you might be interested in finding out what's happened to her."

"It might not be the same Faith Sheridan," Worth said.

"Might not be. The report is coming from someplace in South Carolina."

Worth's heart skipped a beat. "Whitewood, South Carolina?"

"Yes, I think that's—"

"Faith told me she was going home to Whitewood when she handed in her resignation to the Constantines last year."

"Well, this news story must be about her. Take a seat." Sawyer indicated a leather wing chair to the left of his desk. "We'll check out the report together."

Just as Worth eased down in the chair, the local

noon anchorman said, "Now to Connie Beck in Whitewood, South Carolina, where a young mother has been missing for the past thirty-six hours and feared to be the latest victim of the Greenville Slayer, who has murdered two women and left two others close to death in the Greenville, South Carolina area."

Every muscle in Worth's body tensed. Faith dead? No, it wasn't possible. Not sweet little Faith. An overwhelming sense of grief sucker punched Worth, then he recalled something that the newsman had said. He'd said Faith was a young mother. Did Faith have a child? Was it possible that when he hadn't shown up on Christmas Eve last year, she'd turned to another man? But if her name was still Sheridan, she wasn't married. Faith was the old-fashioned sort of woman who would take her husband's name when she married.

The face of the attractive brunette reporter, Connie Beck, appeared on screen. Beside the reporter stood a somber young blonde holding a baby in her arms.

"This is Connie Beck, coming to you from Whitewood, North Carolina, where Faith Sheridan, the owner of a local day-care center and mother of a four-month-old child, has been missing for the past thirty-six hours and is feared dead."

Four-month-old child? Mentally Worth counted back. God in heaven! That meant Faith had given birth in late July or early August, which would mean she had conceived sometime in November.

Was it possible the child was his? No! He wouldn't

believe it. Couldn't believe it. Faith knew how to contact him through the Dundee Agency; if she'd been
pregnant, she could have gotten in touch with him.

Worth tried to focus on what the reporter was saying. "Police aren't revealing much about Ms. Sheridan's disappearance, but our sources tell us the police
fear she was abducted when she left the day-care center night before last, and with a serial killer—the
Greenville Slayer—having recently hit in the town of
Sparkman, only twenty miles south of Whitewood,
there's a good chance Ms. Sheridan is his latest
victim.

"With me today is Ms. Sheridan's best friend since
the two were childhood playmates—Ms. Jody Crenson." Connie Beck held the microphone toward Jody.
"Jody, you have something you'd like to show us and
something you'd like to say."

Jody held up a photograph in one hand as she kept
the baby, bundled in a pink blanket, poised on her
hip. "This is Faith Sheridan. If anyone has seen her
or has information about her, please contact the
Whitewood police department. Faith's friends are collecting reward money for anyone with information."
Jody removed the blanket from the baby's head and
the camera zoomed in on the child.

Worth's heart stopped beating for a split second.
Fat, pink cheeks, button nose, rosebud lips. A thick
fluff of dark-red hair curled atop the child's head and
a set of dark-brown eyes stared into the camera.

She was his! He knew it the moment he looked at
her. Faith's baby was his daughter.

"This is Faith's little girl. Hope needs her mother, so please, if you know anything, anything at all, about Faith's disappearance, we need your help." Tears spilled from Jody's eyes.

"Thank you, Ms. Crenson." The reporter caressed the baby's rosy cheek, then turned back to the camera, which focused on her. "It is feared that Faith Sheridan is the fifth victim of the Greenville Slayer. This man murdered one woman and left two for dead in the Greenville area, all within the past two months. Only three weeks ago, his fourth victim was found dead in an abandoned warehouse in Sparkman, twenty miles south of here."

Worth shot up from his chair and bounded out of Sawyer McNamara's office. He had to get to Whitewood as quickly as possible. Every instinct he possessed urged him to find out what had happened to Faith and to see the child he knew had to be his.

Sawyer came out in the hallway and called to Worth, "What's wrong with you? Where are you going in such a hurry?"

Worth slowed for a moment, glanced over his shoulder and replied, "I'm going to Whitewood to find out what happened to Faith."

"I knew she had a major crush on you after you rescued her last year, but I didn't think you reciprocated her feelings."

Worth didn't explain himself to anyone, didn't justify his actions to anyone, not even his boss—not unless those actions directly related to a current case.

But he did owe Sawyer some sort of explanation. "I'll need some time off. I don't know how long."

Sawyer eyed Worth suspiciously. "Sure. Take however long you need. And call me if there's anything I or the agency can do to help you."

"Thanks."

Worth hurried into his office, tossed his overcoat across his arm, then went by Daisy's desk on his way out.

"Call the airlines and get me the first available flight to Whitewood, South Carolina. And arrange for a rental car."

"Yes, sir."

"Call me on my cell phone to let me know about my reservations."

"I'll take care of the arrangements for you, Mr. Cordell."

Ten minutes later, Worth found himself stuck in downtown traffic. Twenty minutes later just as he entered his one-bedroom apartment, his cell phone rang. Daisy rattled off details of his flight and he registered the information mentally, then set about packing. His plane left Atlanta in less than three hours.

Margaret Tompkins and Lindsey and George Dawson sat around the table in Jody Crenson's kitchen. Half-eaten sandwiches and empty coffee cups littered the table, along with piles of money.

Margaret punched the final numbers into her adding machine, then announced, "We have collected two thousand, six hundred and forty-two dollars and twenty cents.''

"George and I want to add a thousand dollars to that," Lindsey said as she bounced a wide-eyed Hope on her knee.

"With my thousand, that will bring our total to nearly five thousand." Margaret wiped away a tear. "I feel as if we should be doing something more. I want to go out and search this town, house by house."

"The police have pretty much already done that," Jody said. "Everyone in Whitewood knows Faith and if anyone has seen anything, this reward money—" Jody eyed the stack of bills and rolled coins in the middle of her kitchen table "—should entice even the most reluctant to come forward."

"I simply can't believe that anyone would harm a sweet child like Faith." A portly, fifty-something George Dawson had been little Hope's substitute grandfather since the day she was born and both Lindsey and Margaret shared the grandmother role, while Jody was simply Aunt Jody.

"If—and I'm only saying if—the Greenville Slayer—" Jody's voice cracked with emotion.

She could not—would not—allow herself to believe Faith was dead. Her dearest friend had been through so much in the past year. Surely God wouldn't be so cruel as to take her away from little Hope when the child didn't have a father. Well, she did have a father, but the heartless bastard had taken advantage of Faith and hadn't even bothered to call to say he was sorry. Jody would never forgive the man for standing up Faith a year ago on Christmas Eve. The poor kid had sat on a bench in the town square and waited for four hours—in the snow. When Jody had found Faith at midnight, she'd been suffering from hypothermia and had been practically delirious. A week's stay in the hospital battling pneumonia and nearly a month's recuperation at home had come at the same time evil bouts of morning sickness had hit Faith.

Jody had wanted to call Worth Cordell and demand he take responsibility for his child, but Faith had told her she wouldn't ask Worth for anything.

"Obviously he doesn't love me," Faith had said. "If he did, he would have shown up at the square on Christmas Eve as we'd planned. I don't want him to feel obligated to me just because I'm pregnant. If he doesn't love me, my baby and I are better off without him in our lives."

"Don't you worry, Faithie, you've got people who care about you. We'll help you," Jody had told Faith, and the people gathered here tonight in her kitchen had made Jody's prediction come true. Jody, Margaret and the Dawsons had stood by Faith through her pregnancy and rallied around her and little Hope like the family they had become.

Margaret stood and placed her arm around Jody's shoulders. "It's all right, dear, we know exactly how you feel. Faith is like a daughter to me. I refuse to believe that she's dead."

"So do I," Lindsey added. "We can't give in to

our fears. We have to believe in a miracle. For Hope's sake, if for no other reason.''

"I'll take the money to the bank in the morning,'' George said. "And open an account for the Faith Sheridan Reward Fund. And Lindsey will contact the newspapers and the local radio and television stations first thing tomorrow.''

"Thanks.'' Jody offered George a fragile smile. "I don't know what else we can do. We've circulated flyers in Whitewood and all the neighboring towns and the local police have been more than cooperative.''

Hope began whimpering. Lindsey lifted the baby and laid her on her shoulder. "Margaret, warm her bottle for me, will you?''

Margaret got up immediately, retrieved a bottle from the refrigerator and put it in the microwave. "She doesn't seem to like that formula. Sweet little thing is used to mother's milk.''

"Faith is such a good mother. She puts Hope's needs first. Always.'' Fresh tears trickled down Lindsey's cheeks.

The unexpected sound of the doorbell froze everyone for an instant. "I'll get it,'' Jody said. "It might be Reverend and Mrs. Simmons. They mentioned arranging a prayer vigil for tomorrow evening.''

Jody rushed out of the kitchen, through the living room and to the front door. She turned on the porch light, then peered through the window in the door. She didn't recognize her guest. He was tall—very tall—with dark auburn hair, broad shoulders and wore a tan trench coat. She eased open the door.

"Yes, may I help you?"

"Are you Jody Crenson?" he asked, his voice a deep, husky baritone.

"Yes, I am. Who are you?"

"I'm Worth Cordell," he replied. "I believe I'm the father of Faith Sheridan's child."

Jody glared at the big man as shock radiated through her body.

"You're about a year late, you son of a bitch!"

Then she slammed the door in his face.

Chapter 2

Worth rang the doorbell repeatedly. He hadn't come this far just to be turned away by one of Faith's friends. If as he suspected, Faith's child was his daughter, then he had certain responsibilities, as well as certain rights. More than anything he wanted Faith found alive and well, but either way, the child was going to need him.

The front door swung open and a stout, balding, middle-aged man stood there glaring at Worth. Three women hovered behind the man, all of them glowering.

"I'm Worth Cordell. May I come in and talk to y'all. Please."

"Let him come in," an elderly, white-haired lady said as she moved forward and planted her hand on her hip.

"Thank you." Worth entered the living room, then closed the door behind him. "I stopped by the police station and a Detective Rollins told me Faith had friends who were caring for her child and were collecting reward money for information concerning Faith's whereabouts."

"Won't you sit down, Mr. Cordell?" The elderly woman nodded toward the sofa.

The man, the older woman and Jody Crenson flanked Worth as he moved toward the sofa. He felt like a condemned man on his way to the gallows. The third woman, a plump, motherly brunette, held back, staying halfway across the room, but her dark eyes bored into him. Worth's gaze zeroed in on the baby she held on her hip. His heartbeat accelerated as he stared at the little girl. She looked a great deal like his little sister Norma had looked as a baby. Curly red hair and chocolate-brown eyes. Oh, God! No doubt about it—this child was his!

"Sit," the man ordered.

When Worth sat, the threesome formed a semicircle around him.

"I'm George Dawson," the man said, then indicated with a hand gesture first to the older woman, then to the younger. "This is Margaret Tompkins and Jody Crenson." He glanced across the room. "That's my wife Lindsey and…" George cleared his throat. "The baby is Faith's little girl, Hope. We're Faith's friends."

"We're Faith's family." Jody frowned at Worth.

"You said you went by the police station," Margaret said. "Did you learn anything new about Faith's whereabouts?"

"No, ma'am, I'm sorry, there's nothing new to report."

"What are you doing here?" Jody asked.

"I saw your interview on the news at noon today," Worth replied. "I felt I had to come, to see if I could—" All eyes focused hostilely on him. "Faith was...is... I had no idea she had a child."

"If you had bothered to show up last Christmas Eve, she would have told you she was pregnant," Margaret said.

"Why didn't you show up, Mr. Cordell?" Lindsey asked.

"Because he's a low-life scum who didn't care anything about Faith." Jody jumped up out of her chair. "He used Faithie and dumped her. I don't think we should even be talking to him."

"Is Jody right, Mr. Cordell?" Margaret asked.

Worth suddenly understood how a man felt when surrounded by a lynch mob who had already tried and convicted him without a hearing.

"I cared about... I care about Faith. I honestly believed that she was better off without me. If she's told you anything about me, y'all know how we met and—"

"You rescued her from rebels in Subria who had kidnapped her and the Constantine child," George said. "Yes, we know about that. And we know how you make your living. But Faith told us what a good man you were. She's never said one unkind thing about you. Not even when you didn't keep your promise to her.''

''I was in the hospital.'' Worth felt a sudden need to defend himself. ''I'd been critically wounded on a job assignment. They kept me highly sedated, so I didn't come out of it and know where I was until Christmas Day last year.''

''Why didn't you call Faith then?'' Lindsay asked.

''Because he'd never meant to show up at the square on Christmas Eve—'' Jody snapped her head around and pierced Worth with her sharp glare ''—did you?''

''I had planned to meet Faith, to explain why— Look, what does all this matter now? I stayed away because I truly believed Faith was better off without me. I had no idea she was pregnant, that I was a father. If she'd told me, I—''

''You really don't know Faith at all if you think she would have tried to use a baby to trap you into marriage,'' Jody said. ''She loved you. She thought you loved her.''

Worth didn't know how to respond, didn't have any idea how to defend himself against their accusations. He was guilty as charged. After being released from the hospital last year, he should have contacted Faith; instead he'd taken the easy way out.

''I'm sorry I wasn't here when Faith needed me. If I could change things, I would, but I can't. But I'm here now and I intend to stay until we find out what happened to Faith.'' Worth glanced at the baby who had laid her head against Lindsey Dawson's shoulder and fallen asleep. ''May I see my daughter?''

''What makes you think she's yours?'' Jody asked.

Margaret shook her head. ''Jody, dear, you mustn't—''

''He can't waltz in here now and claim Hope. He has no right to assume he can play daddy when it's convenient for him.'' Jody looked from Margaret to George to Lindsey. ''Are y'all forgetting what this man put Faith through?'' Jody turned to Worth, her eyes narrowed, her nostrils flared. ''Faith went to meet you in the square that night. It was raining and the rain turned to snow. She waited for you for four hours, sitting out in the snow. When I found her she had hyperthermia and wound up in the hospital with pneumonia. And she was pregnant!''

A guilt-ridden pain tightened in Worth's gut. He should have known she'd wait for him hour after hour. Damn it—he should have known!

''Our little Faith is such a romantic,'' Margaret said. ''She convinced herself that you were her white knight, her rescuer and protector. She never considered the possibility that you were just an ordinary man or that you weren't as much in love with her as she was with you.''

Lindsey Dawson came forward, but when she started to hand Hope to Worth, Jody grabbed the child away from Lindsey.

"Maybe you aren't Hope's father," Jody said. "You have no proof that you are. We aren't about to turn Hope over to you."

"If I'm not Hope's father, then who is?" Worth asked.

"Now isn't the time to play games with this man," George said. "Jody, let him hold Hope."

Reluctantly Jody handed the sleeping child over to Worth. As his muscles tightened, his body went rigid. He hadn't held a baby since he'd been a kid and held his little sister. Norma had been eight years younger than he—his half sister—and he'd taken care of her when his stepmother had been too drunk to look after her own baby. And that had been just about all the time.

Worth held little Hope as if she were made of spun glass. He didn't think he'd ever seen anything as beautiful. She looked like an angel. Tiny, helpless and sweet beyond belief. His child. He didn't need anyone to tell him she was his. Didn't need any blood or DNA tests. Faith had been a virgin when they'd made love, and there was no way she would have turned to another man so quickly after they'd been together. Jody was right—he didn't know Faith all that well. They'd shared a very brief relationship, having been together for only a few days. But he did know how good and kind and sweet Faith Sheridan had been. Had been? God, she couldn't be dead!

Worth closed his eyes as he held Hope against his heart. The clean, delicate fragrance unique to babies assailed his senses. And an overwhelming feeling of possessiveness claimed him. This tiny bundle lying so trustingly in his arms had been born from the passion he and Faith had shared.

"I...uh...I've checked into the Whitewood Motel out on the strip," Worth said as his big hand cradled Hope's small, round head. "I'm planning on staying in Whitewood until we find out about Faith. I'd appreciate it if y'all would let me know when you hear something from the police." Reluctantly Worth handed Hope back to Lindsey.

"We'll let you know as soon as we hear anything," George said.

Worth stood. "I'd like to come by and see my daughter tomorrow."

"Hope will be at Toddle Town Day Care," Margaret told him. "Lindsey is helping out there temporarily...until Faith comes back." Margaret choked with emotion.

"Toddle Town?" Worth asked.

"Faith's business," Jody replied. "She owns Toddle Town Day Care and keeps Hope there with her. Hope is used to everyone who works there and they're all giving her lots of special attention."

"May I come by tomorrow to see Hope?" Worth looked to Lindsey.

She offered him a tentative smile. "I suppose that would be all right."

"Thanks."

George walked Worth to the door, then stepped out

onto the porch behind him. When he reached up and put his hand on Worth's shoulder, Worth tensed.

"Son, you've got to understand how the ladies feel. Our little Faith was counting on you and you let her down. My wife and Margaret and Jody aren't going to make things easy for you. You'll have to prove yourself to them."

"I understand. And thank you, Mr. Dawson."

"Call me George."

"Thanks, George."

Barney Jeffries crept down the alley between Clanton and Mooresville Streets in Sparkman. In the morning the sanitation department would empty all the Dumpsters in town, so he had only tonight to sort through the trash and find any usable items discarded by others. In his experience, this particular Dumpster usually yielded the most bounty. Once he'd even found a gold wristwatch that he'd been able to hock for nearly fifty bucks. Some idiot's loss had been his gain.

As he neared the Dumpster, Barney looked around for something he could use as a step stool. A stack of empty crates piled up in the corner by the back door of Dottie's Diner caught his eye. After dragging one of the crates across the alleyway and to the Dumpster, Barney climbed up, tossed back the lid and crawled over inside of the huge garbage bin. The stench would bother most people, but not Barney. He'd grown used to the odor and even the worst smells didn't turn his stomach. A man had to possess a strong constitution in order to go rummaging around in other people's trash.

Barney removed his flashlight from his back pocket and shined the light left to right, back to front, searching for any tidbits that might rest on top. He did a double take when he saw the white arm lying limply atop a black garbage bag. Holy-moley! He aimed the light at the arm. Human. And by the size, either a child or a small female. Oh, this wasn't good. This wasn't good at all. He moved the light up the arm to the shoulder. A sinking feeling hit him in the belly. The light moved over the shoulder, up the neck and onto the face. A woman. A young woman with her eyes closed. She was dead. Had to be dead. Otherwise why would somebody have dumped her in the trash? His hand shook so badly he dropped his flashlight. Better get it, he told himself. If the police found it, they'd check for fingerprints and he'd be in deep trouble.

When Barney reached down to retrieve his flashlight, which had fallen by the woman's hip, he noticed her chest rise and fall. She was breathing. She wasn't dead!

"Hey, lady." He nudged her hip with the flashlight. She didn't respond. "I can't help you. If I do, they'll run me in for sure and put me in jail. I'm sorry. Really, I am. But I tell you what I'll do, I'll call for help. I swear I will."

Barney crawled out of the Dumpster, hopped down

on the crate and then onto the concrete pavement. Leaving the Dumpster lid open, he hurried out of the alley. He glanced all around, then ran across the street to a pay phone. Taking a dirty rag from his coat pocket, he lifted the receiver, inserted a quarter in the slot and dialed 911. When the emergency operator responded, the machine coughed up his quarter, which he quickly rammed into his pocket.

"Yeah, there's a half-dead woman in a Dumpster over on Clanton and Mooresville." Before the operator could say a word, Barney hung up the phone, dashed out of the booth and scurried up the street as fast as he could go.

Worth slept fitfully, tossing and turning, dreaming about Faith. His subconscious played half a dozen different horrific scenarios inside his brain. Each time he was within arms reach of Faith, a moment away from saving her, she disappeared. Vanished. And each time, Worth awoke in a cold sweat.

Tossing back the covers, he rose from the double bed in Room 214 of the Whitewood Motel, a two-story U-shaped structure on the strip outside of town. Sitting on the side of the bed, Worth rubbed his hands up and down his thighs, then dropped his hands between his knees. Although common sense told him that even if he'd shown up at the town square last Christmas Eve and even if he'd married Faith, he couldn't have prevented what happened to her. If some crazed serial killer had gotten his hands on her, it would have happened regardless of what Worth had or hadn't done. But the illogical, emotional part of his nature ached with guilt and told him that if Faith had been with him instead of trying to make it on her own, all alone, she wouldn't be missing right now.

Worth stood and walked across the room to the window overlooking the parking lot. He opened the blinds and glanced outside at the first light of dawn spreading across the eastern sky. Memories of another dawn over a year ago flashed through his mind. The morning after he and Faith had made love for the first time. Her first time shouldn't have been in some dark, dank cave in a barbaric country half a world away from her home. And it shouldn't have been with a emotionally battle-scarred former Ranger who wasn't capable of genuine love. Faith had deserved so much better.

He closed the blinds and shut his eyes. He could almost hear her voice, almost feel her soft, smooth skin. How sweet she'd been, how incredibly sweet. And how shy. That morning before they'd headed out for the rendezvous point to meet the rescue chopper, she'd been worried that because she was dirty, her gown tattered, and her hair a mess, he'd think she was ugly. She had told him that she'd always been skinny and unattractive. How wrong she'd been. And he'd made his feelings perfectly clear.

You have no idea how appealing you are to me. You're not skinny—you're delicate. And you have beautiful eyes and a cute little nose and the most de-

licious mouth I've ever tasted. If we didn't have a helicopter to catch out of this hellhole today, I'd take you back inside that cave and make love to you until neither of us could stand up for a week.

He should have known there might be consequences! After all, he didn't have a condom handy that night. Why hadn't he at least picked up the phone and called her after he got out of the hospital last year? He could have at least seen how she was. Damn! Had Jody Crenson been right? Had Faith been too proud to tell him about his child?

Faith had wanted love and commitment. Moon, June and happily-ever-after. He'd tried to be honest with her, tried to tell her that he was the wrong man for her. Yeah, he'd tried all right—just not hard enough. He had made love to a woman who, because of her romantic nature, had waited her whole life for the man of her dreams before giving her innocence. But because she'd feared dying a virgin if they couldn't escape from Subria, she'd begged him to make love to her. He had resisted, at least at first. But what man could resist such alluring temptation?

The ringing telephone brought Worth from the past to the present rather quickly. He stomped across the room, lifted the receiver and said, ''Worth Cordell here.''

''Mr. Cordell, this is George Dawson.''

Worth's heartbeat went wild.

''They've found Faith,'' George said. ''She's alive, but just barely.''

"Where...when...how?"

"Come to Memorial Hospital. Drive through downtown Whitewood, go half a mile on Main Street until you reach Underwood Lane, turn right and go one block."

"Thanks, George. I'm on my way."

"Mr. Cordell?"

"Yes?"

"You'd better hurry."

Chapter 3

When the elevator doors swung open on the second floor of Memorial, the only hospital within a forty-five mile radius and served Whitewood, Sparkman and South Lake, Worth rushed out and, following the arrows pointing the way, hurried down the corridor to the ICU waiting room. Jody glanced up at him, a somber expression on her face, but not with the hostility he'd seen last night. Margaret offered him a soft smile. George rose from the green vinyl sofa and came to meet him.

Grabbing Worth's arm, George said, "She's alive, but just barely. They told us she came out of surgery about an hour ago. We don't know much, only that they had to stop some internal bleeding."

"Where was she found? What happened to her?" Worth asked.

GET 2

HOW TO GET YOUR
2 FREE BOOKS AND FREE GIFT!

1. Peel off the MIRA sticker on the front cover. Place it in the space provided at right. This automatically entitles you to receive two free books and an exciting surprise gift.

2. Send back this card and you'll get 2 "The Best of the Best™" novels. These books have a combined cover price of $11.98 or more in the U.S. and $13.98 or more in Canada, but they are yours to keep absolutely FREE!

3. There's <u>no</u> catch. You're under <u>no</u> obligation to buy anything. We charge nothing – ZERO – for your first shipment. And you don't have to make any minimum number of purchases – not even one!

4. We call this line "The Best of the Best" because each month you'll receive the best books by some of today's most popular authors. These authors show up time and time again on all the major bestseller lists and their books sell out as soon as they hit the stores. You'll like the convenience of getting them delivered to your home at our special discount prices . . . and you'll love your *Heart to Heart* subscriber newsletter featuring author news, horoscopes, recipes, book reviews and much more!

SPECIAL FREE GIFT!

We'll send you a fabulous surprise gift, absolutely FREE, simply for accepting our no-risk offer!

5. We hope that after receiving your free books you'll want to remain a subscriber. But the choice is yours – to continue or cancel, anytime at all! So why not take us up on our invitation, with no risk of any kind. You'll be glad you did!

6. And remember...we'll send you a surprise gift ABSOLUTELY FREE just for giving "The Best of the Best" a try.

Visit us online at
www.mirabooks.com

® and TM are trademarks of Harlequin Enterprises Limited.

BOOKS FREE!

The Best of the Best™ — Here's How it Works:

Accepting your 2 free books and gift places you under no obligation to buy anything. You may keep the books and gift and return the shipping statement marked "cancel." If you do not cancel, about a month later we will send you 4 additional novels and bill you just $4.49 each in the U.S., or $4.99 each in Canada, plus 25¢ shipping & handling per book and applicable taxes if any.* That's the complete price and — compared to cover prices of $5.99 or more each in the U.S. and $6.99 or more each in Canada — it's quite a bargain! You may cancel at any time, but if you choose to continue, every month we'll send you 4 more books, which you may either purchase at the discount price or return to us and cancel your subscription.

*Terms and prices subject to change without notice. Sales tax applicable in N.Y. Canadian residents will be charged applicable provincial taxes and GST.

If offer card is missing write to: The Best of the Best, 3010 Walden Ave., P.O. Box 1867, Buffalo, NY 14240-1867

BUSINESS REPLY MAIL
FIRST-CLASS MAIL   PERMIT NO. 717-003   BUFFALO, NY

POSTAGE WILL BE PAID BY ADDRESSEE

THE BEST OF THE BEST
3010 WALDEN AVE
PO BOX 1867
BUFFALO NY 14240-9952

NO POSTAGE
NECESSARY
IF MAILED
IN THE
UNITED STATES

"Come on outside." George led Worth into the hallway. "The ladies are terribly emotional right now. As a matter of fact, I am, too. Been crying a bit myself. Faith has become like a favorite niece to Lindsey and me. And Hope is like a grandchild."

"What did the police tell y'all about Faith?"

"The Sparkman police received a call from a 911 operator on duty who had gotten an anonymous phone call from a downtown pay phone telling them to look in a certain Dumpster for a woman's body."

"A Dumpster?" Bile rose to Worth's throat. Someone had thrown Faith in a Dumpster? He gritted his teeth as his hands instinctively clutched into tight fists.

"It seems she was beaten. Severely beaten. And thrown in the Dumpster. The police estimate she'd been there, unconscious, for the past forty-eight hours and if she'd stayed there another night, she would have died."

Worth grabbed George by the shoulders. "Do they have any idea who—"

"Detective Rollins of our Whitewood police department told me that the M.O. of the crime fits the M.O. of the Greenville Slayer. All of his victims have been found in similar places—Faith and another woman who died were put in Dumpsters; two were found at landfills; and another was actually discovered in her own garbage can inside an abandoned warehouse."

"My God, this guy is a real psycho." Worth tightened his hold on George's shoulders. "Have y'all spoken to the doctor? What odds are they giving that Faith will live?''

''I spoke to the nurses and they didn't say much, but I got the impression they don't think her chances are very good.''

''Have they let any of you see her?''

''Not yet. But they've told us we can go back, one at a time, during visitation.''

''When?''

George checked his watch. ''In about fifteen minutes.''

''I want to see her.''

George nodded. ''You care about Faith, don't you?''

''Yeah, I care.'' *Admit it,* Worth's inner voice told him, *you care a hell of a lot more than you thought you did.* Ever since he saw that noon news account about Faith missing, he'd been figuratively holding his breath. And when he heard she was still alive, he had released that breath with great relief. *You wanted Faith to be alive because you need a chance to make things right with her.*

Jody came out into the hall. ''I just called Lindsey to check on Hope.'' Jody glanced at Worth. ''They're at Toddle Town and as soon as Hope goes down for her morning nap, Lindsey is coming to the hospital.''

''I should be thanking all of you for taking care of Hope,'' Worth said. ''She's a lucky little girl to have so many people care about her and her mother.''

''You don't need to thank us,'' Jody said. ''We're

Hope's family, the same way we're Faith's family. You, on the other hand, are a stranger to Hope.''

"I'm Hope's father and I don't intend to remain a stranger to her.''

"Well, you'd better wait and see what Faith has to say about it. She might not want—''

George put his arm around Jody's shoulder. "We all know what Faith wanted. Worth being here when she wakes up is going to be the best medicine possible. Why don't we put aside any misgivings about Worth and give him a chance to prove what kind of man he really is.''

Jody glared at Worth. "I'll give you a chance, but so help me, if you hurt her again, I'll—I'll make you wish you'd never been born.''

Worth smiled. "I understand. Faith brings out the protector in everyone, doesn't she? She's so small and delicate, so kind and caring.''

Jody swallowed hard. "She's too good for her own good most of the time.''

Worth nodded. "She's too good for me. Don't think I don't already know that. It's one of the reasons I believed she was better off without me.''

Margaret joined the others in the hallway. "It's about time for visitation. Maybe we should check with the nurse in charge. I won't rest easy until I've seen our girl.''

"I want to see her, but...if she was beaten as badly as they say she was, it'll be hard for us to see her in that condition.'' Jody hugged Margaret and both women brushed away tears from their eyes.

Worth led the others when they entered the intensive care unit en masse and swooped down on the nurses' station.

"May I help you?" A plump, pleasant-faced nurse asked. Her name tag read Wilson.

"We'd like to see Faith Sheridan," Jody said.

"Are you family?"

"Yes, all of us are family."

"Then you may go back, two at a time. But you mustn't stay longer than five minutes." Ms. Wilson rose from her desk and looked directly at Worth. "Are you her husband?"

"No, I'm...I'm her—"

"He's her fiancé," George said.

"Yes, and the father of her baby," Margaret added.

Ms. Wilson blushed and Worth suspected that the middle-aged lady didn't quite approve of unwed parenthood. "I must warn you...all of you—" She glanced from one to the other in turn, then back at Worth. "Ms. Sheridan is in a coma. And she won't look like herself. She's badly bruised. Her face is swollen and her nose was broken and...just be prepared."

"Oh, dear, dear, I don't know if I can bear to look at her." Margaret rung her hands.

"You don't have to see her," Jody said. "It won't be easy for any of us."

"No, no, I must see her."

George placed one hand on Margaret's shoulder and the other on Jody's. "You two go on back to see her, then Worth can go. I'll wait for Lindsey and we'll go in during the next visitation period.''

Worth and George hovered near the doorway while Jody and Margaret disappeared inside cubicle four. Worth crossed his arms over his chest and leaned back against the wall. Neither he nor George said a word. He figured they were both trying not to think about what they'd find when they saw Faith or how savage they'd feel. Worth wanted to get his hands on the man who'd tried to kill Faith. He wouldn't have to think about what he'd do; he'd just do it. With one quick snap of the bastard's neck, he'd rid the world of a monster.

Within three minutes Jody and Margaret emerged from the cubicle. Jody held on to Margaret who was weeping uncontrollably. Tears streamed down Jody's face as they approached George and Worth.

''Must be really bad,'' George said, then moved forward to help Jody with Margaret.

''You can't imagine how horrible she looks,'' Margaret said between gulping sobs. ''The fiend who did that to Faith must be found and punished.''

''I'll take the ladies to the waiting room,'' George said. ''You go on back to see Faith.''

Worth took a deep breath, squared his shoulders and marched toward cubicle four. Before opening the door, he paused, willed himself to remain calm and in control; then he opened the door, entered the cubicle and walked straight to the bed.

He'd thought he was prepared for the worst, but he'd been wrong. Despite all the death and destruction he had encountered as an army Ranger and as a Dundee agent, nothing had prepared him to see the mother of his child lying in a hospital bed, hooked up to wires and tubes, her every breath monitored. And dear God in heaven, her sweet face and delicate body had been battered almost beyond recognition. Purple bruises covered her arms, chest, throat and face. She had a busted lip, both eyes were swollen, and her nose had been broken.

Worth stopped dead still. If the police didn't find the Greenville Slayer, he would—if it was the last thing he ever did.

Forcing himself to move, Worth eased to the bedside. Except for the rise and fall of her chest, Faith appeared lifeless. Unconscious. In a coma. Without even thinking about what he was doing, Worth touched her slender hand, lifted it a couple of inches off the bed and held it tenderly.

"Oh, Blue Eyes. This shouldn't have happened to you." Emotion lodged in his throat. "You're going to be all right. It'll take time for you to recuperate, but I'll be here with you. And when you get to come home, I'll care for you and nurse you back to health. I promise that you can count on me. You and Hope."

God, how he longed to lift her into his arms and hold her. He wished that he could take away all the suffering she had endured. If it were within his power, he'd gladly suffer for her.

"I'm here and I'm staying. Do you hear me, Faith? I'm not going to leave you."

He hoped that on some level she understood him,

that somehow she knew he was here with her, making her promises that he intended to keep. Faith needed him. Perhaps even more than she'd needed him in Subria. And Hope needed a father.

Worth Cordell wasn't the kind of man who shirked his duties.

Jody Crenson entered the ICU waiting room carrying a bag from the downstairs deli. Worth Cordell sat slumped in a chair by the windows, his arms crossed over his chest, his eyes closed. Jody had wanted to hate the man who'd broken Faith's heart, but seeing his devotion to Faith these past two days had softened her attitude toward him. The guy hadn't left the hospital in forty-eight hours; he'd been cleaning up in the rest room and eating from a vending machine. He looked like hell. His clothes were rumpled and his face was darkened with beard stubble.

As she approached him, Worth opened his eyes and stared at her.

"Hi," he said. "How's Hope doing?"

Jody set the bag down on the table beside his chair. "I called Lindsey as soon as I got off from work to check on Hope. She's doing all right. But we all figure she's missing her mommy. She's not sleeping good and her pediatrician has already changed her formula again." Jody nodded in the direction of the ICU. "Any change in Faith's condition?"

Worth shook his head, then got up and walked across the room to the coffeepot on the table in the corner. "Want any coffee?"

"Sure, fix me a cup, please. Black." Jody pointed to the paper sack. "I brought you a sandwich and some chips."

"Thanks." Worth poured two cups of coffee, handed Jody a cup, then sat and held his cup with both hands.

"If you want to shower and shave, you're welcome to come to my house or—"

"George has already offered to let me stay with Lindsey and him, but I'd rather wait until Faith comes to. I don't want to leave. Not yet." Worth sipped on his coffee.

"Sooner or later, you'll have to leave," Jody told him. "Faith could stay in a coma for weeks. The doctors don't know for sure when she'll come out of it."

"She squeezed my hand, you know. Last night."

"Yes, I know, but—" Jody stopped herself before she said something negative. By nature she was a pessimist, so she always expected the worst—of people and of situations. But there was no reason for her to take away Worth's hope that Faith would recover.

"The local police don't have enough staff to post an officer here 24/7," Worth said. "That means I'm not leaving her here unprotected."

"Unprotected? What are you saying? How is she—? Oh, my God, you think the person who did this to her might come after her here in the hospital."

"Local TV and newspapers have reported that she's alive and in a coma," Worth said. "If this guy thinks she might identify him when she wakes, then he very well could come after her.''

"I've been so caught up in Faith's condition and everything going on here at the hospital that I never thought about... Oh, Worth.''

"The police don't think we have anything to worry about." Worth finished off his coffee and set the cup on the table. "The other two victims who survived couldn't ID the guy. They said they never got a good look at his face because he came up from behind them, knocked them out, then kept them blindfolded and tied up while he—" Worth swallowed hard.

Jody laid her hand on Worth's arm. "I'm really glad you're here.''

"Even if I am a year late?''

"Better late than never. Besides, Faith needs you to be her protector again. From what she told me, you're very good at the job." Jody pointed to the sack. "It's roast beef on whole wheat. Eat up.''

Worth glanced past Jody to the door. Jody followed his line of vision. One of the ICU nurses entered, a wide smile on her face. Nurse Malone.

Worth shot out of his chair. "Has something happened?''

"It most certainly has," Nurse Malone said. "Faith has come out of the coma. She's awake.''

Jody let out a deep breath, grabbed Worth and hugged him. Worth lifted Jody off her feet and swung her around several times.

"What's she saying? How is she?" Jody asked.

"Did she ask about Hope? Does she want to see me? Does she remember who attacked her?"

"Dr. Tracy is with her," the nurse told them. "We've telephoned the police to let them know she's conscious. Right now, Faith seems to be slightly disoriented, but that's not unusual in cases such as this."

"When can we see her?" Worth asked.

"Dr. Tracy will come out and speak to y'all after he finishes his examination. I'm sure he'll allow y'all to see Faith very soon."

The minute Nurse Malone left, Jody rushed to the pay phone on the wall, then glanced over her shoulder. "I'll call Lindsey and George, then Margaret. They'll be so thrilled to hear the good news."

"I'm sure they'll want to see Faith," Worth said. "But you should probably tell them that you'll call them back after we see Faith and give them an update."

"Yeah, sure. We can take turns caring for Hope and staying here at the hospital. And with one of us here all the time, you could go home and shower."

"Do I stink?" Worth grinned.

"No, you don't stink, but you do look pretty grungy."

Jody lifted the receiver, but before she could dial the number, Worth clasped her shoulder. She glanced up at him.

"Do me a favor, will you? Tell the others that if after the police talk to Faith, they still don't post a guard at her door, I want to call in one of my Dundee co-workers to come to Whitewood and share bodyguard duty with me until Faith is released from the hospital.''

"You really are concerned about this guy coming after Faith again, aren't you?''

"Yes, I'm concerned. And I've learned from experience that it's better to be safe than sorry.''

"Okay, I'll tell the others. I don't know what hiring a bodyguard will cost, but together we should be able to cover the expense.''

"I'm picking up the tab,'' Worth said. "Faith is my responsibility. I'll take care of her.''

Jody stared quizzically at Worth. "Is that all Faith and Hope are to you—a responsibility?''

"Don't put words in my mouth.''

"Whatever you do, don't tell Faith you'll take care of her because she's your responsibility. She'd kill me if she thought I told you, but...under these circumstances, I think you should know.''

"Know what?''

"Faith is still in love with you.''

Worth followed Jody into cubicle four. Dr. Tracy had told them Faith appeared to be suffering from temporary amnesia, which was fairly common in patients who had received head traumas similar to hers. He estimated the amnesia would eventually clear up entirely and her memory would return in bits and pieces. His prediction was that within a few weeks Faith should regain most, if not all, of her memory. But in the meantime, she didn't even know her own name.

Jody neared Faith's hospital bed. Worth held back, staying just inside the doorway.

"Hi, there," Jody said. "Dr. Tracy tells me that you're having a problem with your memory."

Worth inched a little closer to the bed, close enough so that he could see Faith. Her swollen, bruised eyes were open and she stared at Jody with complete puzzlement.

"Do I know you?" Faith's voice sounded incredibly weak.

"Oh, Faithie." Jody swallowed her tears. "I'm Jody Crenson. I'm your best friend. We've been buddies since we were kids."

"Jody? You're my friend."

"That's right."

"I've had an accident," Faith said. "The doctor told me that I'm going to regain my memory and he told me that I had two friends waiting to see me."

"Yeah, that would be me and Worth."

"Worth?"

Jody motioned to Worth, then said to Faith. "Yeah, this guy hasn't left the hospital since they brought you in. He's been awfully worried about you. We all have."

As Worth came up beside Jody, Faith asked, "Are you my husband?"

Jody gave Worth a concerned look.

"We aren't married," Worth said. "Not yet."

"You're my fiancé?"

"Something like that." Worth reached down and

took Faith's hand. "It's good to see you awake, Blue Eyes. You've been asleep for days."

"Blue Eyes?"

Worth chuckled. "That's what I called you when we first met. Well, actually I called you ma'am at first, but once I got a good look at those beautiful blue eyes of yours—"

Faith squeezed his hand. "Your voice seems familiar. I've heard it somewhere before."

"I've been talking to you while you were unconscious," Worth told her. "Maybe you heard me."

"What—what kind of accident did I have?" Faith looked up at Worth. "Was I in a car wreck?"

"Not exactly, but I don't think now's the time for you to worry about that. You just concentrate on getting well and regaining your memory. Don't worry about anything else. I'm going to take care of you."

"Because you love me," Faith's voice was a mere whisper.

"Yes, because he loves you," Jody answered for him. "We all love you. The whole family."

"Family?"

"You'll meet them later," Jody said. "There's George and Lindsey, who are like…well, they're like your aunt and uncle. Then there's Margaret. She's like your…sort of a grandmother to you. And there's—"

"There's plenty of time later to talk," Worth interrupted. Now wasn't the time to tell a woman who had no memory that she was the mother of an infant. He knew that despite her amnesia, Faith's maternal instincts were probably undamaged and the minute she heard she had a kid, she'd go nuts worrying about the child.

"Yeah, Worth's right. You need to rest and get well." Jody backed away from the bed. "I'm going to call the family and give them a current update."

Worth stayed with Faith, her little hand wrapped securely in his grasp. "You're going to be all right and your memory will return. I know it has to be frightening for you, but trust me to take care of everything. Whatever you want, whatever you need, I'll make sure you get it."

"I'm so tired," Faith said. "And I hurt. I ache all over."

"I'll see if they can up the dosage on your pain medication."

When Faith grasped Worth's hand tightly, he was amazed by her strength. "Don't go," she pleaded. "Don't leave me."

He leaned over and gently kissed her bruised forehead. "I'll stay right here until the nurses run me out."

Someone behind him cleared their throat. Worth glanced over his shoulder and recognized Nurse Malone and Detective Rollins standing in the doorway.

Chapter 4

"Dr. Tracy said that I could speak with Ms. Sheridan," Detective Rollins said.

"He's allowed five minutes." Nurse Malone followed the policeman into the room. "I'm to stay with him while he questions her."

Faith clung tenaciously to Worth's hand. "Why do the police want to question me? Is it about the accident?"

Worth could see not only the fear and uncertainty in Faith's eyes, but he could sense how nervous and upset she was. "Don't worry. Remember that I'm here and I won't let anyone hurt you." Worth eased Faith's hand from his, then turned to meet Detective Rollins.

"Would you mind stepping outside, Mr. Cordell?" the policeman asked.

"Yes, I would mind," Worth replied. "I'm sure you've been told that Faith has amnesia. She's not going to be able to tell you anything. Not now."

"I understand, but I need to speak with her all the same." Rollins was somewhere in his late thirties, with a short, stocky frame, dark hair and mustache and a professional manner about him. "If you want to stay, Cordell, it's fine with me."

Rollins came forward, Nurse Malone at his side. Worth rounded the foot of the hospital bed and took a stand. Faith's gaze sought and found his. He offered her a supportive smile and when she returned his smile, an odd sensation hit him square in the gut. Faith didn't remember him, didn't know him at all, yet on some instinctive level, she trusted him. It was as if her subconscious recognized him as her protector.

"Ms. Sheridan, I'm Jerry Wayne Rollins, a detective with the Whitewood police department and I need to ask you a few questions."

Faith looked to Worth. He nodded. She turned to the detective. "All right."

"Ms. Sheridan, do you remember what happened to you?"

"You mean the accident?"

"Do you think you had an accident?"

"I don't know. I—I assumed that since I'm badly injured and in the hospital, I must have... Wasn't I involved in a car wreck?"

Rollins glanced at Worth. He knew she had to be told, but why now? Couldn't it wait? It would be different if she could remember anything, but she couldn't.

Rollins looked to Nurse Malone. "The doctor said it was all right to explain things to her."

"Yes, it's all right," the nurse replied.

"Ms. Sheridan, you weren't in a car wreck," the detective said. "You were assaulted, kidnapped and severely beaten."

Faith's blue eyes widened in shock. Her mouth opened in a silent gasp. Then her gaze collided with Worth's.

"Worth?" She held out her hand to him. He rushed to her side and took her hand. "Is he telling me the truth? Is that what happened to me?"

"Yes, that's what the police believe happened," Worth told her.

"Who would do such a thing to me?"

"We don't know for sure," Rollins said. "That's one reason we were hoping you could remember something...anything that might help us."

"I'm sorry. I don't know." Faith frowned, a worried expression forming on her face. She glanced around the room nervously, then tried to lift herself into a sitting position.

Nurse Malone rushed to Faith. "Please, don't move around. You need to lie still and rest." The nurse turned to Rollins. "Perhaps you should go, Detective. I'm afraid Faith is becoming agitated."

Worth followed the policeman out into the main area of the ICU.

"Rollins?"

"Yes, Mr. Cordell?"

"Want to fill me in on what's happening?"

Rollins gave Worth a curious stare. "Such as?"

"Such as why you're here questioning Faith and not somebody from the Sparkman police department? Why you don't have a guard posted here at the hospital? Why—"

Rollins held up a restraining hand. "The Sparkman P.D. and the Whitewood P.D. are working together, along with the Greenville P.D. and the state Bureau of Investigation, but since Dr. Tracy informed us that Ms. Sheridan has amnesia, we saw no point in having anyone other than our department do the initial questioning. And at present, we see no need to post a guard. If the Greenville Slayer is the one who attacked Ms. Sheridan, then she's probably safe. He's made no attempt to harm either of the other two women who survived his brutal attacks. Not while they were recovering or since."

"You're taking a chance with Faith's life on the assumption he won't seek her out while she's here at Memorial. I'm not willing to risk it. Either I or another agent from Dundee's will stay near Faith 24/7 while she's in the hospital."

"That's fine with me, Mr. Cordell. She's your girlfriend and you feel a need to act protective. My job is to do all in my power to find the guy who nearly killed her. If she can remember anything about what happened to her, it might help us."

"When her memory starts coming back, we'll be in touch."

Before the detective was out of sight, Worth heard Faith calling his name. Repeatedly. He rushed back into cubicle four to find Nurse Malone physically restraining Faith.

"Please, see if you can do something with her," the nurse said. "If you can calm her, I won't have to give her a sedative."

Worth all but shoved the nurse aside as he leaned over Faith's bed. She reached for him, one slender arm hooked up to tubes and wires. With the utmost tenderness, Worth encompassed her fragile body in his embrace as he jerked the side rail down and sat on the edge of the bed. Lying there, cuddled against his chest, her fast, erratic breathing began to slow and return to a steady rhythm.

"Don't leave me," Faith pleaded.

Worth rubbed his chin across her temple then kissed the top of her head. "I'll stay right here with you, if you promise you'll relax and rest."

"I promise."

Worth's gaze connected with Nurse Malone's, who smiled and nodded, then left the room. When she returned fifteen minutes later, Faith was asleep, cocooned in Worth's arms.

A week later Worth sent Domingo Shea back to Atlanta. The Dundee agent had swapped out twelve-hour shifts with Worth during Faith's hospital stay, but today Faith had been dismissed from Memorial. Her cuts were beginning to heal and the bruises had faded to pale yellow. The doctors had told Worth and

Faith's "family," it was a miracle that neither of her legs or arms had been broken, only her nose, considering the severity of her beating. She had suffered several cracked ribs, which were also healing nicely.

While the nurse's aide wheeled Faith out to the canopied hospital entrance, Worth pulled his rental car to a stop, hopped out and rounded the hood. He and the aide filled the back seat with the flowers Faith had received once she'd been moved from ICU to a private room. Then Worth swept Faith up in his arms and placed her in the front seat of the car. After securing her seat belt, he thanked the nurse's aide, then returned to the driver's side.

"Ready to go home?" he asked.

"I don't even remember where home is," she said. "But yes, I think I'm ready."

"Everyone's going to be there," he told her. "By everyone I mean—"

"Jody and Margaret and Lindsey and George."

"You've memorized their names."

"Yes, and I can put each name to a face. They've been visiting me every day since I came out of the coma."

Worth pulled onto the street and headed toward downtown Whitewood. The family had agreed that Faith should be told about Hope before she came home and Worth had decided that since he was Hope's father, it was his place to tell Faith about their child. It had been a unanimous decision to wait until Faith had recovered to some degree before telling her that she was a mother.

"You're going to stay with me, aren't you?" Faith asked.

"Yes, I'm staying. We've been over that several times, haven't we? I'm not going anywhere."

"I'm sorry, Worth, but for some reason I can't get over this irrational fear that you're going to leave me."

Was her reaction simply gut instincts or was it a hint of returning memory? Worth wondered. Right now Faith depended on him, needed him, wanted him. But how would she feel once her memory came back and she realized he wasn't the knight in shining armor she thought he was? He had taken her virginity, gotten her pregnant and hadn't shown up for the most important date of her life.

Worth pulled the Camry into Faith's driveway and killed the motor, then turned to her. "There's something I need to tell you."

"Something bad? I'm not sure I want to hear anything else bad. It's been difficult enough coming to terms with the fact that someone nearly beat me to death and that this person might be a serial killer called the Greenville Slayer."

"This isn't bad news," Worth assured her. "It's actually good news."

Faith cocked her head to one side and smiled. "If it's good news, why do you look so somber?"

"Jody and the others have planned a welcome home party for you. Nothing elaborate, just them and us and..." Worth reached out and caressed her cheek.

"There's someone else in your life, someone very important."

"I don't understand." Faith's nose crinkled when she frowned. "Jody told me that my parents are dead, that I have no brothers and sisters, that she and I grew up at the Whitewood Girls' Ranch. Is this important person another friend, someone who couldn't come to the hospital to see me?"

"No, not exactly. You see...you have a...we have a... Hope is our child. She's four months old and—"

"I have a baby? I'm a mother?"

"Yeah. Her name is Hope."

"And she's our child? Yours and mine? She was born four months ago and we aren't...we didn't get married? Why didn't we marry?"

"It's a long story and we'll eventually get around to it," Worth said. "But for now, you need to know that there's a baby in there waiting for her mama, waiting for you."

"Oh. I—I can't believe I have a child and I don't even remember her. What sort of mother am I?"

"You're a good mother. The best. It isn't your fault that you're suffering from temporary amnesia."

"I'm beginning to wonder if it is temporary." Faith sighed heavily. "It's been over a week since I came out the coma and so far, I don't remember anything."

"Not consciously, but I think you do remember a few things subconsciously. Not memories exactly, but feelings."

"What if when I see my child, I don't feel anything? What if I don't feel like a mother? She'll know. She'll sense it and... Oh, Worth, I'm scared.''

"I'm pretty scared myself," he admitted. "You see, Faith, I don't know our daughter and she doesn't know me. I haven't been around since she was born, so I'll be getting to know her for the first time.''

"You weren't with me when she was born?''

Worth shook his head.

"Where were you?''

"You and I had ended our relationship before you found out you were pregnant with Hope.'' Worth knew that he owed it to Faith to be as honest with her as he could be, without undermining her confidence and trust in him. "I got it in my head that you were better off without me, so I did what I thought was best for both of us.''

"You told me about how we met in Subria, when I was working as a nanny for a billionaire's daughter and how you were part of the rescue party who freed me. Was that when our daughter was conceived, when we were in Subria?''

Worth nodded.

"But we barely knew each other. Somehow it doesn't feel right. I don't know why, but I feel as if I'm not the sort of woman who'd go to bed with a man I just met and I wouldn't have a child without a husband.''

"That's exactly the kind of woman you are—the good girl kind who gets married first," Worth told her. "But when we were hiding out in Subria, waiting for the rescue chopper, we both knew we might not make it out alive. We had sex…made love because we thought it might be our last night on earth.''

''We didn't love each other?''

Worth couldn't bear the look of disappointment and regret in Faith's big blue eyes. ''Maybe not then, but later…''

''Later we fell in love?''

''Yeah, something like that.''

''But you didn't know I was pregnant and you left me because you thought I was better off without you?''

''Yeah.''

''And we have a baby together and you've come back because…'' She glared at him. ''When did you come back?''

''What difference does it make when I came back? I'm here now and I'm staying to take care of you and Hope.''

Worth caught a glimpse of the front door to Faith's apartment easing open. Jody peeped outside.

''They're waiting for you,'' he said. ''Are you ready for your homecoming party?''

''I thought I was, but… What if I don't remember how to take care of a baby?''

''You won't be alone. I'll be here and Jody lives next door and Lindsey and Margaret are only a few blocks away. We'll manage. After all, how difficult can it be to take care of one four-month-old baby?''

Worth got out of the car, lifted Faith into his arms, and carried her up the sidewalk, onto the porch and through the open front door. Jody closed the door behind them, then followed them into the living room. Margaret sat on the sofa, Hope in her lap. Lindsey and George hovered in the doorway leading to the kitchen.

"Welcome home," they all called out in unison as Worth seated Faith on the sofa beside Margaret.

Everyone held their breaths as Faith studied Hope, looking her over from curly red hair to pink booties. When Faith held open her arms to her child, a collective sigh reverberated throughout the room. Hope gurgled and gooed when Faith took her and held her.

"She's beautiful, isn't she?" Faith looked from one person to another and each person smiled and said that yes, Hope was the most beautiful baby in the world. "She looks like you." Faith's gaze rested on Worth, who stood only a few feet away. "She has your eyes, your chin and…" Faith wound one of Hope's red curls around her finger. "Was your hair this color when you were a baby?"

Worth grinned. "Yeah, it stayed that color until I was about ten, then it started turning darker."

"Hello, Hope, my precious baby," Faith said. "I wish I could remember you. I wish I could…" Tears gathered in the corners of Faith's eyes.

"Hey, we've got supper ready," Lindsey said. "And for dessert there's ice cream and a cake. Anybody hungry?"

"Why don't we go ahead and put the food out?" Margaret suggested as she rose from the sofa. "Then we can make ourselves scarce for tonight. I think Faith and Worth and Hope need some time alone."

"No, please, y'all don't have to leave," Faith said. "I'm sorry if I'm not making y'all feel welcome. It's just that I—"

"It's okay, Faithie," Jody said. "It's going to take you time to adjust. Having a houseful of people on your first evening home was probably a bad idea. Margaret's right—you need some time alone with Worth and Hope."

"We'll be nearby if you need us," George said.

Suddenly everyone disappeared into the kitchen, leaving Worth and Faith alone with their child. Worth sat beside Faith.

"Lindsey left us a to-do list," Worth said. "Things like how to fix Hope's bottles, her regular nap times, her pediatrician's phone number. Stuff like that."

"How could I have forgotten this precious child?" Faith hugged her daughter to her and Hope grasped a strand of Faith's long, dark hair.

Worth put his arm around Faith and pulled her to his side. "You'll remember her. If not tomorrow or the next day, then soon."

"What if I never—"

"Dr. Tracy said it's temporary. You might not ever remember all the details about your attack, but you will regain almost all your memory. Just give it time, Blue Eyes, and it'll come back to you."

"I don't know why, but when you call me Blue Eyes, I get a funny feeling. It's almost as if I can remember that I liked your calling me that."

The foursome emerged from the kitchen. When

Worth started to stand, George motioned for him to stay put.

"Supper's warming in the oven," Lindsey said. "There are four bottles already prepared and in the refrigerator."

"We're heading out now," Jody said. "Remember, I'm right next door, if you need me."

Their company left in a whirlwind and when they were gone, utter silence filled the apartment. Then suddenly Hope began whimpering.

For a split second, Worth wanted to call the others back, to ask them not to leave him. What the hell did he know about taking care of a woman recovering from severe injuries and a helpless little baby? Heaven help him, he was out of his element playing nursemaid and daddy.

"She's hungry," Faith said as she loosened her robe and began unbuttoning her gown. She stopped abruptly, her hand hovering over her left breast. "Did I breast-feed Hope?"

"Yeah, I believe you did."

"But I don't have any milk. It must have dried up when I was in the hospital."

"I'll get her a bottle." Worth jumped up and headed for the kitchen. His heart beat ninety to nothing. What was wrong with him? Why was he letting one fragile, petite woman and one tiny baby scare the hell out of him? He'd taken care of wounded comrades, had rescued people in great danger, administered first aid when a medic wasn't available. He'd been a Ranger, a tough guy through and through.

Why did the thought of being totally responsible for Faith and Hope put the fear of God into him?

Don't think about it, he told himself. Just do what you have to do. He couldn't deal with the reasons that were staring him right in the face. Emotions were a weakness he hadn't allowed himself since he'd been a kid. Caring about somebody meant risking being hurt and rejected. He had to find a way to take care of Faith and Hope without getting in over his head in some touchy-feely quagmire of sentimental feelings.

Chapter 5

With each passing day Faith regained her strength, but Worth insisted she not overdo. Lindsey, Jody and Margaret took turns bringing over home-cooked meals, so all Worth had to prepare was their breakfast each morning. He'd become a whiz at scrambled eggs and toast. He did all the chores, even though Faith kept insisting she could help. Keeping the apartment clean and the laundry done had been a piece of cake compared to caring for Hope. It hadn't taken him more than twenty-four hours to realize a four-month-old needed something almost continuously. He'd lost track of how many disposable diapers they'd been through in five days, how many bottles Hope had gulped down and how many miles he had walked holding her in his arms, usually in the middle of the night.

With a towel wrapped around his waist and tucked into his jeans, Worth stood at the sink, one hand supporting Hope's back while the other maneuvered a small washcloth over her soft, chubby body. She gurgled and laughed and slapped at the water in which she sat. Worth had learned the hard way that when giving Hope her bath, he'd better prepare himself for a bath, too. Her plump, dimpled hand reached for the yellow rubber duck that he'd discovered was a necessity during bath time. As he rinsed his daughter with lukewarm water, he wondered if all infants loved water the way Hope did. His little girl was definitely part fish.

"Need any help?" Faith stood in the bathroom doorway.

"Hey, there, Mommy." Worth glanced at Faith and smiled. "We're almost finished here. How about getting our towel for us?"

Faith lifted the folded hooded towel from the vanity, opened it and held it for Worth. He slipped Hope's head into the hood then wrapped her in the terry cloth and handed her to Faith.

"Can you manage her okay? She's a chunk."

"She weighed nine pounds when she was born," Faith said as she took her child and carried her into the bedroom.

Worth let the water out of the sink, dried off the vanity and set the rubber duck back in the mesh bag of bath toys hanging on the wall. When he joined mother and daughter, Faith had Hope lying on the bed with a diaper on and was struggling with the wiggling infant as she tried to pull on her one-piece pajamas.

Worth placed his hand on Faith's shoulder. "Do you realize you just remembered something else?"

"I did, didn't I? I remembered Hope weighed nine pounds when she was born." Faith sighed. "My memory is coming back in bits and pieces, not whole chunks. I recall unconnected, independent facts and incidents."

Worth squeezed her shoulder. "But every day you seem to recall more and more of these tidbits. Pretty soon those whole chunks of memory will return."

"I hope so." Faith managed to finish dressing Hope, then sat on the edge of the bed and placed Hope in her lap. "I've started keeping a list." She nodded to the dressing table under the double windows across the room. An ink pen lay atop an open notebook. "Every time I remember something, I write it down."

"That's a good idea." Worth sat beside Faith. "Doing that should help you see how much you're recovering."

"It's odd what I remember and what I don't. I remember Jody and Margaret, but my memories are of them from years ago. But I don't remember anything about Lindsey and George. Or you." When she looked at him with those luminous blue eyes, Worth could not control his reaction. From the first moment he'd looked into her eyes in a country halfway around the world, he'd felt an unbidden attraction and an instant desire to protect her.

"You've known Jody and Margaret most of your life. Those memories are returning first."

Faith shook her head. "I know Dr. Tracy said it wasn't unusual to remember my childhood first, but I've had flashes of memory about more recent events. I remember giving birth to Hope, how much she weighed, how happy I was. And I'm having quick bursts of thoughts. I see myself sitting on a park bench and it's snowing."

"I'll go to the kitchen and warm Faith's bottle." Worth rose to his feet. He wasn't sure he wanted her to remember that night.

"I should ask Jody about it—about my sitting on a bench in the snow—because I hear her voice calling my name while I'm sitting there. I wonder if it's a real memory."

"It's real," Worth said. "Let's get Hope down for the night and I'll tell you what I know about that memory."

Faith smiled. "All right."

She smiled more and more often these days; and every time she focused one of those brilliant smiles on him, he wanted to kiss her. Actually, he wanted to do a lot more than kiss her. After the first time he made love to her, he'd become addicted to Faith; and during their brief affair over a year ago, he'd made love to her several times. But Hope must have been conceived the first time, in the cave where they'd hidden from the Subrian soldiers—the one time he hadn't used a condom.

In the past year, since they'd said goodbye at the

airport in Golnar and she had concocted a plan for them to rendevous at the square in Whitewood on Christmas Eve, Worth had tried to forget Faith. He'd lost track of how many times he had fought the urge to pick up the phone and call her. And each time he had stopped just short of dialing her number. He'd convinced himself that they were better off without each other.

But for now, until she fully recovered, and he was sure she was in no danger from the maniac who had nearly killed her, Worth knew he was needed here. Faith needed him. And so did Hope.

Faith studied Worth Cordell as he laid Hope down in her crib and stood over her, a gentle, loving expression on his face. If only she could remember this man. She must have been very much in love with him. After all, they shared a child. And even without any memories of him or their love affair, Faith felt an undeniable attraction to the big man who took such good care of Hope and her. Every time she looked at him, butterflies fluttered in her tummy. His every word, every deed, every tender touch seduced her.

Not once had he mentioned loving her—now or in the past—but his actions spoke to her heart. He acted like a man in love. Why else would he be here, caring not only for his child, but for his child's mother? Sometimes when he thought she wasn't looking, Faith would catch a glimpse of Worth staring at her, a hungry longing in his eyes. Whenever he touched her, either on purpose or by accident, she felt an instan-

taneous connection. When she questioned him about
why they weren't married, she sensed his reluctance
to discuss any details of their past, so she hadn't
pushed him. Soon enough she would remember everything, or so the doctor kept telling her.

Faith eased up beside Worth and placed her hand
on his back. He tensed, then relaxed. It was as if her
touch burned him.

"She's so very precious," Faith said as she gazed
down at her sleeping daughter. "I want to remember
everything about her, from the moment I knew I was
pregnant."

Worth slipped his arm around Faith's waist.
"When you do remember, I want you to share those
memories with me. I wasn't around to share them
with you."

Taking the opening he'd given her, Faith asked,
"Will you tell me about my memory of sitting on the
bench in the snow? There has to be a reason that it
seems to be so important to me, some reason that it's
my strongest memory."

Worth picked up the baby monitor, then led Faith
out of the bedroom, leaving the door open behind
them. When they reached the living room, he set her
down on the yellow-and-blue striped sofa sleeper,
where Worth slept every night. Before joining her, he
placed the monitor on the oak end table to his left,
then lifted his arm and spread it out across the sofa
back behind Faith's head.

"When I left Golnar, you returned to your job as
the nanny for Phila Constantine, to work out a two-

week notice.'' Worth lifted his arm off the sofa, then rubbed the tops of his thighs nervously. He purposely avoided making eye contact with her. Faith concluded that what he was going to tell her must be difficult for him. ''At the airport in Dareh, Golnar, we said goodbye, but you came up with an idea that would give us both time to think about our feelings.''

''What sort of idea?''

''Actually it was a plan to give me time to sort through my feelings,'' Worth admitted. ''You were pretty sure of your feelings.''

''I was in love with you,'' she said, and realized she knew without a doubt how she'd felt about him. Not exactly a memory, but a certainty coming from an inner past knowledge.

He nodded. ''You said that if I—if we decided we loved each other, we'd meet in the Whitewood town square at eight o'clock on Christmas Eve. You showed up. I didn't.''

''You didn't meet me?''

''No, I...uh...I couldn't meet you. I'd gotten shot on an assignment and wound up in the hospital. I didn't regain consciousness until Christmas Day.''

''Then you called me and explained and—''

He shook his head. ''No, honey, I decided that Fate had played a hand in my decision, that I'd been right about your being better off without me in your life.''

''You didn't meet me and you didn't call me later to explain.''

''I thought I was doing the right thing,'' he told

her. "I had no idea you were pregnant. If I'd known... I'm sorry, Faith."

"Was it snowing that night, the night I waited for you?"

"Yeah, Jody said it snowed that night."

"It must have been very difficult for me. I must have expected you to show up. I had the most wonderful news to tell you, didn't I?" A vague, cloudy memory surfaced, then gradually became clearer. "I couldn't wait to go to the square that evening. It was raining, but I didn't care. I walked from the house to downtown. I knew you'd be there because I believed you loved me as much as I loved you."

Worth looked directly at Faith. "Are you actually remembering that night?"

"Yes, parts of it. I remember how I felt. I remember being very happy. And I remember the snow. It was terribly cold and I could hear the church bells chime out the hour."

"You shouldn't have waited," he told her.

"But I did wait. I waited and waited, but you didn't come." Anger combined with sadness and Faith understood she was experiencing the same emotions she'd felt that night. "I loved you so very much." Her gaze locked with his. "Did you love me? Did you love me even a little bit?"

"Faith...I..." He sat there beside her, staring at her, his mouth open, but no other words came out.

"No, you didn't love me, did you? And you don't love me now. You're here out of some misguided sense of obligation, not love."

She felt his rejection as keenly as she'd felt it that night and the pain spread through her at an alarming speed. She didn't think she could bear sitting here, so near to him, seeing the truth in his eyes.

Faith surged up off the sofa and ran toward the bedroom, then she remembered her sleeping child and turned back toward the kitchen.

Knowing she was going to cry, she didn't want to risk waking Hope. But before she reached the kitchen door, Worth caught up with her. His big hand clamped down on her shoulder. She froze instantly.

"Faith, please…"

"Please, what?"

When he grasped her shoulders and began turning her to face him, she thought about rejecting him, but something within her succumbed immediately. He didn't say anything, just looked at her. Why was it that, if this man had been little more than a stranger to her in the past and was no more than that to her now, she understood him so well? He wanted to say the right things to her, but he was afraid to speak, afraid he'd say the wrong thing and hurt her even more. He might not love her, but he cared. She was important to him—very important—whether he realized it or not.

"All my memories aren't going to be happy ones," she told him. "Some of them are bound to hurt me. Especially if…when I remember about the attack. You can't protect me from the truth." She lifted her hand and caressed his cheek. "I know you want to

protect me, want to cocoon me in some safe place
where I can't ever be hurt again.''

Worth said nothing for a moment, and then, as if
giving into some inner struggle, he lowered his head
until his lips met hers. Faith held her breath, uncertain
and yet expectant. When he kissed her, she responded
without giving a thought to the consequences. On
some instinctive level, she remembered the feel and
the taste of this man. His body heat seeped into her
skin; his passion consumed her. Giving herself over
to the moment, she dissolved into Worth, becoming
one with him as sensation alone dominated their
actions.

She could feel everything; all her senses were
heightened. His mouth was warm and moist, his kiss
powerful and demanding. Her body longed to know
his complete possession. Whimpering, she opened her
mouth, allowing him admission. His tongue thrust inside like a velvet-tipped hot poker, exploring as it
raked softly against the smoothness of the interior.
Tingles spiraled upward from her feminine core. Her
nipples peaked. Her body pulsated with need.

It had been this way before, this overwhelming desire to be with him. With Worth. Only with Worth.
He was the other half of her, a part of her soul.

But he doesn't love you, a taunting inner voice said.

Yes, he does. Yes, he does! Her heart defended him.
He loves me. He just doesn't know it yet.

Suddenly Worth ended the kiss and gently pushed
Faith away from him. After taking several deep

breaths, he said, "I'm sorry, honey. I shouldn't have let things get out of hand."

"It wasn't your fault. I wanted it to happen just as much as you did."

"Yeah, I figured that out." He shoved open the kitchen door and held it for her. "How about something to drink? Some tea or cocoa or—"

Faith laid her hand on his chest; he went rigid as a stone statue. "You want to make love to me, don't you?"

"Faith..."

"Don't you?"

"Yes."

"I want us to make love," she told him. "I don't know if it's right or wrong. All I know is that...I love you. With or without my memory, my feelings are the same. During the time we've spent together, I've fallen in love with you all over again. Don't you see, that must mean we're meant to be together."

"Faith, honey, you're not fully recovered, physically, mentally or emotionally. If I took you to bed now, I'd be taking advantage of you."

She rubbed the palm of her hand over his chest, caressing the cotton material of his sweater, when what she longed to touch was his naked chest. "What are you so afraid of?"

"I don't know what you mean." He lifted her hand from his chest and gently released her.

She smiled to herself. This was the way he'd acted once before...in the cave, when she'd asked him to make love to her. He'd been afraid then, too. Afraid of her.

"I remember," she told him. "The first time we made love, I asked you and you said no, at least you did in the beginning."

"You remember?"

She nodded. "Not everything, just how reluctant you were. You were afraid to make love to me then just as you are now. You're afraid of the way I make you feel, afraid that you might love me."

"Don't do this. Don't build up some imaginary fairy-tale romance around you and me. I'm no Prince Charming, believe me. I'm the last guy a sweet, gentle, loving woman like you needs."

"Why do you say that?" She wanted to put her arms around him and hold him close, but she sensed his need to keep some physical distance between them.

"Faith, you don't know me. The real me. You never did. You have no idea what I'm capable of doing. I was a soldier, a special forces soldier. Do you know what that means? I've killed people. Men and women..." He swallowed and glanced away, focusing his gaze on the floor. "And children. Do you hear me—on my last assignment for the Rangers, I was part of an ugly battle between our guys and the native rebels. They came at us from all sides—men, women and children, some of them no more than ten or eleven."

"Oh, Worth, how terrible for you. You're such a

kind man. That type of brutal killing must have been very difficult for you.''

When she reached out to him, he grabbed her wrist and hauled her up against him. ''Damn it, Blue Eyes, don't you understand—I've been a hard-ass son of a bitch all my life. I'm a white-trash redneck from Arkansas who knew how to hot-wire a car by the time I was twelve. I'm not good or kind or caring. I'm none of those things.'' He cupped her face between his big hands. ''But God help me, I want to be. For you. And for Hope.''

''I wish you could see yourself through my eyes,'' Faith said. ''To me you are all those things—good, kind, caring, gentle and loving. Ever since I woke up in the hospital and I saw your face, I somehow knew that as long as you stayed with me, I'd be all right.''

''You see something in me that no one else ever has.'' He kissed her forehead, her cheeks and then her lips. Sweet, tender kisses, his passion held in check. ''Maybe love *is* blind.''

''I see you perfectly, Worth Cordell. I accept that you have flaws. Everyone does. Just look at me.''

''I am looking at you,'' he told her. ''All I see is how wonderful you are.''

Just when Worth's lips touched hers again, the doorbell rang. They halted before they actually kissed. Worth groaned, then slowly released her. Feeling slightly unsteady on her feet, she leaned back against the door frame.

''I'll go see who it is,'' Worth said.

She waited for him to get to the door before she

walked across the living room and came up a few feet behind him. He turned on the porch light, glanced through the peephole and then opened the door. Detective Rollins stood on her front porch.

"May I speak to you and Ms. Sheridan?" Rollins asked.

"Come on in." Worth nodded, indicating a welcome.

"Thanks." Rollins entered the living room; Worth closed the door. "I've got some bad news and I wanted to deliver it in person."

"What kind of bad news?" Faith asked as she inched her way closer to Worth.

"You might want to sit down," Rollins suggested.

"Oh, God..." Tremors shivered through Faith's body.

Worth reached out, slipped his arm around her waist and pulled her to his side. "Out with it. Can't you see you're scaring Faith."

"Sorry, ma'am. It's just I hate like the devil to have to tell you this." Rollins inhaled and exhaled deeply. "The Greenville Slayer's second victim, Gloria Clemmons, who survived the ordeal, just as you did, has been found murdered in her own home."

"How was she..." Faith's voice trailed off as tears lodged in her throat.

"Blunt trauma to the head," Rollins replied.

"Any suspects other than the obvious?" Worth asked.

Rollins shook his head.

"Why would he kill her?" Faith asked. "She couldn't identify him."

Rollins stuck his hands in his coat pockets and rocked back and forth on his heels. "We figure he came back to finish the job."

"That means...oh, Worth—" Faith buried her face against his chest as he wrapped his arms around her. "He's going to come after the other woman who survived, isn't he? And he's going to come after me."

Chapter 6

After Detective Rollins's visit three days ago, Worth and Faith had discussed the precautions they would take to keep Faith safe, but she had been adamantly opposed to leaving town with Worth. He'd wanted to whisk Faith and Hope out of harm's way and take them back to Atlanta with him. But in the rational part of his brain, he'd known what Faith had pointed out to him—that if the Greenville Slayer wanted to kill her, he'd find her no matter where she went. Rollins had hinted at using Faith as bait to catch the killer, but Worth had dismissed the idea before the detective had been able to fully explain it to Faith. She had told Rollins that she would seriously consider the idea, but no way was Worth going to let Faith put herself in more danger.

This morning they'd driven into town to finish

Christmas shopping and purchase a live Christmas tree. The big day was coming up in less than a week—Hope's first Christmas. She wasn't old enough to understand the concept of Santa Claus, but it really didn't matter. Faith and Worth were knee-deep into the Jolly Old Saint Nick fantasy. They'd practically bought out the local toy store.

This afternoon Worth had gotten up on a ladder and strung white lights across the edge of the front porch roof, as well as around several large shrubs in the front yard. Since Jody was on Christmas holiday break from her job as an elementary schoolteacher, she'd volunteered as a baby-sitter while Worth and Faith put up the tree and decorated it.

Faith stood across the room and surveyed their handiwork. "It's beautiful. All it needs is the angel on top." She lifted the tree topper from its cushioned bed in the box, then walked across the room and handed the golden-haired angel to Worth. "When I was a little girl I thought all angels had blond hair and blue eyes."

Worth leaned down from his perch on the ladder, took the angel in one hand and clutched Faith's chin with the other. "Some angels have blue eyes and dark-brown hair."

Coming in from the kitchen, with Hope on her hip, Jody cleared her throat. Faith jumped away from Worth as if she'd been caught doing something naughty.

"Oops. Sorry. Was I interrupting something?" Jody asked.

"Not a thing," Worth replied. "I was just getting ready to put the finishing touches on the tree." He placed the blond angel in the flowing white gown atop the tree. "Is she straight?"

"Perfect," Faith said.

"Hey, I was wondering if y'all want me to order pizza for supper?" Jody asked. "It's nearly five and I'm starving."

"Is it that late?" Faith checked her watch. "The day has gone by so fast." When Faith held out her arms, Hope came to her immediately. "You order the pizza and I'll fix Hope's bottle."

"We like cheese pizza," Jody said. "What do you like, Worth?"

"Meat Lovers Supreme," he said. "Order one of each. I can eat a medium all by myself."

Jody sized him up, from head to toe. "I don't doubt that for a minute."

When Faith disappeared into the kitchen, Worth stepped down off the ladder, folded it and put it away in the closet. Jody lifted the receiver and dialed the phone on the end table by the sofa. While Worth gathered up empty boxes in which Faith stored Christmas ornaments, Jody ordered supper.

Worth picked up the remote, turned on the television to check the local news and weather and laid the remote on the sofa arm. The forecasters had been predicting snow for today, but none had materialized. No snow, sleet or even rain.

"She's doing great, isn't she?" Jody plopped down

on the sofa by Worth. "She's regaining more of her memory every day."

"Yeah, she's recalling more and more about her past, her friends, Hope and even me. But she still can't remember anything about the day she was attacked."

"Maybe it's better if she never remembers," Jody said. "It's not something I'd want to remember."

"If she could ID her attacker, I'd want her to remember. That guy needs to be stopped before he kills someone else."

"I know you're concerned about what happened to that other woman, another of his victims who survived. But Faith has you to protect her. Or is that the problem—are you getting tired of hanging around, playing knight in shining armor?"

"I thought you and I had buried the hatchet," Worth said. "You still don't trust me, do you?"

"I trust you to protect Faith, but I don't quite trust you not to break her heart again."

Before Worth could reply, Faith emerged from the kitchen.

"When she finishes her bottle, I need to give Hope a quick bath and change her clothes before we leave." She handed Hope and her bottle to Worth. "I'll go get things ready, so when she's through, bring her into the bathroom."

"Where are y'all going?" Jody asked.

"We're taking Hope to the mall this evening to see Santa Claus and get her picture made with him," Faith replied. "Why don't you come with us?"

"Sure, I'd love to." Jody glanced at Worth. "That is unless I'd be a third wheel. After all, a trip to see Santa is sort of a family thing, isn't it?"

"You're family. You're Hope's Aunt Jody," Faith said as she headed toward the bedroom.

"Faith's right," Worth added. "We want you to come along."

Suddenly Worth heard the television announcer mention something about the Greenville Slayer, but since he had the sound turned down low on the TV, he didn't catch exactly what had been said. Readjusting Hope in his arms, he reached for the remote on the sofa arm, then upped the volume for the television. Before focusing his attention on the TV screen, he glanced over the sofa to Faith, who stood dead still by the open bedroom door.

"The Greenville Slayer has struck again and this time it's another repeat attack," the announcer said. "Lois Helton, the Greenville cosmetologist, who survived a brutal attack two months ago, and her husband were both shot and killed in their home today. Police estimate the murders occurred around three this afternoon. The police officer guarding Mrs. Helton was critically wounded and is not expected to survive."

"Oh, God!" Jody gasped.

"He's killed both women who survived," Faith said. "It's only a matter of time before he comes after me."

Worth checked Hope's bottle. She'd drunk three-fourths and was still guzzling away. With Hope in his arms, Worth stood and went over to Faith. He looked directly at her, his gaze demanding her eyes to meet his.

"We'll cancel the trip to see Santa," Worth said. "Next year, Hope will be over a year old and she'll enjoy getting her picture made with Santa more than she would have this year."

Faith nodded. "Does this mean I'm going to be a prisoner in my own house? I've been remembering what it felt like to be held captive in that horrible basement in Subria when I was abducted with Phila Constantine last year. It's a terrible feeling. Not one I want to experience again."

"I wish I could say that it won't be necessary to curtail all your normal activities even more than we have already, but we can't take any chances," Worth told her. "Not with your life on the line."

"It'll be only temporary. Just until the police catch the killer," Jody said, as she jumped up off the sofa and looked back and forth from Faith to Worth. "And you have a big plus the other women didn't have— you've got your own professional bodyguard right at your side."

"You're right on both counts." Faith reached out and took Hope from Worth. "I am lucky to have my own bodyguard. And this insanity isn't going to stop until the killer is caught and put behind bars."

"I know what you're thinking," Worth said. "Forget it. I won't let you do it. Do you hear me, Faith?"

Snapping her gaze back and forth from Worth to

Faith, Jody asked, "What's he talking about? What won't he let you do?"

"The police suggested setting a trap for the killer and using me as bait." Faith pressed a tender kiss on top of Hope's head.

Jody gasped. "I'm with Worth on this one. No way, Jose!"

"Can't you both see that it's the only way!"

"No it's not the only way," Jody said. "You're getting back more and more of your memory all the time. You'll probably remember the attack and be able to ID the attacker—tomorrow or the next day or—"

"Or never." Faith turned away and walked into the bedroom.

"Hell! Do something," Jody told Worth. "I know Faithie, and when she's determined, nothing can stop her."

Worth and Jody followed Faith into the bedroom. She sat down in the white rocker beside Hope's crib, removed the empty bottle from the baby's mouth and set it on the floor; then she rocked back and forth as she crooned a soft lullaby.

"You can't do it," Jody said.

"Sh— Be quiet," Faith whispered. "I don't want to discuss it. My mind's made up."

"Then unmake it," Worth told her. "Think about Hope. Think about your friends…your family."

"I am thinking about Hope and about my family. You can't guarantee me that he won't try to harm Hope. And with your standing between him and me, he could hurt you. This man won't stop killing until someone stops him.''

"Why does it have to be you?" Jody asked.

"Because I'm the only one left. If I don't do all I can to stop him, he'll kill again and again.''

"We need to talk about this before—'' Worth said, but was interrupted by the shrill ring of the telephone. "I'll get it.''

He stormed across the room to the phone on the nightstand, then picked up the receiver. "Cordell here.''

"Mr. Cordell, this is Detective Rollins. I have some more bad news.''

"Yeah, we already know. Your bad news is being broadcast on all the local TV stations.''

"We're going to send a patrol car to stay outside Ms. Sheridan's apartment, around the clock, starting tonight,'' Rollins said.

"Who is it?" Faith asked.

Worth placed his hand over the mouthpiece. "Detective Rollins.''

"Tell him that we're coming to the police station first thing in the morning to discuss his plan.''

"No, Faith.''

"Yes, Worth.''

After removing his hand from the mouthpiece, Worth said, "Rollins, Ms. Sheridan and I will see you in your office in the morning. She wants to discuss your plan to capture the killer.''

Worth heard Rollins's indrawn breath, then silence for a couple of minutes. "If she agrees to do this—

to put herself directly in the line of fire—I swear to you, Cordell, I'll do everything in my power to keep her safe.''

"She's not doing this unless you agree that I'm part of the team. I want to be there, close by, participating. Not in the background.''

"I believe that can be arranged.''

Worth hung up the receiver, then turned to Faith. "We'll have to arrange for someone to take care of Hope until this is all over.''

"I can—'' Jody said.

"No.'' Faith shook her head. "I'll pack some of her things in the morning and we'll take her to Lindsey. She can stay with Lindsey and George until...'' Faith looked at Jody. "You're in the apartment next door. If this guy finds out where I live, I don't want Hope anywhere around here.''

"You're right,'' Jody agreed. "The best place for her is with George and Lindsey.''

The doorbell rang. A collective gasp filled the bedroom, then utter silence.

"You two stay here,'' Worth said, then left the bedroom and headed for the front door.

He peered through the viewfinder and saw a teenage boy carrying two boxed pizzas. A relieved sigh swept from his lungs to his lips.

After paying the delivery boy, he carried the pizza into the kitchen, then called out, "Pizza's here. Let's eat.''

Worth ate. Jody and Faith nibbled. They tried to engage in idle chitchat, but it took more effort than it was worth to keep up the pretense of a normal evening. At eight, Jody hugged Faith and said goodnight. At eight-thirty Faith and Worth gave Hope her bath, then Worth gave her a bottle and rocked her to sleep while Faith showered and got ready for bed.

By nine-thirty Worth was sacked out on the sofa bed in the living room. The latest David Baldacci bestseller he was trying to read wasn't doing much to help take his mind off the reality of Faith's situation. He wasn't Faith's husband, but did that mean he didn't have a right to be part of the decision making? He cared about Faith and the thought of her dying scared the hell out of him. Hope needed her mother. Faith's friends needed her. The whole world needed a kind, caring person like Faith.

And you need her, an inner voice told him. *Faith has become very important to you, as vital to you as the air you breathe.*

Worth slammed the book shut and tossed it aside, then slid down until his head hit the pillows. After turning out the lamp on the end table, he pulled the covers to his neck and stared up at the dark ceiling. He lay there listening to the quiet sounds of night. Solitude. Loneliness. He felt both, despite being a part of Faith's life. He had lived with solitude and loneliness since he'd been a kid. When his mother died and his father remarried, he'd been alone. He might have lived with his father and stepmother, but he'd never been a part of their family. The only family he'd ever had was his half sister and he'd lost her years ago. A drug overdose at a wild college party. He hadn't loved anyone since he lost Norma.

He hadn't meant to care so much about Faith, but little by little he'd fallen under her spell. And she had turned to him these past couple of weeks for protection and emotional support, just as she'd done when he'd rescued her in Subria. She'd called her feelings love then and she believed herself in love with him now. But Worth had his doubts. Somewhere in that gentle heart of hers she had confused hero-worship with love. Faith needed him; but did she really love him?

And then there was Hope. His daughter. He'd never thought about fathering a child and had been careful to always practice safe sex—except that one time with Faith. Maybe he should regret the fact that he'd gotten Faith pregnant, but how could he? That tiny baby girl had wrapped him around her little finger. Whenever he looked at her, his heart swelled with love. He was glad to be Hope's father. He loved her and wanted to be a part of her life from now on.

But what about Faith? *Admit the truth,* he told himself. *You want to be a part of Faith's life, too.*

An earsplitting scream surged from the bedroom and reverberated through the house. Worth bounded out of bed and raced toward the bedroom, his only thought was to reach Faith and Hope. Hope's whimpers burst into gulping cries. With his heart racing like mad, he skidded to a halt when he saw Faith sitting straight up in bed, a look of sheer terror on her face. He rushed to her, grabbed her shoulders and shook her gently.

"What's wrong?" he asked.

She flung her arms around him. "A nightmare. A terrifying nightmare."

Worth soothed her, stroking her back and whispering reassurances. "It's okay. It's okay."

The phone rang. Hope cried louder and louder.

"You get Hope," Faith said. "I'll answer the phone."

When Faith picked up the phone, Worth headed toward Hope's crib in the corner of the bedroom. As he lifted his daughter into his arms and placed her on his shoulder, he heard Faith reassuring Jody that everything was all right, telling her that she'd simply had a nightmare. Worth walked the floor with Hope, humming to her as he patted her back. His big hand covered her upper torso. She was tiny and helpless—and his. Did every father feel this way—loving, possessive and protective?

In his peripheral vision he noticed Faith get out of bed and head for the bathroom. He laid Hope in her crib and rocked her back and forth until her droopy eyelids closed.

"Go back to sleep, sweetheart. Daddy's here and everything is all right." He bent over the crib and kissed his daughter's forehead. "I need to take care of your mama now."

He met Faith as she came out of the bathroom, her face moist and her hair slightly damp. "Are you really okay?"

She nodded. "A splash of cold water in my face helped."

"You should go back to bed and try to rest."

She crawled into bed, then held out her hand to him. "Stay with me. Please."

"Faith, I'm not so sure it's a good idea."

She smiled faintly. "I seem to remember your saying something like that once before, or is my memory wrong?"

Worth sat down on the edge of the bed. "Do you remember that night?"

"Most of it. I remember how dark the cave was and how cold I felt...until I curled up to your back. Then I got hot pretty fast."

"You were a regular hussy." He reached out and pushed several loose strands of her hair away from her face. "Want to tell me about the dream?"

"He killed me. In my dream, he killed me."

"Faith..." Worth scooted over in the bed and pulled Faith into his arms. "He's not going to kill you. Whatever happens, I'll be there to take care of you."

She wrapped her arms around his waist and snuggled close, burrowing her nose against his neck. "How could you have ever thought I would be better off without you?"

"We shouldn't let this happen again," he told her, but made no move to release her. "You were afraid of dying that night, when I made love to you for the first time. And now, tonight, you—"

"Hush." Lifting her head from his shoulder, she

placed her index finger over his lips. "I seem to recall that we made love several times after we were rescued. We couldn't get enough of each other. Those memories are coming back to me now and I know how much I loved you then…and how much I love you now."

"But Faith…"

She tapped her finger on his lips. "It's all right. You don't have to say you love me. For some reason, you find it difficult to say the words. But I know how you feel. Your actions—in the past and in the present—have proven to me how much I mean to you."

She brought her arms up and around his neck, then pressed her body to his. He couldn't deny that he cared about her because he did. And he couldn't turn away from the need he saw in her eyes. She wanted him the same way he wanted her.

He spread kisses in her hair, over her face, down her neck. "I'll try to be gentle. I don't want to hurt you."

She sought his mouth, then whispered against his lips. "Don't hold back. Make love to me the way you did before. I know you won't hurt me."

He laid her back into the mattress and came down over her, bracing himself with his knees as he kissed her. The kiss grew hotter, wilder and more intense. They devoured each other, hunger urging them to take everything, to enjoy every millisecond of their passion. Faith's fingers skimmed his chest with inquisitive touches, acquainting herself with every inch of flesh, every muscle. With unsteady hands, he reached between them and unbuttoned her pajama top, then spread it apart to reveal her small, high breasts. When his lips suckled one tight nipple, she moaned; when he licked and stroked the other nipple, her hips rose off the bed. With her mound pressed against his erection, she wriggled and squirmed, rubbing herself up and down in an enticing manner.

"Keep doing that and I'm going to lose it before I'm inside you," Worth murmured against her ear, then grasped the waistband of her pajama bottoms and tugged.

She lifted her hips enough for him to easily maneuver the pajamas down her legs and over her feet. As he tossed the pajamas to the foot of the bed, he kissed her again. Deeply. Savagely. And when she gasped for air, he painted a trail from mouth to breasts. She whimpered and writhed beneath him. His tongue slid over her rib cage, down her belly to her navel. She held her breath. He moved southward, pausing at the edge of her triangle of dark hair. When his mouth captured her tenderness, his hands covered her breasts and kneaded, then tweaked her nipples.

Faith keened deep in her throat when his tongue delved and retreated, then delved deeper. He found her most sensitive spot and stroked her, harder and harder, until she clutched his head and held him in place while he finished the job. He felt her body tighten; he worked harder and faster. Faith cried out as her climax splintered through her. While she was in the throes of fulfillment, Worth rose up and over her, took her slender hips in his hands, lifted her and thrust his sex to the hilt within her.

As he hammered into her, seeking his own satisfaction, she clung to him and within minutes began undulating to the rhythm he'd set. When the moment came, his ears rang and his body trembled from the force of his release. But before the pleasure subsided, Faith reached the pinnacle a second time. As the aftershocks rippled through them, Worth fell exhausted into the bed beside Faith, pulled her into his arms and lifted the sheet and comforter to cover them. She snuggled against him.

"I love you," she whispered a moment before she fell asleep in his arms.

Chapter 7

They dropped Hope by Lindsey and George Dawson's before heading out to the police station. Worth had done everything in his power to dissuade Faith from offering herself as bait in the police's trap, but she'd been unmovable in her conviction that it was the only way to regain control over her life. He understood how much that meant to Faith, especially since her captivity in Subria last year. Nothing made a person want to exert control over their life as much as having all power taken from them.

Detective Rollins met them at the door to his office and welcomed them, then ordered coffee.

"Detective MacMillan from Sparkman, Detective Roberts from Greenville and Agent Colter from the state bureau will be working with us on this plan," Rollins said. "I'm expecting all of them here by ten this morning. I'd rather wait until they arrive before we discuss the details.''

"That's fine with me," Faith said. "I—" She glanced at Worth. "We don't mind waiting."

"None of us like the idea of using you to lure this guy into our trap," Rollins said, "but we admit that the law enforcement of three towns and the state of South Carolina are no closer to nabbing the Greenville Slayer now than we were right after the first murder."

"I intend to play a vital role in any scenario that requires Faith to risk her life." Worth reached across from his chair to Faith's and grabbed her hand.

"You'll have to humor him." Faith squeezed Worth's hand. "It's the only way I could get him to stop fighting me about my decision. If Worth isn't involved, then neither am I."

"Your assistance isn't needed and won't be appreciated." Rollins's gaze met Worth's. "But I've given you my word. I'll explain to the others that your involvement isn't debatable."

"I'm not exactly a civilian," Worth said. "I know how to conduct myself under dangerous conditions."

"I had you checked out, Cordell. I know your background."

One of the police officers brought a tray laden with coffee cups into Rollins's office and offered a cup first to Faith and then to Worth.

Rollins glanced through the open doorway as he lifted his cup from the tray. "I see our team has arrived a little early."

Worth and Faith followed Rollins's line of vision. Three men in plainclothes stood outside the office. Rollins motioned to them.

"Come on in. Ms. Sheridan is already here."

The threesome entered, Rollins made introductions and once they were seated, Agent Carter laid out a simple yet potentially dangerous plan.

"There's a good chance this guy is already keeping tabs on Ms. Sheridan," Carter said. "If he is, he's aware she's never alone, that you're with her at all times and a police car is stationed in front of her apartment."

"Lois Helton's husband was with her when she was killed," Worth reminded them.

"Lois Helton's husband was sixty-five years old," Detective MacMillan said. "If this guy's gotten a good look at you, Cordell, he's probably been intimidated by your size alone."

"Bottom line is we have to make it appear that Faith is alone," Agent Carter said. "It's probably the only way to bring him out into the open. And we believe if she goes alone to Toddle Town on some pretense, he'll be less suspicious than he would if it appeared you'd left her alone at her apartment."

The minute Worth heard the details, his survival instincts kicked in. He didn't like the sound of it. It wasn't a bad plan and the odds were they'd catch their guy; but there was a downside—they couldn't give Worth a hundred percent guarantee they could keep Faith safe.

"You want me to go to Toddle Town alone?" Faith asked.

"We'll send a policewoman with you," Detective Roberts said. "She'll wear street clothes and you two can act like a couple of old friends. We'll have Toddle Town under surveillance and our men will already be in place when this guy follows you there."

"What makes you think he's watching me? And if he is, why do you think he'll follow me?" Faith looked around the room at each lawman.

"We don't know for sure, and it might take more than one try for this plan to work," Rollins explained. "If you'll go to Toddle Town every day at the same time, stay for say two hours and then go home, it will set up a routine and make our killer less suspicious. If he's watching you—and the odds are that he is— he might keep tabs on your activities for several days or even a week or so before he strikes. And by setting the trap at Toddle Town, we know it's a place he's familiar with. It's where he abducted you the first time."

Faith turned to Worth. "What do you think?"

"It's too dangerous. I don't like it."

"Other than that, what do you think? It's a good plan, isn't it?"

"If we don't factor in the possibility that you could get killed, yeah, it's a good plan."

Faith looked at Rollins. "When do we start?"

"How about late this afternoon?"

"That soon?" Faith sucked in a deep breath. "All right. Let's do it."

* * *

Six days until Christmas. On day one, Faith and policewoman Dale Carruthers drove up in Faith's SUV, parked and headed straight to Toddle Town's front entrance. They carried on a conversation, both appearing perfectly natural; Faith even managed a realistic-sounding laugh. Once inside, they set about taking down Christmas decorations and straightening up the individual rooms. They spent two hours trying to act as if they weren't waiting for a killer to strike. Since the high temperature for the day was supposed to be thirty-four, it had been easy enough to hide the bulletproof vests they wore beneath bulky sweaters. SWAT team members were stationed across the street in the upstairs of a dry cleaners and various police officers joined the downtown Christmas crowds on Hickory Avenue. Disguised as a city work crew repairing a broken pipe line, Worth, Rollins and Macmillan stood around in coveralls and thick jackets, their bulletproof vests and their 9 mm weapons well out of sight.

After two hours, Faith and Dale locked the front door and walked to the SUV. No sign of their guy. Five minutes later, the fake work crew got in a city truck and drove away. Worth didn't like the fact that there would be a good fifteen minute interval when he wouldn't be with Faith. He knew that Officer Carruthers was well trained to defend Faith, but his gut instincts warned him that no one, not even the entire SWAT team, could protect Faith the way he could. Hell, it wasn't personal to anyone else.

And the fact that it was personal for him was as much a disadvantage as an advantage. The minute he saw Faith in imminent danger, not only would his trained instincts kick in, but so would his natural emotional instincts. It was as basic as the fact he would be protecting his woman and not a client.

Day two came and went in pretty much the same manner as day one, without even a hint of their killer being in Whitewood, let alone him following Faith.

Day three. Saturday. Another no-show. Tensions mounted for everyone involved. Worth could see how nervous Faith was and how valiantly she tried to hide it. They took a day off on Sunday. Worth attended church with Faith and Hope, which was a strange event for him. He hadn't been inside a church since his mother died when he was six. After church they ate lunch at the Dawsons', joined by Margaret and Mr. Tippins, as well as Jody and Jody's on-again/off-again boyfriend, Tommy Kenyon. Old Horace, the Dawsons' beagle, slept soundly in front of the fire the entire time.

Later on at home, while Hope took a late afternoon nap, Worth made slow, sweet love to Faith. Although Hope had stayed with Lindsey for the past few days, Worth and Faith decided to bring her home with them today. Each moment they shared together as a family became more precious with each passing day. Tomorrow afternoon, they would return Hope to the Dawsons. Three days of nerve-racking waiting had taken a toll on both Faith and Worth. He wasn't sure how much longer either of them could endure the uncertainty.

In the aftermath of lovemaking, they lay in bed together, naked and sated. Worth idly stroked Faith's slender hip.

"I remember so much about my life," Faith said. "Almost everything."

"But not the attack?"

"I remember everything that day, up to when I locked the door to Toddle Town and walked toward the parking area. Then it's all a blank until I woke up in the hospital."

"What about everything before then—from your childhood up to that day?"

"I still have a few holes in my memory, but not many. It's odd, but I still can't recall everything about the night I waited for you in the square. I remember going to the square. I can hear the church bells and even see the snow, but I don't remember leaving the square and going home. I've lost several days there, maybe even a week or so. I remember being in the hospital after Christmas. I think I had pneumonia. Is that right?"

"Didn't Jody tell you about—"

"Jody told me she thought it was best if I waited for my memories to return instead of her filling in the blanks."

Worth pulled Faith to him and kissed her. "Jody's right. Give it a little more time. You'll remember."

He hoped she never remembered all the details of the night she had waited for him for four hours. He couldn't bear the thought of her experiencing that kind of emotional pain again. If her memories of that night remained vague, he knew that sooner or later, he'd have to tell her. But selfishly, he wanted it to be later. A part of him feared that when she recalled all the details, she would hate him and not be able to forgive him for disappointing her.

Three days to Christmas. Faith spent Monday morning wrapping presents and trying her best to pretend her life was normal. She'd put on a CD of *All Time Favorites* and the mellow voice of Bing Crosby crooning ''White Christmas'' filled her apartment. The aroma of gingerbread cookies baking in the oven wafted out of the kitchen and a spicy scent permeated the air. Worth sat on the pallet on the living room floor with Hope, watching her waver back and forth as she shook the rattle in her hand. Faith loved seeing Worth with his daughter; she could tell by his every action that he adored their child. But her big, strong, macho guy couldn't put his feelings into words. She knew, in her heart of hearts, that Worth loved them. Even if he didn't know it yet; even if it took him a while longer to come to terms with emotions alien to him.

Worth lifted Hope into his arms and stood, then walked over to the sofa where Faith sat with a gift box half-wrapped in bright-red paper. ''If this afternoon's stint at Toddle Town is a bust, I want you to put an end to it. We've all given it our best shot. This guy has eluded the law for months now, which means he's not stupid. He's probably suspicious about why I'm letting you go to Toddle Town every day without me."

"We can't give up." Faith clipped off a piece of tape and used it to secure the folded edges of her package. "Today could be the day he shows up. Or tomorrow."

"Or next week or next month? Honey, you can't keep doing this day after day. It's going to wear you down."

"What's our alternative?"

"I get Dom Shea back here and we keep you and Hope under guard 24/7 until the police nab this guy."

Faith placed the wrapped gift atop the stack she'd made in the floor in front of the sofa. "For how long? We can't live that way indefinitely. Besides, I'm not doing this just for myself, you know. I'm putting myself out there as bait so we can stop this lunatic before he kills another woman."

Suddenly a loud singsong siren went off. Faith stilled instantly. A smoke detector. The kitchen? Were the cookies burning? Then she realized it wasn't her smoke detector. The sound wasn't loud enough.

"That must be Jody's smoke detector," Faith said. "You'd better go check it out. I'm pretty sure she spent the night with Tommy last night and probably isn't home yet."

"You stay here." Worth handed Hope to Faith. "I'll check it out. Where's your key to Jody's apartment?"

"I don't have a key," Faith said. "Jody keeps an

extra taped to the back of the wreath on the front door.''

''I'll have to talk to her about leaving a key where just anybody could find it.'' Worth went to the closet, got his jacket, then checked the pocket for his Glock. After slipping into the jacket, he headed for the door. ''Lock the door behind me and don't open it to anyone except me. Not even Officer Deloney out there.'' Worth nodded to the unmarked vehicle across the street.

''Do you think—''

''I don't think anything in particular,'' he told her. ''Just lock the door.''

As soon as Worth went outside, she closed the door behind him and locked it.

''Well, Miss Sweetie Pie, let's go check on those cookies while your daddy's gone.''

Faith entered the kitchen, placed Hope in her bouncy seat in the middle of the table, then picked up her oven mitts and put them on. Just as she bent over to open the oven door, she heard a loud crash. Her first thought was that Worth had broken something next door. Gasping, she jerked around to check on Hope. In her peripheral vision, she caught a glimpse of the back door to her apartment. Something had shattered the glass pane.

Oh, God! Oh, God! Faith dashed toward Hope, grabbing her, just as a hand reached through the empty space where the glass had been. The gloved hand twisted the doorknob. They kept the door deadbolt locked and the key was on the kitchen counter.

With her heartbeat thundering in her ears, Faith started to run toward the living room. A gunshot rang out. A bullet whizzed over her head and entered the wall. Faith dropped to her knees, cradling Hope in front of her. Another shot ripped into the floor not a foot from Faith. She began crawling on her knees, trying to place herself out of the shooter's line of vision.

Worth stood in Jody's kitchen gazing at the open back door when he heard the crash. He was halfway out the door when he heard the gunshots. Damn! Racing outside onto the back porch, his thoughts jumbled with fear, recriminations and pure rage, Worth saw the man shooting through the broken pane in Faith's back door. Then he heard the scream! His blood ran cold. Faith screaming in agony.

Worth pulled out his Glock, prepared himself for battle and charged. The guy spun around, his eyes wild as he scowled at Worth.

"You're too late. She's dead," the gunman said. "And you're next."

An evil, crazed grin spread across the guy's face as he pointed his pistol at Worth. Thank you, Worth thought. Thank you for making it so easy for me to kill you, you son of a bitch!

Before the killer got off another shot, Worth aimed and fired. The bullet hit the guy right between the eyes. He reeled backward and fell onto the porch in a dead heap. Worth barely glanced at him as he rushed past and into the house. When he saw Faith sprawled out on the floor, facedown, his heart stopped.

No, please, God, no!

He ran across the room, dropped down on his haunches and grasped Faith's shoulder. She grunted, then rolled over, Hope still secure in her arms. Hope yelled at the top of her lungs.

"Where are you hit?" Worth asked. "Just lie still. I'll call 911."

"I'm all right. I don't know how he kept missing me, but he did. He didn't shoot me." Faith held Hope out to Worth. "Take her while I stand up."

A sense of unparalleled relief washed over Worth, a tidal wave of thankfulness. With one hand he lifted Hope up and braced her on his hip, then reached down, grabbed Faith's arm and pulled her to her feet. He wrapped mother and daughter in his arms.

Officer Deloney came running around the side of the house, his pistol drawn. The minute he saw the dead man sprawled out on the porch, he skidded to a halt.

"Is everybody okay?" Deloney asked.

"We're safe," Faith said as she clung to Worth. "Finally, we're safe."

Chapter 8

The police, an ambulance and a fire truck showed up after Officer Deloney put in a 911 call. Before the first emergency vehicle pulled into the driveway, every neighbor within two city blocks showed up in the yard. Although Faith insisted she was perfectly fine, Worth demanded she allow the paramedics to check her.

"Really, Worth, I'm all right," Faith insisted, but her voice quivered slightly. If Worth didn't have his arm around her waist, she wasn't sure she could stand.

"Either you let them check you out or I'm taking you straight to the hospital right now." She gazed up at Worth and realized how deadly serious he was. His tense, strained expression told her he was fighting to control his emotions.

Worth kept gently jostling Hope in an effort to

soothe her. Her yelping cries had softened to sobbing whimpers.

"All right," Faith agreed. "But first, let me sit down before I fall down."

George and Lindsey Dawson came rushing in the back door, allowed entrance by their nephew, one of Whitewood's policemen.

"Merciful heavens," Lindsey said. "Are y'all okay?" She glanced from Faith to Hope to Worth. "Give me that baby and you see to Faith. She looks like she's about to keel over."

Without hesitation Worth handed his daughter to her honorary grandmother, then caught Faith in his arms just as she swooned in a faint.

"Damn," Worth cursed under his breath.

"Poor thing," George said. "She's been through so much. That child deserves nothing but happiness for the rest of her life. Nobody should have to experience so much tragedy in one lifetime."

Worth turned to the two paramedics standing in the kitchen. "I'll put her in the ambulance and ride along with y'all. And I'd suggest we get going before she comes to." He turned and looked at Hope nestled securely in Lindsey's loving arms. "Take care of—"

George slapped his hand down on Worth's back. "No need to tell us to take good care of Hope. We'll bring her on to the E.R. and wait with you until the doctor checks Faith out."

"Thanks. I don't know what Faith and Hope would do without you two."

Worth carried Faith through the house and out onto

the front porch. Suddenly the throng of neighbors congregated in the yard quieted and every eye focused on them. Inquiries buzzed from various lips. "Is she all right? Was she shot? What can we do to help? We'll pray for her. We care so much about Faith."

Just as one of the paramedics opened the back doors to the ambulance, a sleek, silver sports car skidded to a halt on the street in front of the duplex. Jody jumped out of the Corvette and flew across the yard, parting the crowd like Moses parting the Red Sea.

"Faith, Faith, Faith!" Jody screamed. "Oh, God, Worth, what happened? Is she—?"

"She's all right," Worth said. "She fainted. I think she may be suffering from a mild case of shock. We're taking her to the E.R. to get checked out. Lindsey and George are bringing Hope."

"What the hell happened?" Jody asked, her voice tinged with hysteria.

One of the paramedics interrupted. "Sir, we're ready to go."

Worth crawled into the back of the ambulance, laid Faith on the gurney, sat beside her, then looked back at Jody. "Get Tommy to bring you to Memorial and I'll fill you in on the details. But don't worry about the guy who tried to kill Faith. He's dead."

Jody's mouth gaped open. "Oh. You—you—?"

"Yeah," Worth replied just as a paramedic closed the ambulance door.

When the ambulance was only minutes from her apartment, Faith roused and looked up at Worth. "Where's Hope…what—?"

When she tried to sit up, Worth grasped her shoulders, forcing her to stay put. "Lie still, Blue Eyes. Hope's fine. She's with Lindsey and George. You've had quite a scare. You need to relax and stay calm."

"Me?" Faith smiled. "Worth Cordell, you're the one who needs to relax and stay calm."

"I am perfectly calm," Worth said through clenched teeth.

"No, you're not, so don't try to lie to me. I can see the expression on your face and in your eyes. I know you well enough to be able to read what those brown eyes of yours are saying."

"Damn it, Faith, what do you expect? I'm not going to fall apart on you just because I'm still shaking like a leaf inside. When I realized there was no fire in Jody's apartment, that somebody had gotten into her place and set off the alarm as a distraction to get me away from you—" Worth clutched his knees tightly as he leaned over the stretcher on which Faith lay. "If anything had happened to you..." He swallowed hard and glanced away.

Hope lifted her hand and laid it atop his on his knee. "You saved me...again. It seems to be your fate to be my hero. I guess I'm just one of those women who needs her own personal protector."

Worth gazed deeply into Faith's blue, blue eyes. He'd never cared as much for another human being as he did Faith and the intensity of his emotions scared him. He'd never been in love, not really. Just a teenage infatuation that had gone bad. He wasn't sure he knew what being in love was all about. What he felt for Faith was the most powerful emotion he'd ever known. Possessiveness, protectiveness and a huge dose of pure male lust. When he was near her, he wanted to look at her, touch her, taste her, absorb her. No matter how many times he made love to her, he wanted her again. He realized that he could never get enough of her. But was what he felt real love? Hell, if it wasn't, it was the closest thing to love he'd ever felt.

"You've gotten awfully quiet," Faith said as she lay there looking up at him. "You're not worrying about me, are you?"

"Just thinking," he replied.

"About what?"

"About us."

"Oh."

"Be quiet and rest until we get to the hospital. We'll have plenty of time to talk later." When she nodded, Worth took her hand in his. "Everything is going to be fine."

"As long as you're with me."

A tinge of uncertainty alerted Worth to his deepest fears. Did Faith love him or was she mistaking her need for a protector with genuine love?

In less than ten minutes the paramedics unloaded Faith and carried her into the emergency room at Memorial Hospital. Worth followed, staying as close to Faith as possible. By the time the doctor had given Faith a clean bill of health, Jody and Tommy, Lindsey and George, with Hope, as well as Margaret had arrived at the E.R. and were congregated in the waiting area.

"I'm perfectly all right," Faith announced as she held out her arms for Hope.

"That's just what we wanted to hear," Margaret said.

When Faith brought Hope close and kissed her rosy cheeks, Worth put his arm around Faith.

"Y'all are coming home with us," George said. "We've got plenty of room in our big old house and we can go get anything you need from the apartment."

"Oh," Faith sighed. "I guess we can't go home right now, can we? Do you suppose the police are still there?"

"They might be," Worth said. "But even if they aren't, there's no way we'll be going back to that apartment."

Faith shivered. "You're right. I don't think I can ever go back into the kitchen without thinking about..."

"Let's get you to the house," Lindsey said. "I have a nice pot roast cooking and I made a fresh sweet potato pie this morning."

George chuckled. "My wife thinks all of life's problems can be solved with a good, hardy meal."

Lindsey glanced around at Margaret, Jody and Tommy. "Y'all are invited to come to supper, too. After a day like this, we should all be together."

An odd sensation seeped through Worth, a bittersweet realization that for the first time since he'd been a small child, he was part of a family. Faith's family. And he didn't want to lose that good feeling, didn't want to lose Faith and Hope.

Faith doesn't need you now, an inner voice reminded him. *She got along for the past year without you and if you left today, she'd get by just fine.* But what about Hope? Every child needs a father. But he couldn't use Hope as an excuse to remain in Faith's life.

"What are we waiting for?" Margaret asked. "I've got my car here. Faith, you and Worth and Hope can ride with me." She turned to George. "Get Hope's car seat for me."

In no time at all the entire group arrived at the Dawsons' home. Cars lined their driveway. Faith was seated in a big recliner in the den and Hope stayed in her mother's lap while the other ladies put supper on the table. Just as George brought Worth and Tommy a bottled beer apiece, Detective Rollins showed up at the front door and asked to speak to Worth.

Worth stayed in the foyer, keeping his voice low during their brief conversation.

"We'll need you to come down to the station. Later tonight if possible," Rollins said. "There's no doubt in anyone's mind that you killed the guy in self-defense, but—"

"I understand," Worth replied. "I've been through this before. In my profession, being willing to kill to protect a client is part of the job."

"How's Faith doing?"

"Truth be told, I think she's doing better than I."

Rollins nodded. "It's rough on a man to see the woman he loves at risk. Thank God you were there with her."

Worth walked the detective out to his car, then joined the others in the dining room for a late supper.

"We'll all have Christmas here," Lindsey said. "George and I will bring your gifts from your place over here and put them under our tree tomorrow."

"This is Hope's first Christmas, so I want everything to be perfect," Faith said.

Margaret patted Faith's hand. "We'll make sure the day is perfect for Hope."

Worth noted that Faith hadn't touched her meal. She had simply moved the food around on her plate. She was such a tiny thing, slender and delicate. Something in him—that caring, protective part of him—wanted to spoon-feed her, but he knew she'd veto the idea.

Later that evening while Faith settled into bed in the Dawsons' guest room, Worth helped Lindsey give Hope her evening bath.

"Why don't you settle down in that rocking chair with her?" Lindsey suggested. "I'll warm her bottle and bring it to you."

An hour later, long after Hope had finished her milk, Worth sat in the semidark room, slowly rocking his daughter and humming softly to her. Faith had fallen asleep within minutes of going to bed, her sleep the results of a mild sedative given to her in the E.R. Worth rose from the rocker, placed Hope in the crib that Lindsey kept at her house, then walked down the hall to find his hosts.

Undoubtedly everyone else had gone home; he found George and Lindsey alone in the den. When he entered the room, they both glanced up at him.

"Are our girls asleep?" George asked.

Worth nodded.

"I've made up the bed for you in our elder son's old room," Lindsey said.

"That's mighty kind of you," Worth replied. "But I won't be staying tonight. I've got some things I need to do."

"You aren't leaving," Lindsey said, alarm in her voice.

"Now, honey…" George cautioned her not to interfere.

"I'll be back," Worth said. "In the morning, tell Faith that I'll see her tomorrow night. Tell her to meet me in the town square at eight o'clock."

"Oh, my." Tears gathered in Lindsey's eyes. "You're going to…oh, Worth, what a sweet thing to do."

"I have a great deal to make up for…to Faith and to Hope. Tomorrow night, we'll start all over again. And this time I'm going to do it right."

With Hope bundled in a pink snowsuit, Faith entered the town square at seven-fifty. She knew that her family was across the street, waiting and watching from the storefront windows at Margaret's Goodies. Faith's heart beat wildly as she headed toward the bench where she'd sat and waited for Worth a year ago tonight. As she drew closer, she saw him approaching from the other side of the square. Worth Cordell was the best-looking man on earth. Big, tall, rugged. And about as masculine as a man could be. The closer he came, the more erratic her heart beat. She increased her pace, as did he, until they were practically running toward each other. When only a couple of feet separated them, they both stopped abruptly; their gazes locked and held.

"Hello, Blue Eyes."

"Hello."

"You told me that if I realized I loved you, then I should meet you here tonight," he said.

"Yes, I did, didn't I?"

"Well, I'm here. And I love you, Faith."

She swallowed tears of happiness. This was the moment she had been waiting for, dreaming of, for what seemed like a lifetime. "You know I love you. I have since that first night we were together."

Worth delved his hand into his coat pocket and brought out a tiny jeweler's box, flipped open the lid and held it out to Faith.

The marquise-cut diamond solitaire shimmered in the muted glow from the streetlights in the square. For a split second, her heart stopped.

"Will you marry me?" he asked. "Marry me as soon as possible."

"Oh, Worth. Yes, yes, I'll marry you."

When Worth opened his arms, she walked into his embrace. He slipped the glove off her left hand, then removed the ring from the box and slid it onto her third finger. With Hope snuggled between them, Worth leaned down and kissed Faith. Hope squirmed and whimpered.

"I think she's trying to tell us that we're smothering her." Faith laughed.

Worth chuckled as he took his daughter, held her up so that her cheek lay on his shoulder; then he draped his arm around Faith's waist and led her through the square. Just as they neared the street, snowflakes began falling. Tiny flakes at first, but they soon grew larger and more dense. By the time they walked across the street, the snow had already begun to stick to the grass.

"This is the happiest moment of my life," Faith said.

Worth halted, kissed Hope's cheek, then kissed Faith again. "Mine, too. And I promise you that I'm going to do everything I can to make sure the rest of your life is filled with happiness."

"How could it be anything but happy, with the three of us together. And who knows, maybe by this time next year, we could give Hope a baby brother."

"Are we planning on having a large family?" Worth asked.

"How does three children sound to you?"

"It sounds just fine to me. I've found out with Hope that I like being a daddy."

Faith snuggled against Worth, then whispered, "Margaret has a little party planned for us at her shop, but act surprised when we walk in and everyone is there.''

"Sounds like your family was pretty sure of me."

"Oh, Worth, my darling, everyone, including me, knew that you loved me. You were the only one who seemed to be clueless.''

"I always was a slow learner," he said. "But once I learn a lesson, I never forget it.''

Worth, Faith and Hope entered Margaret's Goodies and found their family waiting to celebrate with them. They drank hot chocolate, sang Christmas carols and stood by the windows watching a white blanket of new-fallen snow cover the town of Whitewood.

This Christmas was only the beginning, the first magical moments of happiness destined to last a lifetime.

* * * * *

Available now: A brand-new,
longer-length book
in Beverly Barton's bestselling series,

THE PROTECTORS.

Don't miss

ON HER GUARD,

featuring Ellen Denby,
CEO of Dundee Security,
and the man she loved—and never forgot.
Only from Silhouette Books.

A RANCHER IN HER STOCKING

Leanne Banks

* * *

This story is dedicated to the special people
who have always helped make Christmas
such a magical, loving time—my family.
To Mama, Daddy, Karen, Janie, Tony, Adam and
Alisa, thank you from the bottom of my heart....

Dear Reader,

What would you like in your stocking this holiday season? Do you remember what you wished for as a child? I was blessed to have a warm, close-knit family, and holiday seasons were filled with Christmas carols, delicious food, cold weather, a warm home with a tree all of us decorated and the anticipation of the big day. I remember that my parents put candy, little toys and sometimes little-girl jewelry in the Christmas stocking my mother made with my name on it. I also remember making a Christmas wish list with toys and dolls. As I've matured, my wish list has changed, and my appreciation for my family has grown. I've learned the secret that giving makes me feel like I'm receiving at the same time.

In "A Rancher In Her Stocking," the heroine is determined to experience and spread the spirit and joy of the season despite some tough obstacles. Unfortunately, she didn't always have a wonderful childhood holiday experience, so now she's made a promise to herself to always make the best of the holidays. Her unsinkable attitude won my admiration…along with the heart of a tough loner rancher. She found the best surprise of all in her stocking: love.

During this holiday season, I'm hoping you get all the really good things in your stocking—safety, good health, joy and love.

Merry Christmas and happy holidays!

Leanne Banks

www.leannebanks.com

Chapter 1

Christmas gave him heartburn.

Lucas took a deep swig directly from the bottle of antacid as he stood in the darkened kitchen of his ranch. It was midnight here in Kent, Missouri, and he'd just driven one hundred miles to finalize the sale of several hundred head of cattle to a rancher who wore a Stetson that played "Jingle Bells" every time the man touched it—and he touched it a lot. Lucas usually enjoyed talking with Ben Ericson, but the constant reminder of the holiday season had made his gut knot and burn.

Lucas had a legitimate reason for disliking Christmas, but he didn't want to stop the holidays for anyone else. He just wanted to be left alone.

He heard a sound from the stairs and figured he must have awakened his longtime housekeeper, Flora.

Screwing the lid on the medicine bottle, he strode into the hallway, ready to reassure Flora.

From the side of the steps, he watched a pair of slim, silky legs descend the stairs, and his words stopped in his throat. Lucas took in bare feet, trim ankles, shapely calves and flashing glimpses of creamy thighs as a short silk robe caressed ivory skin.

No disrespect intended to his housekeeper, Lucas thought, but Flora sure as heck didn't have legs like that!

He craned his neck to get a better look. His gaze skimmed up the curve of the mystery woman's hips and waist, lingered on the swell of her breasts, then wandered higher to a face that somehow managed to combine the look of a wide-eyed elf with a full mouth designed to fuel a man's most forbidden fantasies. The fact that her auburn hair stuck out in no less than eight different directions didn't stop a surge of unbidden heat inside him. Lucas cleared his throat.

The woman gasped and jerked her head toward him, clutching her robe to her throat. "Who…oh…are you Debra's brother? Are you Lucas Bennet?"

Lucas pulled his brain out of his jeans. Debra was his sister. So she was behind this. "Yes, I'm Lucas. And you are…?"

The woman bit her lip as she descended the rest of the way down the stairs. Her face wasn't classically beautiful in the same way as his former wife's. This woman was more well, *cute,* he guessed, but her rapid-fire change of facial expressions was compelling. "You didn't get the message she left on your cell phone, did you?"

Lucas shook his head. After hearing "Jingle Bells" until he was gritting his teeth, he hadn't wanted any noise. He'd turned off the radio in his truck, as well as his cell phone and cherished blessed silence.

The woman winced. "Oops. Well, I had a problem with my house and uh—"

"Problem?"

"There was a fire," she said, a trace of sadness darkening her eyes. "It will take some time to figure out what's salvageable and what isn't."

"Sorry," he murmured, immediately wanting to know more. Lucas was a volunteer fireman for the community. "Do you know what caused it?"

She lifted her shoulder in a gesture of uncertainty. "They mentioned something about faulty wiring."

"Were you there at the time?"

She shook her head. "It happened while I was at school. I'm Amy Winslow, the new elementary schoolteacher. Your sister Debra wanted me to stay with her, but her house is crowded since her mother-in-law is visiting, so she assured me that you had plenty of room and wouldn't mind my staying here temporarily."

He felt her green gaze search his face and swallowed an oath. His sister knew damn well that all he wanted during the holidays was to be left alone.

"If I had family, I could go home, but..."

Lucas could have sworn he felt the weight of a noose around his neck. "No family?"

She shook her head, her auburn hair fluttering

around her face. "My parents have been gone a long time. If my staying here is a problem..." she began, her voice trailing off uncertainly.

Lucas stifled a groan. It definitely was a problem, but Lucas knew how hard the small rural community had worked to attract a schoolteacher. Most teachers fresh out of school couldn't be less interested in accepting a position in a small community deep in the ranch country of Missouri, where a hot time in town was defined as the monthly dance at the community center. Now that the small community of Kent had a teacher, folks would do everything they could to keep her, and Debra would expect him to do his part. Plus it would be flat out cruel to turn the woman away.

She looked as if she were determined to remain calm, but Lucas had seen enough people rendered homeless from fires to know that shock would follow. Amy technically had no one.

He shelved his own needs. "It's not a problem. I've got plenty of room."

"It's just until I find another place to live," she promised, and Lucas blinked as a plump calico cat scampered down the steps and rubbed against Amy's ankles. Her gaze locked with his, guilt glinting from her eyes. She bit her lip and quickly picked up the cat. "Oops. Debra told me you don't like cats. I'll try to keep Cleo in my room."

"Cleo," he echoed, still staring at the cat. Lucas had never understood the appeal of cats. Felines reminded him of fickle women. He was a dog fan through and through.

"I'll just be here through Christmas," Amy reassured him earnestly. "I'm a big believer in Christmas, so I'll make sure it looks, sounds and smells like the holiday season."

Lucas's gut twisted. "That's not necessary."

Amy shook her head emphatically. "Oh, I absolutely insist." She tilted her lips in a lopsided smile, and her entire face lit up. "I love Christmas. It's my favorite time of the year."

Lucas sighed. *Oh, goody,* he thought. He was stuck with a Christmas nut whose body could rewind the clock of every man in town. Maybe he should sleep in the barn.

The following morning, Lucas rose earlier than usual and wandered into the kitchen for his first cup of coffee. Amy stood by the counter sipping a cup of coffee and nibbling on a piece of toast. Her hair damp waving from a recent shower and face scrubbed clean of makeup, she wore a pair of low-slung jeans and a chunky celery-green sweater. She looked like she was thirteen years old.

Except for her mouth, he thought, watching as she pursed her lips to blow, cooling her coffee. She turned to look at him. "Good morning."

He nodded. "Mornin'," he said. "You're up early."

"I'm going to my house. A fireman told me I would probably be able to get a few things today."

"I'll go with you," he said, pouring himself a cup of coffee. His training made safety a priority.

"That's not necessary. I don't want to interrupt your schedule."

"You'll have to interrupt someone's schedule if you're going to go prowling around a house that was on fire yesterday. I'm a volunteer fireman. It may as well be me."

She blinked. "Oh."

"You look surprised," he said, curious despite himself. He took a gulp of the hot black liquid, and felt it burn all the way down.

"I was told that you own the biggest ranch in the county. I wouldn't think you would have time for fire fighting."

"Luckily, there aren't that many fires to put out. We're a small community, and we try to look after each other, so a lot of us cover more than one base."

Amy smiled. "I keep being surprised by the differences between living in the city and the country."

"You miss the city?"

"Not much so far. Every once in a while, I crave a little retail therapy or would like to see a movie before it's two months' old."

He gave her an assessing glance. "Our winters can get a little tough."

Amy heard a combination of doubt and challenge in his deep voice. She wasn't quite sure what to make of Lucas. So far, he seemed the polar opposite of his friendly, outgoing sister. He hadn't cracked a smile since she'd met him; however, he emanated strength, both in his imposing, muscular frame and rock solid character. Here was a man who wouldn't be easily shaken, but something about the way he looked at her made her feel jumpy.

Amy ignored the sensation, met his gaze and was momentarily distracted by the thick fringe of his eyelashes. For such a hard man, he had killer eyelashes. She shook off the thought and answered his doubt. "I can handle a tough winter. I've got a good winter coat, a sturdy pair of boats, lots of warm socks and a humdinger of a recipe for hot chocolate."

Taking another drink of coffee, he gave a nod, but she could tell he wasn't convinced. If Missouri needed a poster boy for the state slogan *Show Me,* then Lucas was their man.

Amy stiffened her already hard resolve. She would *show him* and everyone else who doubted her. "Just curious. Do you have a stainless-steel throat, or is there some secret to how you can swallow scalding coffee?"

His hard mouth twitched, and his eyes glinted with a hint of humor. "Practice." As if to prove his point, he finished the cup. "We can leave as soon as you dry your hair."

"I never dry my hair in the morning," she said. "I can leave now."

"Didn't your mother ever tell you going out in cold weather with a wet head is a great way to get sick?"

"No," she said. "My mother relinquished care of me to the state when I was four years old, and I lived in a children's home until I left for college."

He was quiet for a long moment and studied her.

"Well, you're on my time now. So dry your hair and we'll leave."

"Your time?"

He nodded. "My sister put you in my care. I'll make sure nothing happens to you while you're in my home."

Amy felt a burst of feminist outrage at the same time she was utterly confident that if any man could keep a woman safe, it was Lucas. Irritated, she lifted her chin. "I've been taking care of myself for a long time."

"Every mother in this community will have my head if I let anything happen to the new teacher they're all raving about. If you've been taking care of yourself for a long time, just look on this as a little break," he said with a shrug.

Amy didn't know whether to be flattered by his sideways compliment of her teaching skills or frustrated by his stubbornness regarding her *care*. She sighed, then took one last sip of her coffee. "Give me two minutes," she said, unwilling to expend any more of her energy on an argument. This was temporary, she told herself as she strode upstairs, and it was Christmas. The supposed season of peace...even if Lucas generated anything but peace.

On the way to Amy's house, Lucas called the volunteer fire chief so he would know what to expect. As soon as they walked through the front door, he was bombarded with the scent of smoke and the sight of charred Christmas decorations. Sooty packages sat beneath a small scorched Christmas tree, a nativity on the fireplace mantel, and the staircase rail was lined with red ribbon and greenery limp from water sprayed from a firefighter's hose. The decorations were tasteful, but Lucas still felt the burn of pain beneath his ribs.

Amy stood perfectly still as she took in her flame-ravaged home. He almost reminded her to breathe, but she shook herself and fled past him. "I just want to check on a few things," she said, rushing up the stairs.

He followed her up the staircase into a bedroom where half the room had been blackened by the blaze. Amy skipped the jewelry box on the dresser, the clothes closet, and fell to her knees beside her bed, digging out two boxes. She opened one and gave a sigh of relief. "Photos survived." She peeked in the other box, which was dark around the edges and smiled. "All okay." Snapping the top on the box before he could get a look at what it held, she looked up at him. "If I can get the gifts downstairs, I should be set."

"What about some clothes or your jewelry?"

"Oh," she said with a blank expression, as if she'd been so intent on rescuing other items that clothing hadn't occurred to her. She rose to her feet and turned to the closet. "I should get a suitcase," she mumbled to herself, pulling out a piece of luggage from inside. She covered her nose. "The smoke smell is so strong."

Lucas nodded, opening the suitcase for her. "You

might want to choose wash-and-wear now. The insurance company will help cover smoke damage for everything. You should probably go ahead and schedule a professional cleaning.''

''I'd love to schedule the cleaning, but I imagine a lot of people are taking off for the holidays,'' Amy muttered as she pulled a few pieces of clothing from the hangers, then turned to her dresser. With both hands, she scooped up a couple of nighties and silky underwear and bras.

Lucas felt an odd twist in his gut at the sight of the sensual intimate clothing that she would wear next to her naked skin. A forbidden, *unbidden* image of her dressed in ivory satin panties and bra slithered across his mind, raising his body temperature.

She dumped the lingerie into the suitcase, then quickly grabbed her photo album and the mystery box. As if she were on autopilot, she reached for the suitcase, but Lucas shook his head. ''I'll carry it.''

He followed her down the stairs and watched as she gathered the charred gifts from beneath the tree. Biting her lip, she tried to stack them to carry them outside and Lucas saw an accident waiting to happen.

''Stop.''

At the sound of his voice, Amy immediately halted and met his gaze. Lucas saw a world of vulnerability in her eyes. ''You'll be okay,'' he told her, reading her need for reassurance.

She nodded, but her eyes looked far less certain. ''Of course I will. It's just unsettling to be—'' Her voice wavered and she gave a weak smile. "Unsettled."

Lucas could tell Amy was no wuss. Her back was ramrod straight, but he couldn't help wondering how much weight her slim shoulders should bear. Her chin was set with determination, but her eyes showed a storm of emotions he suspected she would never confess. The urge to embrace her hit him in the stomach like a knockout punch.

He walked closer and stopped a mere step away from her. "It's normal to feel unsettled, even a little afraid," he told her.

Amy took a deep breath, her gaze surveying the damage to her home. "I just want a safe place of my own. My own home. Now it's such a mess, and I don't even know if I'll be able to move back in." She closed her eyes for a few timeless seconds, then opened them and met his gaze. "But it's Christmas, and I refuse to whine."

She whirled around and Lucas felt a rumbling suspicion that he'd just encountered something a hell of a lot stronger than a house fire. That something was the indomitable will of Amy Winslow.

After Lucas dropped Amy off at the ranch, he drove his truck out to check the livestock. Pulling to a stop, he got out and inhaled the cold winter air. Lucas liked the cold at Christmas. It numbed him, and blunted the pain. His marriage to Jennifer hadn't been perfect, but he'd made promises, and Lucas believed in keeping promises. She hadn't been happy living on the ranch. Four days before Christmas, she'd left a note telling him she'd made the two-hour drive to St. Louis and would return late that night.

But there'd been an ice storm, and a semi had crushed her car, killing her. He'd buried her on Christmas Eve. He'd also officially buried his interest in celebrating Christmas.

Hearing a car slowly move toward him, he turned his head and spotted his sister's SUV. His sister, Debra, was the bane of his existence, but he would die for her. After all, she was his youngest sister. She'd bugged the devil out of him when he was a teenager, tagging after him, horning in on phone conversations. Even though Debra was younger, once their parents died, she acted as if it were her place to watch over his social life. After Jennifer died, Debra had relentlessly tried to lure him into enjoying the season when all he wanted was to be left alone.

Debra, six months pregnant with her third child, stopped the car, got out and walked toward him. She had that busybody glint in her eyes, but her face was slightly pale. She didn't get enough rest for a woman in her condition. When Lucas looked at her, he still saw his little sister in pigtails instead of a grown mother of three. "So when will you be speaking to me again?"

"Never," he said. "You need to get more rest."

"Yeah," she said, standing next to him. "Easier said than done. I think I'm suffering from overexposure to my mother-in-law. Two women in the same kitchen is like—"

"Like having two dictators with different strategies make battle plans. War or détente?" he asked, looping his arm around her shoulder.

"Détente if it kills me."

"I would never wish you pain, but you deserve a truckload of discomfort for sending me Kent's answer to the unsinkable Molly Brown. You know that all I want for Christmas is to be left alone."

Debra sighed. "Left alone so you can punish yourself for Jennifer's death. When are you going to stop blaming yourself?

"She was my wife, my responsibility."

"She was an adult, too."

Lucas shrugged and moved away. He couldn't explain his harsh sense of failure and disappointment in himself to his sister, and he wasn't going to try.

"Well, your overdeveloped sense of responsibility is one of the reasons you were chosen to house Amy Winslow," she said. "That, and the fact that everyone knows you've turned into a monk."

Lucas gave her a double take. "What are you talking about?"

Debra crossed her arms over her bulky coat and arched her eyebrows. "You weren't the only volunteer to have her as a guest."

Lucas looked toward the heaven for help. "*I* didn't volunteer. I was *drafted!*"

"Well, there were plenty of volunteers. Men, some single, a few, married, wanted to have Amy in their houses for Christmas. Every single one of them was wearing a wolfy gleam in their eyes, champing at the

bit to get their paws on her. I could tell what they
wanted, and I knew Amy needed to be protected.
That's why I volunteered your house. She'll be as safe
with you as she would be with a monk, since you've
obviously decided you're never going to have sex
again.''

Chapter 2

The wreath on his front door was the next sign that Lucas's home had been invaded. It was a cheerful combination of greenery, holly berries and bells, topped off with a bright-red bow. Lucas frowned.

He would allow the wreath, but drew the line at a tree. No Christmas tree allowed.

Lucas felt the familiar twist in his gut and opened the door to the sound of children's voices and Christmas music on the stereo. "What the he—" He walked toward the kitchen and entered the doorway.

Five little kids, faces smeared with various colors of frosting and big smiles, crowded around his kitchen table as Amy helped them decorate cookies and his housekeeper removed a pan of cookies from the oven. Lucas's gaze automatically swung back to

Amy. She wore a red apron, and one cheek was smudged with red and green frosting.

A little girl spotted him first. "Who's he?" she asked.

Flora, his housekeeper, whipped around, and her eyes grew wide with surprise. "You're early!"

"He's big," another little girl said.

"He looks mean," a little boy said.

Amy winced at the little boy's words and shot Lucas a wary glance. "He's not mean, Ryan. He's just surprised. This is Mr. Bennet's home," she said, then turned directly toward Lucas. "Before the fire, I had promised my special readers that if they met the goals we'd set then we would celebrate with a cookie-decorating party. I didn't want to disappoint them, and Flora said you probably wouldn't mind."

She did? Lucas threw Flora a sharp glance, but his housekeeper just busied herself at the kitchen counter.

"Wanna cookie?" a little girl asked, holding up a cookie decorated with a large blob of green frosting.

Every eye in the room gazed at him expectantly. Lucas withheld a sigh. "Sure," he said, and was rewarded with bright smiles from both the little girl and Amy.

Eating the too-sweet cookie, he felt a tug on his jacket. Ryan, the little boy who had said he looked *mean,* looked up at him. "Can you draw a reindeer? I wanna put a reindeer on my cookie."

With that, Lucas washed his hands and got sucked into decorating cookies with Amy's special readers for the next thirty minutes. Amy helped the little rascals clean up, and sent each of them home with a dozen cookies and a smile on their face.

As soon as they left, she turned to Lucas. "Thank you. I get the impression Flora thought you wouldn't mind the invasion as long as you didn't know about it, but you did. The kids loved having you there."

"It's no big deal," he said gruffly, uncomfortable with the gratitude in her eyes.

"Yes, it was," she insisted. "It takes a real man to be willing to draw reindeers on cookies for first graders."

The husky sound in her voice did strange things to his stomach. It was probably those damn cookies, he told himself. Although Amy was attractive, Lucas wasn't open for business. Besides, as his sister pointed out, he was supposed to be protecting her...instead of thinking about licking the tiny smudge of frosting off the corner of her lips or wondering what kind of sounds she made while making love.

Feeling an unwelcome rush of heat, Lucas bit back an oath and shrugged. "I have some numbers to crunch in my office," he said, and walked away from temptation.

That night Amy dreamed she settled into a new home, only to see it devoured again and again by flames. The dream upset her so much she woke up, her heart pounding and filled with dread. She inhaled several deep breaths before she realized she was in Lucas Bennet's house and she was safe.

The irrational threat of the dream, however, hung over her, just as it had last night. Glancing at the clock, she made a face at the hour: 2:00 a.m. Wide-awake, she knew she wouldn't go back to sleep any-time soon, so she tossed back the covers and slid out of bed. Maybe hot chocolate would help. She pushed her arms through her robe and quietly crept down-stairs to the kitchen.

She mixed the ingredients to her special recipe into a saucepan, thinking she could stand an extra shot of Kahlúa. As much as she was determined to pretend otherwise, being displaced by the fire dug up painful childhood memories.

Amy found routine and longtime possessions com-forting. Unlike many of her friends, she didn't yearn for the excitement of travel and new experiences. She longed for a home of her own, and six months ago, she had decided to make her home in Kent, Missouri. She couldn't remember a time when she hadn't wished for her own family and a safe place.

Her friends and colleagues in Baltimore had thought Amy was nuts to accept a position in no-where, Missouri, but in the warm, rural community of Kent, Amy had seen the seductive possibility of at least part of the life she'd envisioned for herself.

She hadn't, however, envisioned a fire destroying her home during the Christmas season. Amy had spent her entire life battling the knot of apprehension in her chest that she shouldn't count on much of any-thing. The fire had brought back that familiar knot of apprehension. She absently rubbed her chest and took a deep breath. Pouring the hot chocolate into a mug, she tossed in a few marshmallows and wandered toward the picture window in the large den. The moon gleamed over the frost-covered ground.

Cold outside. Cold inside, Amy thought and shivered.

"It's either a little early or a little late, isn't it?" a male voice said from behind her.

Surprised, she turned to see Lucas walking toward her in a pair of jeans and an unbuttoned shirt that revealed his muscular chest, the shadow of chest hair, and his washboard flat abdomen. His brown hair was attractively sleep-mussed and his eyelids lowered in a sexy half-mast. With his thumbs hooked through the loops of weathered jeans, his casual gate belied the masculine power he oozed. A complex, intriguing man, he operated the largest, most successful ranch in the area, pitched into the community by serving as an on-call volunteer fireman, guarded his solitude, yet wouldn't turn his back on a first grader asking for help. If he weren't so remote, Amy could be entirely too susceptible to his strength and... Her gaze took in the length of him and felt her heart hammer at his rugged appeal.

Dismayed by her involuntary response, she took a quick sip of her chocolate and immediately singed her tongue. A tiny yelp escaped her throat, and she fanned her tongue.

The corner of his mouth tilted upward. "Too hot?"

Amy's gaze lingered on the smooth bare skin of his chest that his shirt didn't cover. He had no idea.

"Yes. I forgot to pick up that stainless-steel lining for my mouth and throat in town today. Which store carries it?"

His half grin grew. "There are only five stores within the town limits."

He moved closer, and Amy felt a flutter of nerves. "I'm sorry I woke you. I tried to be quiet."

He pushed his hand through his hair. "I think I smelled chocolate."

"There's still some left in the pot if you want a mug."

"Thanks. Maybe in a few minutes," he said with a shrug of his impressive shoulders. "Why're you up?"

Amy lifted the mug to her lips and took a tiny, careful sip. "I woke up and couldn't go back to sleep."

"What woke you?"

Amy resisted the urge to squirm beneath his intent gaze. "Nothing important," she muttered.

"What woke you?" he repeated.

Amy sighed. "It was just a silly dream."

"But it bothered you enough to keep you awake," he concluded. "What was it?"

"I dreamed my new home kept catching on fire, again and again. Just as I relaxed and started to think everything was going to be okay, the fire would start again."

He nodded slowly and gave her a considering glance. A strange silence hung between them for a few seconds. "You wanna go for a walk?"

Amy did a double take. "Excuse me? A walk at this time of night?"

He nodded again and gave her that almost smile. "Might as well. We're both awake. A walk in the cold will—"

"Wake us up even more," she interjected.

"Then maybe returning to the warm house will make us sleepy."

She stared at him, wondering why his suggestion appealed to her. "I'll need to change," she said.

"Not on my account," he drawled. "But you might be more comfortable."

Amy's heart tripped over itself and she did another double take. *Was he flirting with her?* No, she immediately answered herself. Absolutely not. She didn't think Lucas was capable of flirting, and his sister had insisted that since he wasn't interested in romance, Amy would be perfectly safe with him. Her gaze encompassing his partly bare chest, she took a careful breath. "I'll go change."

Three and a half minutes later, she scurried down the steps as she shoved her arms into her coat sleeves and pulled on a hat. Lucas waited for her at the front door wearing a Stetson, jacket and boots, in addition to his jeans and shirt. He opened the door and dipped his head for her to proceed.

The cold air hit her face like a wall of ice. She breathed in quickly and her lungs felt frozen. Her expression must have revealed her shock.

"A little nippy?" he asked with a sexy edge of humor in his voice that surprised her.

"A little," she said, then corrected herself. "A lot."

"You're just not used to going out in the middle of the night in Missouri," he said, walking beside her down the steps to the front walkway.

"Why are you?" she asked.

"Because farm animals and ranch problems have their own timetable. It's not like school. The bell doesn't really ever ring for recess here."

"How long has the ranch been in your family?"

"Five generations," he said, leading her down a pathway along a pasture where the ground glistened with frost.

"Now, that's cool. Having all that history must feel great."

"Sometimes," he said. "It depends if you want to follow the family plan."

Although she didn't know Lucas very well, she couldn't imagine him doing anything but ranching. "Did you ever want to do something else?"

"I thought about it a few times when I was in college and after my wi—" He broke off suddenly and turned quiet.

"After your wife died," she said quietly. "Debbie told me that was rough for you."

"Yeah," he said, narrowing his eyes as a dozen emotions passed through them.

"I'm sorry."

He shoved his hands in his pockets. "What made you come to Kent?"

"Because the community really needed me. I received other offers, but I could tell Kent really needed me. I could see myself belonging, and that's something I've wanted my entire life.''

"But what about the lack of entertainment?"

She smiled. "Entertainment is a matter of taste. I couldn't walk along a path at 2:00 a.m. and see this kind of view in Baltimore."

"True," he said. "But there aren't a lot of singles' bars in town, either."

"I don't think I'll find what I want in a singles' bar," she said wryly.

He stopped. "What do you want?"

"Not that much. To feel needed and wanted. To make a place for myself."

"I bet you'll get bored as hell after you've lived here awhile."

His doubt in her pinched. She frowned. "You don't know me well enough to make that judgment."

"I know the winters here are long, and you're a city girl used to creature comforts."

"It all depends on what creature comforts are important to me."

He adjusted his hat but still wore a doubtful expression on his face. "Okay, I'll bite. What creature comforts are important to you?"

"A warm fire. A safe home of my own. People calling my name when I walk down the street. Friends who stay in my life for a long time."

"What about family?"

The question cut at a tender place she tried to keep

hidden. She crossed her arms over her chest. "My friends will be my family," she said. "And Cleo."

"Your cat?" he queried, raising an eyebrow in disbelief. "Why don't you just get married? You're attractive. You should be able to find a guy to marry you."

Amy tilted her head at his backhanded compliment. "Thank you—I think. I don't want to be married unless it's to the right person. It looks like a lot more pain is caused by being married to the wrong person than by being single. But I could say the same to you. You may be grouchy and remote, but you're attractive. You should be able to find a woman to marry you," she said with the sweetest smile she could muster.

He frowned. "I didn't say I wanted to get married."

"Neither did I."

The vapor from her breath mingled with his as she met his gaze. She noticed that they had stopped walking and he was standing entirely too close to her. She told herself to pull away, but her feet refused.

"Are you ready to go to bed now?" he asked in a low voice.

Her heart hiccuped in her chest. *Bed.* In a flash, an unwelcome visual flitted through her mind of Lucas, naked, hot and anything but grouchy and remote. Amy found the image too appealing, too tempting. After his cool reception of her, she liked the idea of getting him hot and bothered. A distant mental warning bell sounded. Bad idea, she told herself. This was not a man to taunt.

He gently chucked her chin with his forefinger. "Cleo got your tongue? You think you can go back to sleep now?"

Fat chance. "Sure," she said, even though she was certain she was awake enough to paint the house. "I'll probably drift right off as soon as I get warm again."

"Good," he said, and they made the return walk in silence.

As soon as they entered the house, she was compelled by politeness to thank him. "It was nice of you to suggest a walk when you probably could have gone back to sleep with no problem."

His eyes glinted with mischief. "I guess I'm just a nice, grouchy, remote, but attractive man."

Amy bit her lip to keep from smiling. He was throwing her description of him right back at her. "I guess you are," she returned and reached out to squeeze his arm. "Thanks."

He glanced down at her hand on his arm, and when his gaze met hers, she could almost swear she saw the barest hint of sexual intent. She moved her hand away as if she'd touched a hot stove.

Lucas didn't sleep well the rest of the night. It was almost as if someone had stuck a splinter in his side since Amy had shown up. His peace and solitude had been completely disrupted, and her assessment of him got under his skin. He wasn't all that grouchy, he thought. He just didn't like Christmas.

Every time he closed his eyes, he saw her face.
Changeable green eyes wanting to trust and that full
mouth of hers that could produce an innocent smile
one moment, and remind him what he'd been missing
the last few years the next. This woman, he concluded, got on his nerves.

The next morning, he rose early and threw himself
into work. The natural rhythm of caring for the animals and repairing a stretch of fence calmed him, and
he didn't return to the house until evening.

The wreath on the door greeted him, then as soon
as he entered, he heard Christmas music playing on
the stereo, and the cat appeared, rubbing against his
ankles.

His housekeeper, Flora, met him wearing a wary
expression. "I couldn't say no to her."

His gut knotted. "What do you mean?"

Flora shrugged helplessly and pointed toward the
den.

Carefully stepping over the cat, Lucas strode to the
den, fully prepared to do what Flora had been unable
to do. He stopped midway into the room at the sight
that beheld him. Perched on a ladder, Amy strung
lights around a large Christmas tree. The scent of pine
filled the air.

The tree felt like a knife between his ribs. He remembered all too well taking down the tree his wife
had decorated before she'd died. He swore under his
breath.

Amy must have heard or felt him. Her gaze shot

to his, her eyes rounding at his presence. Startled, she
wobbled on the ladder, losing her balance. "Oh, no!"

Lucas's heart stopped, and he rushed toward her,
grabbing her and falling backward at the same time.
He landed on the floor bottom first with her cradled
on top of him. They lay in silence for a few breath-
shattering seconds.

Amy lifted her head and looked down at him, her
bangs falling over one eye. "Are you okay?"

Lucas felt a twinge in his backside. "As long as I
don't sit down for the next month."

She winced. "I'm sorry."

His heart still hammered in his chest, but his other
senses began to engage. He inhaled her sweet, sultry
scent and felt the soft pressure of her breasts against
his chest. The weight of her lower body rested intimately against his.

Her gaze locked with his, and he watched her eyes
darken with gradual feminine, sensual awareness. She
licked her lips.

"I should move," she murmured.

"Uh-huh," he said, but neither of them did.

Chapter 3

Amy fought the delicious, seductive sensation that urged her toward Lucas. He was so solid, so strong, so... She wondered how he kissed and stared at his mouth for a long moment. Glancing back into his eyes, she saw that he'd caught her. Her cheeks heated. Hoping he couldn't read her mind, she began to carefully back away, the same way she might back away from a lion.

Holding her with his gaze, he followed her up on his elbows.

A dozen tingly, odd sensations coursed through her, and she cleared her throat to break the silence. "You move fast for such a tall man."

"I didn't want you to hurt yourself," he said.

His intent expression made her knees unsteady, but she forced them to work anyway, standing. "There you go with that overdeveloped protective streak again," she joked.

He didn't smile. His face was dead serious. "No falling," he said. "I don't want you on the ladder unless someone is right beside you."

"But—" she protested.

"But nothing," he said, pulling off his suede jacket. "I'll put the rest of the lights on the tree, then you can decorate up to the ladder level and stop."

"But—"

He leaned his head so that he was two breaths away from her. "This is nonnegotiable."

Amy's throat went dry at the sensual combination of velvet and steel in his voice. Confused, she gave a tiny nod, wondering what was wrong with her. She'd never been attracted to domineering men.

He didn't appear satisfied. "Repeat after me. Lucas, I will not climb the ladder unless another person is helping me."

"Are you always this bossy?"

"When it's important," he said, without one iota of apology. "I'm waiting."

She sighed and rolled her eyes. "Okay, I won't climb the ladder unless I have help. There. Are you satisfied?"

"It'll be one less thing to give me heartburn," he muttered turning toward the ladder. As he climbed it, Amy couldn't help observing that Lucas had an incredible backside. He quickly strung the rest of the lights, and descended the ladder. "All yours."

She plugged in the lights. The tree lit up, and she

nodded in approval as a wave of bittersweet nostalgia passed over her. "Thank you. Ever since I lived at the children's home I've always had a Christmas tree. Even when I went to college, I had one of those little tabletop artificial ones in my dorm room. I think of Christmas as the time of year when most everyone is a little nicer. I think the season brings out the best in people. A little light in the darkness, kinda like the lights on the tree."

She looked at Lucas and suddenly felt self-conscious at her disclosure. "Sorry. Didn't mean to get all soppy on you."

He looked at her thoughtfully. "No apology necessary," he said, then a glint of pain sliced through his eyes.

His expression tugged at something tender inside her. She was filled with the odd longing to wipe away his grief. She balled her fists to keep from reaching out to embrace him. He wouldn't appreciate it, she told herself. He didn't want a hug, even if she wanted to give one.

"Enjoy the tree, Amy," he said, and left her staring after him, her hands feeling strangely itchy and empty.

Lucas successfully avoided his on-site Christmas fairy during the next twenty-four hours by sticking to outside work. The cold weather suited him, numbing him to the pain that sneaked up on him at odd moments. It was dark when he returned to the house. The first thing he noticed was a cluster of about ten cars spilling from his driveway. Even before he opened the front door, he heard a chorus of voices singing a Christmas carol.

Lucas sighed, pushed the door open, and the sound of the season assaulted him. There was no way he could escape Christmas with Amy in his house. Amy's cat, Cleo, scampered out of the den and rubbed against his legs.

The music ended and laughter filled the air.

Amy appeared in the doorway with an uncertain expression on her face. "I asked Flora if you would mind if some Christmas carolers met here for a little practice. Everyone was originally supposed to meet at my house, but you know what happened." She glanced down at his feet and her lips twitched. "Look at Cleo marking you. She likes you."

Lucas glanced down in consternation as the cat continued to wind around his ankles. "Marking me?"

She nodded. "Cats rub against you and mark you to show they like you."

Lucas had no idea how to respond. Why in the world did he feel vaguely pleased that Amy's cat liked him? This was insane. He removed his hat and slapped it against his thigh in frustration.

"Flora shouldn't have said the Christmas carol practice would be okay with you, should she?" Amy asked in a low voice as she stepped closer. "I can get everyone to leave."

Lucas sighed and shook his head. He couldn't say no to Amy any better than Flora could. "I'll grab a sandwich and eat it in my room."

"Hey, Amy," a male voice called from the den. "Where'd you go?"

"Are you sure?" she asked, ignoring the man's call. Her gaze tangled with Lucas's for a long moment, and the look in her eyes made his heart thud with a rough, edgy rhythm.

A man strode into the doorway, breaking the odd moment stretching between Lucas and Amy. Lucas immediately recognized him—Dan Arthur, a local attorney. And he was looking at Amy the same way a cat looked at a canary.

"You disappeared," Dan chided her, looping his arm over her shoulders. He glanced up at Lucas and nodded. "Seasons greetings, Lucas. Nice of you to give our favorite teacher a place to stay after the fire. I bet you've enjoyed her Christmas decorations. The only thing missing is mistletoe," he said, with a pointed grin for Amy.

Lucas's gaze hung on the man's arm around Amy's shoulders. His stomach knotted with an unwelcome feeling he couldn't quite identify. *Mistletoe.* Dan clearly wanted to do a heck of a lot more than kiss her. Lucas resisted the urge to push Dan away.

Annoyed at the territorial instinct roiling inside him, he swallowed an oath. "Give her time," Lucas muttered darkly, and left the couple in the foyer. He had two words for Dan Arthur, and they weren't *Merry Christmas.*

Hours later, Lucas sat in bed and read an article on ranch management instead of sleeping. The holiday season always unsettled him, but tonight he was equally unsettled by thoughts of Amy.

It was bad enough that the woman had the fervor of Santa's elves when it came to the holiday season, but Amy bothered him in other ways. She wasn't classically pretty, he kept telling himself, but that didn't stop him from studying her face every chance he got. He shouldn't find her sexy, but she projected an earthiness that made him want to strip off those baggy jeans and chunky sweaters and slide deep inside her.

After Jennifer died, he'd ruthlessly pushed aside his sexual needs. His wife had died, so denying himself pleasure seemed just and right. He had failed to protect her, so why should he be happy?

Sighing, he tossed aside the journal and rose from the bed. He wandered to his window and raked his hand through his hair.

A muffled whimper from down the hall penetrated his brooding isolation.

The nightmare had returned. Desperation seeped through her like acid. Her heart hammering, Amy shook her head. "No, no, no." She saw her new home. She was finally settled, surrounded by furnishings she'd chosen that made her feel as if she had at last found home. Then, the flames kicked up, destroying everything. Over and over again, she walked into her home, hopeful, only to see the flames burn her precious dreams to ashes.

"No, no!" she said, watching her photos melt from the relentless fire.

She felt strong hands on her arms, shaking her. The visual of the fire faded.

"Amy."

The male voice immediately diminished her panic.

She blinked and sat up, finding herself in Lucas's arms. Disoriented, she sucked in several deep breaths. "It was the dream. The fire," she murmured, trying to steady herself. "The dream. I'm okay."

"You're safe. There's no fire."

I'm here. He didn't say it, but she felt it, and his presence made all the difference in the world. Amy instinctively sank against him. She couldn't refuse his reassurance. Here was unadulterated strength. At times Lucas might be cranky, but he was solid through and through. His complete reliability got under her skin and touched her where she was most vulnerable. In Lucas's arms, she was a lonely little girl again, wanting to feel safe, believing it was possible.

The feelings sent her equilibrium spinning.

His fingers slid through her hair in a comforting caress, and she closed her eyes. She inhaled his clean, masculine scent. Her palms rested on his chest, and his skin was smooth over the steel of his muscles. His strength again seduced, and she couldn't resist the urge to touch.

The air was cool, but he was warm.

"What was your dream?" he asked in a low voice that sent a delicious shiver through her.

"I keep making a home for myself, but every time I think I'm safe, the fire comes back."

"You hide your fear very well," he said.

She looked up, searching his face in the darkness. "What do you mean?"

"You sing your Christmas carols. You bake your cookies. But your dream tells that you're afraid."

She stiffened in defense. "I'm not—"

He placed his thumb over her lips. "It's normal," he told her. "I've watched a lot of people fall apart when they lose their homes. You haven't."

"I don't want to fall apart. I'm not going to fall apart."

"I believe you," he said. "You're tough."

She sighed and dropped her head against his chest. "I don't feel tough," she whispered.

"You are," he said, sifting his fingers through her hair again.

"But the dream keeps coming back."

"You're expecting too much of yourself. Give yourself some time."

"How come you're so smart about this?"

He chuckled, and the sound rippled through her nerve endings. "I'm just naturally smart."

She smiled at his masculine humor and lifted her head to look at him. "Sorry I interrupted your sleep again."

"I wasn't asleep."

Surprise skipped through her. "Kinda late for a rancher who gets up early every morning. Or do you have special powers? Like your stainless-steel throat. You don't need sleep?"

"No," he said, and his gaze held banked heat. "Contrary to popular belief, I'm very human."

Amy stared into his eyes, and felt a bone deep-connection with him resonate inside her. Her breath hitched, and an electric anticipation sizzled in the air.

His gaze drifted to her mouth as if he were struggling with an inner demon, and Amy's heart hammered against her rib cage. She was acutely aware of his naked chest beneath her palms, skin against skin, the whisper of a chance for more. For a millisecond she wondered if she should move away, but couldn't imagine moving from his warmth.

Lucas lowered his head slightly and Amy gave in to the drugging wanting sensation inside her. She lifted her mouth, and he took it.

His mouth was warm and supple as he rubbed hers. She parted her lips and giving a low sound of approval, he slid his tongue just inside her mouth, tasting and teasing. He coaxed her response with a subtle seductiveness that made her want more. He ran his tongue around the inner perimeter of her lips and she grew hot from the inside out. Her fingers instinctively massaged his well-developed pecs.

He rubbed his tongue with hers, slid his thumb down her neck to finger the tiny strap of her nightgown. Cocking his head to one side, he sought deeper, more intimate access as he continued to toy with the strap. Amy felt her breasts grow heavy with arousal, and she shifted as her blood pooled in all her sensitive places.

Lucas thrust his tongue inside her mouth, simulating how his body would take hers. She suckled his tongue, and Lucas pushed the strap off her shoulder, and skimmed his finger down her breast. At the same time he made love to her mouth, he rubbed his finger over her nipple.

She gasped at the electric sensations that coursed through her.

Pulling his mouth away, Lucas stared at her with fire in his eyes, his nostrils flaring. He nudged her down and replaced his finger with his mouth on her nipple. His tongue laved the turgid tip, and passion roared through her head. He slid his hands to her nightgown and between her thighs.

His hands and mouth were persuasive, but the raw need he emanated made her weak. Sinking her fingers into his crisp hair, she wriggled against him. Giving a low growl, he moved up her body. "So responsive," he murmured, sliding his fingers just inside her panties.

Amy bit her lip. Her body clamored to go further, to sink deeper into him, but some buried instinct of self-protection clanged like a loud bell inside her head. She covered his hand with hers. "Fast," she managed to say breathlessly.

His gaze, full of need and want, wrapped around her for a full moment. He swore under his breath, then shook his head. Pulling away, he moved from the bed in one smooth moment that left her feeling cold and exposed. She pulled her nightgown into place and lifted the covers to her shoulders.

"Crazy," he muttered, raking his hand through the

same hair she'd touched just moments before. "Insane. I don't know what got into me," he said, looking at her. "I heard you when you were having your nightmare, but I didn't intend to—" He broke off. "Put it down to sexual deprivation and forget it happened," he said, and left her staring after him.

Stunned and insulted, Amy lay in bed for a half moment. *Crazy, insane.* She could buy that, but the notion that any woman could have aroused him raised her blood pressure. Tossing back the bedcovers, she jumped out of bed and stalked after him. He'd already closed the door on his room, but that didn't stop her. She rapped smartly on it, then pushed it open.

He stood by the window, the moon spilling over his tall, powerful form. Her heart dipped, but she tried to ignore the sensation. "Sexual deprivation," she said, moving toward him. "Are you telling me that the reason you kissed me had no emotional basis? That you're not attracted to me in the least?"

"Yes, to the first question. No to the second," he said bluntly. "It's been a long time since I've had sex."

"With your sparkling personality, I can understand why."

"I gave up sex after my wife died."

Amy suddenly felt two inches tall. "Oh," she said.

"Don't expect anything emotional from me," he warned. "I have nothing to give."

Amy felt a wave of pain emanate from him. The depth of his wound and his remote attitude grabbed at something inside her. He was so different from the man who had held her and kissed her with such passion just moments ago. "I'm not sure I can agree with that," she said, forcing herself to move toward him even though he couldn't be less welcoming. "If you had nothing to give, then you wouldn't have come to me when you heard me having a nightmare."

"It wasn't personal," he told her in a quiet voice.

A sharp stab slowed her pace toward him. "So you would have comforted anyone having a nightmare. That's okay. Does that mean you would have kissed anyone, too?"

He gave a heavy sigh. "Don't take any of it personally. I'm not used to having a woman like you around the house all the time." He raked his hand through his hair and looked over her shoulder. "I'm sorry it happened."

I'm sorry it happened. I'm sorry I held you. Nothing personal. Nothing personal was her worst nightmare. If there was one thing Amy didn't want with a man, it was a temporary burst of passion. She wanted a relationship that would last, something worth keeping. A knot formed in her throat and she followed his gaze to his dresser where a photo sat. She walked toward the photograph to better see it. A beautiful blond woman wearing a lace wedding dress smiled with happiness and confidence. Perfect smile, perfect features.

"Your wife?" Amy asked even though she already knew.

"Yeah," he said, keeping his distance.

"She's beautiful."

"Yeah," he said, and a silence full of grief and heavy emotions filled the room.

Confused, Amy didn't want to face Lucas at the moment. She didn't want to look at him, nor did she want him looking at her. She wanted to hide. "I'll go now," she said quietly, and left the room. Lucas was a good man. He just wasn't good for her.

Lucas didn't see Amy at all the next day. Long after nightfall, she was nowhere to be seen. That was good, he told himself as he looked outside the window. He didn't need her around messing with hormones he'd thought were dead. He didn't need her constant reminders of the Christmas season. Christmas might be a favorite time of the year for others, but for him it meant loss. He didn't need her around upsetting his routine and making him feel…alive.

Lucas swore under his breath. The phone rang, distracting him from his dark thoughts. He picked it up, and his sister was on the other end of the line.

"You need to go into town to Lucky's," Debra said without preamble.

Lucas glanced at the clock. It was after 10:00 p.m. Lucky's was the only bar in town. "Why?"

"Because the Christmas carolers went there after they finished singing, and Dan Arthur is after Amy. I just know he's going to have too much to drink, and he'll end up doing something lewd and insulting."

Small-town gossip spread faster than a five-alarm fire. "Deb, you're being a busybody," Lucas said.

"I'm protecting my children's education. Amy is

the best teacher we've ever had here, and nobody wants to lose her."

"Then why don't you go to Lucky's?" Lucas asked.

"Because I'm not big or hairy enough to be threatening to Dan. A man needs to do this."

Lucas rolled his eyes. "Don't you think Amy can handle this kind of thing herself?"

"Maybe," Debra conceded. "But just in case she can't, I think you should be there."

"And what exactly am I supposed to do?"

"Look big and threatening to Dan and give Amy a ride home."

Lucas shook his head. "I'm settled in for the night. I'm not going to Lucky's because *you* are afraid Dan Arthur is going to turn into a raging bull in rut with poor little Amy."

"Lucas Bennet, if we lose Amy because you wouldn't do your part in taking care of her, then I promise you I will send all of my children to *your* house every day for you to teach them. Goodbye," she said, and hung up.

Amy wasn't feeling very Christmasy. The cold wind whipped through her as if she weren't dressed in layer on top of layer. Trudging down the lane from town, she adjusted her knit cap and wondered if she should be walking toward Lucas's house or not.

She had thought the outing tonight would take the sting out of his *apology* for kissing her. She snarled in distaste. The Christmas carol part had helped, but sharing a hot toddy with Dan Arthur afterward to fortify her feminine ego hadn't been one of her better choices. Dan had already been pushy, and after a few drinks, he'd become grabby. She'd felt as if she'd been fighting off an octopus, and when she'd decided to leave, he'd protested loudly. He insisted on driving her to his house for them to talk, but Amy knew he didn't want to talk, so she'd left the bar.

Lucas lived too far from town for her to walk the entire way, but Amy thought she might be able to stop at one of her fellow carolers' homes and get a ride. There were no cars on the road because, with the exception of Lucky's, the town had closed.

Fighting her horrid mood, she belted out "Rudolph the Red-nosed Reindeer," as she continued walking against the brisk winter wind.

Thirty minutes later, her voice grew raspy, her jaw shivered, and she couldn't feel her toes. Her nose was running.

A truck, the first vehicle she'd seen since leaving Lucky's, pulled alongside her. Amy was so cold she would consider accepting a ride from her worst nightmare.

The driver-side window whirred downward and Lucas looked out at her.

Her worst nightmare, she thought. Close. She didn't want any more favors from him, even a ride, but the seductive promise of warmth won over pride.

"Want a ride?" he asked.

She nodded and strode to the other side of his truck. He pushed the door open for her and she climbed in. Heat roared from the vents and warmth immediately enveloped her.

"Want to tell me what happened?" he asked.

"Not really," she said, rubbing her hands together and looking away from him. "Mind if I change the heat vents?"

"No."

As soon as he muttered the word, she flipped the controls so that heat flowed from the lower and upper vents. She stuck her face in front of one of them, relishing the warm air.

"Problem with Dan Arthur?" he ventured.

"Yes," she said, feeling she owed him a limited explanation since he'd rescued her from the cold. "He had too much to drink at Lucky's and got a little—" She broke off, searching for the right word. "Pushy." She pulled off her glove and wiggled her hand in front of the vent. "Oh, that's wonderful."

"Dan was wonderful?" he asked.

She shook her head. "No. The heat is wonderful. I don't want to talk about Dan. He's not going to be very happy with me when he finds out I took his keys."

"Why did you take his keys?"

She pulled off her other glove and wiggled her other hand in front of the vent. "You have no idea how good this feels."

The near-sexual purr in her voice slid under Lucas's skin. "Dan's keys," he prompted.

She sighed, pulled off her hat and poked her face in front of one of the vents again. "I couldn't let him

drive, so I took his keys when he went to the bar to
buy a drink for me.''

''If you took his keys, why didn't you just drive
his car home?''

She made a face. ''He's an attorney and he'd probably sue me or call the sheriff if I took his car. He'd
have a tougher time going after me just for keys. I'll
return them tomorrow.''

''I'll take them back for you,'' Lucas said, anger
burning in his gut. ''What kind of man lets a woman
walk miles in the freezing cold at night?''

''Since I sneaked out of the bar, he didn't really
know I would be walking in the freezing cold. In
fact,'' she added dryly, ''he invited me to stay over-
night at his house.''

Lucas scowled. His sister had been right. He felt
Amy's gaze on him.

''I was lucky you drove by,'' she said. ''What
brought you out tonight?''

''Neighbor called. Asked me to check on something,'' he hedged, then pulled into his driveway. He
turned the corner of the drive and stopped in front of
the house. ''Let's get you inside.''

She shot him a gaze full of reluctance. ''I don't
want to.''

He arched a dark eyebrow. ''Why?''

''Your house is cold. It's warm here.''

He heard a tinge of feminine pique in her voice.
Watching her wrap her arms around herself, he suspected she was talking about more than room tem-

perature. She was probably talking about him. "I'll turn the heat up."

When she said nothing, he sighed. He shouldn't care squat if she wanted to camp in his truck the rest of the night. "C'mon. I'll build a fire."

She threw him a look of skepticism laced with a sexual dare that hit him like an unexpected undercut. "Are you sure you know how to build a fire and keep it burning?"

Chapter 4

Stop being nice to me, Amy wanted to say to Lucas after he quickly built a fire in the wood stove insert, then situated her in front of it. *I don't want to like you.* He gave her a blanket, disappeared for a few minutes, then returned to offer her a mug of hot chocolate.

"I used your mix in the glass canister on the counter," he said, leaning next to the mantel.

Amy took a sip and the liquid kicked and burned all the way down. She cleared her throat. "I think you added something."

His mouth lifted in a lazy half grin. "A couple shots of bourbon. I figured you could use it. You've had a rough night."

His hair slightly tousled, he stood in casual attention-getting ease, wearing a flannel shirt and jeans that molded to his powerful thighs. She sighed and took a deep gulp of her cocoa. If he were uglier or meaner, she wouldn't find him so utterly compelling. Maybe if she didn't look at him, that would help keep her defenses in place. "Thank you," she said, closing her eyes and leaning her head back against the chair.

"You're welcome," he said quietly. "Warm enough?"

"Yes," she said, even though she knew he could make her a lot warmer. She took another sip. She'd never been a big drinker, but the sweet cocoa countered the bitterness of the alcohol. She took another sip and felt some of the tension leave her body.

"I walked past your room and noticed you hung some kind of ball over your door."

Amy immediately stiffened and opened her eyes to meet his gaze. "It's not a hint," she told him. "It's not personal."

Confusion wrinkled his brow. "What is it?"

"It's one of my most treasured possessions and, no matter where I've been, I have hung it every Christmas since I was six."

"You still haven't told me what it is," he said.

She paused a moment, reluctance holding her tongue. "It's a holiday kissing ball," she finally admitted in a low voice. "I've been working on it since I was six years old. A lady came to the children's home where I lived and helped us make them." A wave of nostalgia passed through her. "She told me she wanted to keep me, but she couldn't."

"Why not?"

"She was sick. She visited me several times, but then she died that next year."

"That must have been tough."

"Yeah," she agreed. "But she was one of those people that I was lucky to meet even if it was only going to be for a short time. She knew that Christmas was going to be her last, but she was determined to make the best of it. Even though she knew her time was running out, she made sure it counted. I was young, but old enough to be impressed, and I wanted to be like her." She closed her eyes, remembering that wonderful feeling of being wanted. "I felt so special that she could want me."

Amy felt the silence stretch between them and took a long sip from her hot chocolate. "Oops. I'm getting all sentimental and I'm probably making you very uncomfortable, so I'll stop. Tell the truth, that kissing ball is the gaudiest thing you've ever seen, isn't it?"

He looked at her in consternation, then chuckled and shook his head. "It's vivid," he said, as if he were straining to find the right description.

"Don't be kind about my kissing ball," she said. "Martha Stewart would need a tranquilizer if she took one look at it. There's something on that kissing ball from just about every stage of my growing up years."

"Really," he said, looking at her, then leaving the room.

"Where are you—" She broke off and shrugged, then took one last swallow of her hot cocoa.

He returned to the room with the kissing ball dangling from his hand. "Inquiring minds want to know. Why the black ribbon and skull and crossbones?"

Surprised by his interest, but too relaxed by the cocoa-with-kick to be overly self-conscious, she smiled. "My very brief Goth period."

"Goth," he echoed in disbelief.

"Yeah, it's when I died my hair black, wore all black clothes and a black leather choker and bracelets."

He wrinkled his nose in distaste.

"Mercifully brief," she said, and pointed to the tiny pony charms. "That was my pony period. I asked Santa for a pony for Christmas. He said I was a little too young to care for one by myself, but perhaps when I was older, I could have one. Shrewd guy. Knew how to cover his posterior without totally mashing my dreams."

Lucas nodded. "What about the sparkles?"

"Magic phase. I wanted to change the world," she said with deadpan seriousness. "By being a fairy."

Lucas cleared his throat to cover a chuckle.

She narrowed her eyes at him. "You're not laughing, are you?"

Lucas took in the sight of her hair sticking out in at least four different directions, smudged mascara beneath one eye, and her bad-girl mouth trying to be stern but not succeeding. She wasn't pretty, but she was fascinating. Her Christmas Pollyanna attitude got on his nerves, but he understood it a little better now. And she was right about the kissing ball. It was the most gosh-awful conglomeration of color, fabric, and doohickeys he'd ever seen, but through her stories it, too, became oddly fascinating.

He'd hated the lost look he'd seen in her eyes when he'd picked her up on the side of the road. That was why he'd started the fire and fixed the cocoa. That was why he'd asked her about the kissing ball—to distract her. For himself, he couldn't be less interested.

"What about the lace?"

She winced. "Bride stage. I wore a veil for about three months."

"When did that stage end?"

"When I found out that boys pay more attention to football games than they do to girls. Tommy Vincent kissed me in the coatroom at school, but when I asked him to come to my birthday party, he said he would rather play ball with his friends than eat cake and ice cream with mine."

"Kissed you in the coatroom," he repeated, filled with the unsettling image of kissing the grown-up Amy in a coatroom.

She nodded. "I have never had a face that would launch a thousand ships," she said, referring to the legendary beauty of Helen of Troy, "but when Tommy Vincent kissed me, I felt like the bomb. A good kisser can knock a girl off her feet."

It irritated him for her to think less of herself. She wasn't classically pretty. She was more, better in some strange indefinable way. "Don't you remember that beauty's in the eye of the beholder?"

"Or in the case of my situation tonight, beauty's in the eye of the beer holder," she wisecracked with a gamine grin, then met his gaze and sighed. Her smile fell and hints of seductive emotion glinted in her eyes. "You should go to bed, now."

"Oh, really," he returned, surprised at her abrupt suggestion. "Why?"

"It's late and you have to get up early because you are a Type A rancher, and..." Her voice dipped and faded. She caught her upper lip with the edge of her teeth and Lucas was distracted once again by hot visuals involving her mouth and his body.

"And?" he prompted.

"For a man who I'm sure is distantly related to Ebenezer Scrooge, you are very hot," she said with a feminine frankness that was so sexy he felt an immediate surge of arousal. "You've been very kind, but I shouldn't take it personally."

For one intense visceral moment, even though he'd warned her off him, he wanted her to take it personally. He wanted to wipe out the memory of Tommy Vincent's kiss. He wanted to sink inside her and devour her honest need.

He wanted. And that wasn't good. That now-familiar edgy feeling of deprivation ate at him again. Steeling himself against it, he pushed it aside, but it was getting more difficult.

He handed her the kissing ball and stood. "G'night," he said, taking in the inviting sight of her wrapped in a blanket relaxing in front of the fire. As he climbed the steps, his mind taunted him with a picture of stripping off her clothes and warming her all the way through.

Over the next two days, Lucas vacillated between his usual seasonal brooding and his reluctant attraction to Amy. She was like a bad virus that affected all his senses. When he entered the house, he listened for her throaty laughter. He stood closer to her than he should just so he could inhale her sweet, sexy scent. He didn't know what soap she used, but it reminded him of clean, bare, feminine skin. Every once in a while, she accidentally rubbed against him as she walked past, putting his nerve endings on high alert. When she brushed her tongue over her lips, he remembered how she'd tasted, how she'd felt during that forbidden night when he'd allowed himself to taste and touch her. The trouble with sampling Amy was that a sample hadn't been enough. He wanted to make an entire meal of her.

After Flora set out a dinner he ate by himself in his office, Lucas took his dishes into the kitchen and walked into the den as he flipped through his mail. Although the room was quiet, the tree screamed holiday memories at him, so he quickly headed back to his office.

Amy whipped around the corner with a laundry basket in her arms and slammed right into him.

"Oh!" The laundry flew out of the basket onto the floor.

Lucas instinctively shot out his hands to steady her. Jolted, she looked at him with chagrin. "Sorry, I didn't see you coming." She met his gaze and stood perfectly still, sensual awareness gradually seeping into her eyes. Glancing down at his hands on her waist, she cleared her throat and stepped backward. "Sorry," she said, glancing down. "I've made a mess."

"No harm. Nobody got hurt," he said, bending down to help her collect her clothing. He picked up a wild striped sock and a shirt.

Amy shook her head as she scooped up part of the clothing. "I'm glad I hadn't folded yet. It looks like a laundry bomb went off. Are you going to your sister's house tomorrow night?"

Distracted by the black bra he found in his hands, he tossed it into the basket. He couldn't help remembering how responsive her breasts had been to his touch. "Why would I go to my sister's house?"

Amy looked at him in disbelief. "It's her Christmas party. She said she holds a big bash with food and dancing every year. Don't you usually go?"

Uncomfortable, Lucas shrugged. "It depends on what else I have going on. I'm not a party animal."

"But this is *your sister's* party," she said as if she couldn't imagine him not attending.

Lucas absently picked up a silky garment and glanced down at it. A black thong. His mouth went bone dry. Despite her usual casual attire of jeans and big sweaters, he could easily visualize Amy dressed in the black bra, thong, heels and nothing else. He ran his thumb over the skimpy thong, imagining the way her skin would feel as he slipped the garment from her hips, down her silky thighs.

After a moment, he realized she had turned silent. He glanced up and saw her watching him as he held the garment that touched her where he wanted to. She bit her lip and her eyes darkened with banked desire.

"Do you really wear these?" he had to ask.

She cleared her throat. "They don't cause panty lines when I wear something that fits."

"So the idea is to make you look like you're wearing nothing underneath," he said, feeling a surge of heat. Lord help him, he hadn't thought about women's undergarments in years.

"I guess," she said, pulling the thong from his hands and putting it in the basket. "Debra tells me the party is dressy."

He nodded, rising with her as she stood. "She likes giving everybody an excuse to dress up at Christmas time. The women like it."

"The men don't," Amy concluded with a grin.

"The men don't mind looking at the women," he said.

"Hmm," she said with a nod. "Well, I'll let you get back to what you were doing while I go fold my laundry. And maybe I'll see you tomorrow night at your sister's party."

Or not, he thought as he watched her climb the stairs, her shapely bottom swaying from side to side, conjuring an erotic image with that black thong.

His distraction with her irritated him. After a cold shower late at night, he wondered how to get her out of his system. A rebellious part of him asked him why he shouldn't take what he wanted. They were both adults. It didn't help that he often caught her looking at him with sensual curiosity just before she glanced away.

Lucas told himself that just because he took her to bed didn't mean he had to take her down the aisle.

He didn't want to hurt her or lead her on, though, and he knew she wasn't the kind of woman who separated her body from her feelings. That knowledge, however, was part of the attraction. If a man was able to tap Amy's passion, what kind of lover would she be? The possibilities taunted him like a forbidden fantasy in the midnight hour, luring him, irritating him, frustrating the living daylights out of him.

Reading the newspaper the following evening, he caught sight of Amy as she fluffed her hair and stuck her arms in the sleeves of a winter coat. Her long slim legs were encased in black stockings, and the hem of her little black velvet dress stopped three inches above her knees. He wondered if she was wearing the black bra and thong he'd held in his fingers the night before. Surreptitiously searching for panty lines beneath her dress, he saw none and felt a slow heat build from the inside out.

Her eyes sparkled, and she'd emphasized her full lips with red lipstick. It occurred to him that he couldn't imagine any man in the community of Kent who wouldn't be angling for a kiss from Amy under his sister's mistletoe. The notion irritated him.

She glanced up at him and smiled. "Still undecided about the party?"

"I may go over later," he said, still not willing to commit himself. He hadn't gone to a Christmas party since his wife died.

"You should," she said as she pulled on her gloves. "It'll be fun. Bye." She whirled out of the foyer, leaving her feminine scent in her wake.

Fun, Lucas thought. Christmas hadn't been fun for him for years. Why should it be now?

Debra's face fell when she looked past Amy standing in the doorway to her lovely home. "I'm so glad you came, but I was hoping…"

"That Lucas would come, too," Amy finished for her as she stepped into Debra's beautifully decorated, large home. "He said he might, but I wouldn't put money on it. I've never met a man less inclined to celebrate Christmas than your brother."

Debra squeezed Amy's shoulders and gave a sad smile. "It's true. Ever since his wife died a few days before Christmas, he hasn't—"

"At Christmas," Amy interjected, giving Debra a double take. Her heart squeezed tight in her chest. No wonder Lucas acted like a grinch. Every year represented a painful reminder. "I knew his wife had died a few years ago, but not during Christmas."

Debra nodded as she took Amy's coat. "Lucas has a Superman complex. Even though his wife was miles away when her car crashed, he somehow thinks he should have done something to protect her."

Amy remembered the photograph of Lucas's wife on his dresser and felt her stomach twist. "They must have had a wonderful relationship for him to still be in love with her."

Debra wore a neutral look on her face. "I don't know. Some people suffer from survivor guilt more strongly than others. But I can't solve this for Lucas, although heaven knows I've tried." She gave Amy a once-over. "I'm envious. You wear that tiny black dress so easily, and I look like a model for a dancing Christmas tree ornament."

Amy laughed and shook her head. "You look beautiful. You have the pregnant glow."

"New makeup," she confided and ushered her into the large formal living room filled with the citizens of Kent. "Let me introduce you to a few local bachelors. It'll be fun for me to watch them salivate over you."

"You're exaggerating, but it's nice to hear," Amy said, thinking again of how her appearance couldn't ever compare to the beauty of Lucas's former wife. She frowned at the thought. Comparing appearances had never gotten her anywhere, so she wasn't going to start that again. "Lead on," she said, determined to forget about Lucas.

Within a half hour, three men had asked for her phone number. Unfortunately, since she was temporarily living at Lucas's house, she didn't really have a number except her cell phone. All three men solved the problem by giving her their business cards with home phone numbers scrawled on the back.

Along with several other couples, Debra shooed Amy and Mr. Business Card number three, Frank Ginter, into the center of the room to dance to the sounds of Harry Connick Jr.

Amy looked into Frank's friendly eyes and couldn't help noticing his fair, spare eyelashes. He wasn't as tall as Lucas, and his shoulders weren't—

Stifling a groan, Amy stopped her useless comparisons. She'd told herself not to think about Lucas tonight. She'd told herself to flirt, to focus her undivided attention on whatever was happening at this very moment.

This very moment, over Frank's shoulder she spotted Lucas entering the room dressed in a crisp white shirt, a dark burgundy tie, black slacks and suspenders.

Weeooo. Amy had a thing about a man in suspenders.

She felt his gaze collide with hers and wrap around her like a hot encircling flame.

She stumbled. "Oops."

Frank steadied her with a smile. "No problem. Song's over. Would you like a drink?"

"Good idea," she said, determined to keep her gaze fixed on Frank's kind face. Her ornery peripheral vision caught a half glimpse of Lucas. The man was entirely too watchable. Out of the corner of her eye, she saw Debra give her brother an enthusiastic embrace, which he returned.

Her attention divided, Amy blindly allowed Frank to guide her toward one of the refreshment tables. He whirled around and smiled. "Merry Christmas, Amy." Then he lowered his head and quickly kissed her.

Confused, she stared at him.

"Mistletoe," he said, pointing upward.

She looked up and saw the familiar greenery. "Oh, Merry Christmas," she said because she could think of nothing else to say and turned to get her punch.

Although it took some effort, she managed to escape intense attention by ducking into the kitchen. She spotted Debra ruffling the hair of one of her children as she looked out the window.

"One more treat, then off to bed," Debra said, then met Amy's gaze. "Teacher, please tell this little elf she'll get sick if she eats too many more Christmas cookies."

"Miss Winslow!" the little girl said, her happy face covered with crumbs.

Amy recognized her student and smiled. "Hilary, you look like you're having a wonderful Christmas."

Hilary gave a big nod. "That was our assignment, Mom."

"But if you get a tummy ache from eating too many goodies, it's going to be hard to complete your assignment," Amy reminded the little girl.

"Okay," Hilary said reluctantly. "Did you see that my mom is gonna have a baby?"

"Sure did," Amy said. "Are you excited?"

"I want a sister since I already have a brother."

Debra ruffled Hilary's hair again. "We'll see what we can do. Bedtime in fifteen minutes," she said.

"Oh, *Mom*," Hilary protested.

"Or now," Debra said.

"Fifteen minutes," Hilary said and ran out of the kitchen.

"She's great in class. Whenever I ask questions, her hand shoots up first," Amy said.

"Well, she absolutely loves Miss Winslow. I think you gave a good holiday assignment. I just wish everyone would follow your instructions," Debra said, tilting her head meaningfully toward the window.

Amy stepped closer and saw Lucas standing outside on the patio decorated with tiny white lights. The strong solitary image tugged at her heart. "Tough time of year for him," she murmured.

"Yeah. I keep hoping for a change," Debra said with a sigh. "I should return to the party." She hugged Amy. "I'm glad you came."

"Me, too," Amy said, then her attention returned to Lucas as Debra left the kitchen with a platter. He probably preferred his solitude, she thought, unbidden instinct nudging her to reach out to him.

Go, a soft insistent voice inside her said.

Don't go, the loud, self-protective, practical voice ordered.

Go. She couldn't bear his loneliness.

Don't go. He wouldn't want her intrusion.

Torn, Amy bit her lip. She closed her eyes, but his image remained, stamped in her mind. No escape. Warning bells clanging loudly inside her, she walked out to join him.

Chapter 5

"Hi," she said breathlessly, the winter air freezing her lungs. She had hoped to muster something more original or clever, but she felt edgy approaching him.

Lucas immediately turned to meet her gaze. "Hi," he said. The music playing in the den was piped outside.

No conversational help from Lucas, she thought, wrapping her arms around herself. "Beautiful night," she said, nodding toward the stars. "Freezing, but beautiful."

He nodded. "Why'd you come outside?"

Because you looked lonely and I couldn't bear it. She bit her tongue, then forced herself to smile. "Because I had escaped to the kitchen and saw you out here so I wanted to say hi."

"I saw you with Frank. He made good use of the mistletoe."

"He took me by surprise," she said, and moved closer. "I wasn't sure you would come."

"I wasn't, either. Not a party animal."

"You dress the part well."

He raised an eyebrow and almost smiled. "Is that so?"

Amy rolled her eyes. "As if you didn't know every woman was drooling over you."

He chuckled in disbelief. "The only female I saw drooling was a teething six-month-old baby." He paused. "*Every* woman was drooling," he repeated, studying her intently. "Does that include you?"

Amy felt a rush of discomfort. Her cheeks heated, and she prayed the darkness hid her telltale sign of embarrassment. Keep it casual, she told herself. "I'm not blind. For a cranky rancher, you're pretty amazing eye candy."

He blinked and dipped his head as if he didn't understand. "Eye candy. No one has ever called me eye candy."

She lifted her chin. "Maybe not to your face."

He chuckled again. "Wanna dance?"

Amy's jaw dropped. Shock ran through her. "Pardon me?"

"Dance," he said, moving closer, his eyes full of things that made her heart bump. "Wanna dance?"

"Uh, sure," she said and stood there like a post.

Lucas extended his arms and drew her against him. The sounds of another Harry Connick Jr. song drifted through the outdoor speaker as Amy swayed in rhythm with Lucas. His shoulder was strong beneath her hand, and her head fit just beneath his chin. She inhaled deeply and was convinced the scent of his aftershave was formulated to inspire a woman to strip off her clothes and throw herself at him.

Amy closed her eyes and allowed herself a moment to play a game of pretend. What would it be like to be the woman Lucas wanted more than anything? How would it feel to be the object of his affection?

Bittersweet longing slid through her and twisted her heart. To be wanted by him. To see passion and love in his eyes for her. To hear words of love from his mouth. To be the woman who made him smile.

She wondered if he had danced this way with his wife. She wondered if he longed for his wife tonight. The ache inside Amy spread to her throat and stomach.

As his thighs rubbed against hers, she wanted to lean forward to kiss his throat, to taste his skin. She shouldn't be thinking these things. If she did what was good and safe, she would wipe all these crazy, impossible thoughts from her head. When it came to Lucas, even a few moments of the game of pretend was dangerous.

Yet Amy couldn't find it in herself to walk away. Deep down, she knew he was hurting and lonely.

Following an impulse, she pulled back. ''I think we should leave and try to find some moose tracks ice cream.''

He looked down at her as if she were crazy. "Ice cream? I thought you said it was cold."

"It is," she said. "But sometimes you just need some moose tracks ice cream."

"There's nothing rational in that statement," he said, clearly not convinced.

"That's the beauty of it. Irrational, impulsive enjoyment." She paused. "Or we could always rejoin the party."

He frowned. "Wild-goose chase for ice cream or a party. Great options," he muttered, then shook his head. "We might as well try to find this deer droppings ice cream."

"Moose tracks," she corrected with a chuckle. "We brought separate cars, so—"

"Let's take mine. We can pick yours up in the morning."

"Okay, I need to get my coat."

He shook his head. "If you go back in there, you'll never get out before midnight. Frank will grab you and hold you hostage by the mistletoe."

"I'll freeze," she complained as he led her around the perimeter of the house.

"I'll turn the heater on high."

Lucas figured he had covered about eighty-seven miles and visited seven backwater convenience stores before they'd hit pay dirt. So now they sat in his truck with the heater blasting in the parking lot of Rob's Hop-In. He was so hot he'd tossed his tie and unbuttoned his shirt down to his waist and wanted to ditch the rest of his clothes. His body temperature wasn't exclusively the result of his truck's roaring heater.

Just across from him, Amy sat on the seat in her black stocking feet with her legs splayed to the side, making her little velvet dress ride up her thighs. That was bad enough, but if he watched her lick the spoon from her carton of ice cream one more time, he thought he might explode.

She dipped the plastic utensil into the carton and lifted a heaping spoonful of ice cream. Lucas felt a trickle of sweat roll down his back. He prayed she wouldn't eat it. He prayed she wouldn't lick that spoon with her wicked pleasure-promising tongue.

She smiled and extended the spoon. "Wanna bite?"

He let out a hiss of breath. "Of moose droppings," he muttered, still unable to believe that he'd run all over two counties to get ice cream. He had lost his mind, and it was all because of Christmas. He never should have gone to his sister's party.

"Moose tracks," Amy corrected and lifted the spoon closer to his lips. "Better hurry or it'll drip."

He covered her hand with his and lifted it to his mouth. The creamy combination of vanilla, chocolate fudge, and peanut butter filled his mouth while Amy licked her own lips. He stifled a growl. "Not bad," he said.

"Moose tracks ice cream has magical restorative powers. I discovered it in college," she said, lifting another spoonful of ice cream to his lips.

He guided the spoon into his mouth and a nudge of curiosity. "Who introduced you?"

She furrowed her eyebrow in confusion. "Who introduced me to whom?"

"Who introduced you to Moose Droppings?"

"Tracks," she said again with a mock-glare. "A group of girls in the dorm introduced me."

Lucas relaxed slightly. "Hen party," he said with a wry grin.

She looked affronted. "We were a group of intelligent, liberated women discussing—"

"Men and PMS," he finished and took the spoon from her when she gaped at him. He dipped a spoonful and rubbed the bottom of the spoon on her lower lip. She sucked the ice cream into her mouth and he felt a visceral tug in his gut. He wanted to see her mouth on his flesh.

She lifted her chin. "We were discussing British Literature."

"And?"

"Men," she reluctantly admitted.

"And?"

"Women's issues," she said in a snooty voice.

Lucas threw back his head and roared with laughter.

Amy stared at him.

"What?" he asked.

"You should do that more often," she said.

"Do what?"

"Laugh," she said. "It makes you look so— It's

so wow— You look—'' She broke off and shook her head. ''Then again, maybe you shouldn't.''

''I look what?'' he demanded, curious about the look in her eyes.

''Never mind,'' she said, eating another bite of ice cream.

He covered her hand. ''You started the sentence. Now finish it.''

''I don't want to.''

''Tough. You owe me. I went all over the place to get you ice cream.''

''I thought this was a gift from the heart,'' she said with a mock-lovelorn expression.

''It wasn't. Finish the sentence,'' he said, refusing to be dissuaded.

She rolled her eyes. ''Okay. If you answer one of my questions first, I'll answer your question.''

He nodded. ''Ask your question.''

''Name three things you want for Christmas,'' she said.

Drawing a complete blank, Lucas groaned and wiped his hand over his face. ''All I want for Christmas is for it to be over.''

''Sorry, Ebenezer, that's not an answer.''

Lucas swore. He couldn't remember the last time someone had asked him what he wanted for Christmas. Even his sister knew better than to ask him such a question. Racking his brain, he threw out the first things that came to mind. ''Socks, a new rack for my truck, and... a Maserati.''

Amy stared blankly at him. ''Socks,'' she echoed.

"You want socks and a new rack for your truck for Christmas. That's the lousiest Christmas wish list I've ever heard."

He grinned. "Don't forget the Maserati. Your turn."

She took another bite of ice cream and slowly licked the spoon clean, torturing Lucas with her tongue so much he nearly jerked the plastic utensil out of her hand.

"When you laughed," she finally said in a low voice, "you looked very, very sexy. Satisfied?"

"Not nearly," he said and gave in to what he'd wanted to do all evening. He took her impudent, sassy, drive-him-crazy mouth with his.

With Lucas's lips on hers, Amy felt herself melt into the leather seat. The texture of his mouth was both firm and supple, irresistibly sensual. He nibbled at her with his lips as if he wanted to consume her. His tongue slid over hers, invading, inviting. He tasted like ice cream, felt like sin, and she drew his tongue more deeply into her mouth.

She was peripherally aware that Lucas moved the nearly empty carton of ice cream from her hand and pushed back his seat. Before she knew it, he pulled her onto his lap. One of his hands slid up her thighs, and her head began to spin.

The kiss turned carnal, cranking up her internal heat. He shifted so that his hardness intimately rubbed where she grew damp and swollen. He guided her bottom in a primitive mind-robbing rhythm that snatched her breath and good sense.

"This is crazy," she breathed, but opened her mouth for his kiss.

"Damn, you get me hot." He squeezed her bottom and groaned again, this time in frustration. "Panty hose should be outlawed."

Pulling back, he stared into her with eyes nearly black with arousal. "I want you," he said, his rough bluntness sending a shocking but euphoric adrenaline through her veins.

He lowered his lids, and his outrageous eyelashes concealed his expression. "I want you naked in my bed. Under me. I want inside you."

His raw need echoed inside her. She moaned as he took her mouth again for a quick, illicit caress.

"If it weren't the dead of winter, I would take you right now in this damn truck," he muttered.

The urgency coursing through her turned her equilibrium upside down. Lucas had no idea how much his agreement to find moose tracks ice cream had weakened her defenses. It was a small thing, but his determination to please her filled her head with crazy thoughts. Thoughts like maybe, just maybe, if Lucas wanted her, maybe he could grow to love her. Maybe he could grow to need her.

Dangerous thoughts, but now, in his arms with matching need pulsing from him to her, Amy couldn't turn him away. "Maybe we should go back to the house," she said.

His gaze met hers. "You need to know that I'll do

everything I can to get you in my bed. No-holds-barred.''

Her stomach danced at the possibilities. She inhaled deeply. ''You make me curious what no-holds-barred means.''

''Hang around and you'll find out,'' he promised, reluctantly returning her to her seat. ''Nothing will stop me except you.''

He put the car in gear and drove toward his house. They said little, the air in the truck heavy with anticipation. He slid his hand behind her nape and caressed her with his fingers while he drove. Stopping the vehicle just before he turned onto his driveway, he tilted her chin upward while he lowered his mouth to hers for a scorching kiss that left no doubt of his need and intent.

A trickle of nerves skittered through Amy. ''What about Flora?''

''She sleeps through everything.''

Except a call from the emergency room, Amy learned within three minutes. Dressed in her robe, Flora greeted them at the door with the telephone in her hand.

''My niece has gone to the emergency room. She was in terrible pain. They don't know what's wrong with her.''

''Which niece?'' Lucas asked.

''Valerie. She has five children and—''

''Lives on the other side of St. Louis,'' Lucas recalled.

Flora nodded. "Her mother died a few years ago, and I don't have any children, so Valerie and I have become much closer. I realize I'll never take my sister's place, but if she needs me, then I will have to go."

Lucas squeezed Flora's shoulder. "If Valerie and her family need you, then I'll understand. I know you're upset, but you don't have all the information yet. You may get another call telling you she's fine."

Flora gave a long sigh. "You're right. I'm still worried, but you're right. You have to be the most rational, levelheaded man in the state."

Lucas looked at Amy, his gaze filled with irony, and she could see that he was thinking about how both of them had been anything but levelheaded just an hour ago when he'd wanted to make love in his truck. With Flora's crisis, Amy knew she and Lucas wouldn't be sharing a bed tonight. His gaze, however, promised the time would come.

Flora wrinkled her brown. "Where's your coat?" she asked Amy.

Heat rising to her cheeks, Amy didn't dare look at Lucas. She shrugged. "Crazy, but I walked right out of Debra's house without it." Diverting attention away from herself, Amy motioned toward the kitchen. "Let me fix you something to drink while you wait for your call."

"Oh, no," Flora protested, but allowed Amy to fix her a cup of herbal tea. Lucas and Amy kept Flora company until early morning. When both of them urged her to get some rest, Flora shook her head, insisting she couldn't sleep until she received word on her niece's condition.

Amy climbed the stairs to her guest room and pushed open the door. Lucas snagged her wrist and gently whirled her around to face him. He lowered his head and gave her a French kiss that made her dizzy. Or maybe her dizziness was due to the lateness of the hour. *Wishful thinking.*

"This was just a temporary delay," he told her in a velvet voice that stroked her secret places.

"Or an opportunity to gain a little sanity," she said.

"Can you honestly say you don't want me?" he dared her.

"No, but—" She inhaled deeply and the scent of his aftershave slid past her protests. "But I can't honestly say it would be rational or levelheaded, either."

"You're right. It wouldn't," he said, running his finger over her bottom lip.

Amy barely resisted the urge to slide her tongue over his finger. She'd like to see him at least half as off-kilter as she felt.

"It sure as hell won't be sensible. It will just be unforgettable." He dropped his finger from her mouth, but his gaze lingered on her lips. "'Night, Amy."

She swallowed over her dry throat. "G'night," she said, and wondered how she could say no to this man. Especially when everything inside her wanted to say yes.

* * *

The following morning, Flora learned her niece had suffered appendicitis. The emergency surgery was a success, but her niece would still need help for a few days, so Flora left and assured Lucas she would return as soon as she could.

Not long after Lucas left to tend to the stock and Flora left for her niece's house, the snow began to fall. Amy put a pot of homemade chowder on the burner and did some last-minute shopping on the Internet. Since moving to the community of Kent, she'd learned the value of Internet shopping.

The day wore on, and the snow continued to fall. Amy checked the weather forecast and heard the weatherman admit he had missed the mark with his prediction for a light winter snow. Kent, Missouri, was being hit with a blizzard.

As the hours passed, Amy told herself not to worry about Lucas. If any man could handle himself in a crisis, it was Lucas. When she looked out the window at the whiteout conditions, though, a knot formed in her stomach. What if he had hurt himself and couldn't get back?

Day turned to night, and Amy watched and worried. She ate a bowl of chicken corn chowder. Taking comfort in Cleo, she rubbed her cat and listened for the door. When the clock struck eight o'clock, she couldn't stand the images in her mind of Lucas hurt and freezing. Putting on so many layers of clothing she could barely walk, she grabbed a lantern and stomped through the fresh-fallen snow.

* * *

Lucas finished securing the horse barn for the harsh weather and stretched his back. He always kept a skeleton crew in the winter, and during Christmas most of his ranch hands visited their families. Ordinarily Lucas welcomed the distraction of long hours during the holidays, so he didn't mind the lack of help. This year, a different distraction burned inside him. This year, a warm woman waited for him in his home. He'd slept alone too long.

The door to the barn swung open, making him jump. Someone wrapped up like a mummy appeared in the doorway. A hat covered the head, a scarf shielded the face.

"What the hell—"

"I was worried about you," Amy said in a voice muffled by the scarf. She lowered the scarf slightly. "You were gone a long time and the snow kept falling, and I was afraid you were hurt and freezing to death."

His heart swelled at her concern. "I've been through plenty of these winters. I know how to handle myself."

She lifted a shoulder uncertainly. "I know, but just in case."

He shook his head. "You're not exactly Amazon Woman. What did you think you could do?"

"Rescue you?" she ventured doubtfully.

He turned his head and looked up at the barn ceiling for help from on high. This woman was the physical equivalent of an elf. "You shouldn't have come out. You could have gotten lost. It's not like you could carry me.''

''I might could drag you,'' she said, lifting her chin a millimeter. ''What was I supposed to do—leave you hurt and freezing to death?''

''I wasn't hurt or freezing.''

''How was I supposed to know that?''

Unaccustomed to having anyone check on him, he opened his mouth, then closed it. ''You were supposed to trust that I can handle myself.''

''That thought did occur to me.''

''That's good to know,'' Lucas said dryly as he pulled on his gloves.

''But I just couldn't stand the idea of you hurt and freezing to death.''

She was so wrong, but so earnest. Feeling an odd tug in his chest, he chuckled despite his frustration. ''Next time just sit tight. I'll be okay. Now let's get back to the house.''

As they walked through the windy, snowy night, his houselights shined like a beacon in the darkness. Lucas noticed Amy seemed to struggle with her progress through the snow. ''You need me to carry you?''

In mummy mode again, she shook her head. ''I'm okay, just slow. I put on a couple extra layers, and it's a little bulky,'' she said in a muffled voice. ''Isn't your face freezing?''

''Nah. I haven't been out in the snow for a while.''

''You don't look like you have on many clothes for a blizzard.''

He chuckled to himself. "Looks like I can borrow from you if I need anything."

Slowing, she lowered her scarf a tad and glared at him. "You don't have to be smug."

"I'm warm-natured."

Her gaze darkened in feminine mystery. "Must be nice."

"Comes in handy in the winter."

"I'm sure you do," she said, and the husky tone in her voice affected his anatomy in a way that he'd previously considered impossible in a blizzard.

He helped her make a stiff-legged climb up the front porch steps. "You cleared the steps," he said, surprised.

"I kept coming out to sweep with the broom, so it didn't have a chance to accumulate."

He opened the door and immediately caught a whiff of something mouthwatering. "What do I smell?"

"Chicken corn chowder."

His stomach growled in protest of his hunger.

Amy stomped the snow off her boots, stepped inside the door and began to peel off her clothes. First the gloves and scarf, then the hat, then the jacket. She pulled her wool sweater over her head and her red hair crackled with electricity. Next she ditched her wind pants, sweatpants, and tugged off her turtleneck. She stood before him in a long sleeve black silk T-shirt and a pair of black stretch pants.

Lucas glanced down at the pile of clothes in amazement. "No wonder you couldn't walk," he muttered. "Well?" he said expectantly.

"Well what?"

"Don't stop now."

Chapter 6

Amy's heart somersaulted at the predatory look in Lucas's eyes. This man was hungry for more than food. She pulled off two of three pairs of socks and regarded him carefully. "I'll get your bowl of chowder," she said and hightailed it to the kitchen, fanning her face as she stepped out of his sight.

She bit her lip as she ladled the chowder into a bowl. She poured a cup of coffee and turned around to find him less than a foot away from her. She jumped in surprise, barely saving the chowder from a spill. "I didn't hear you." Her heart was beating too freakin' loudly. "Here," she said, extending the steaming bowl to him. "Eat this."

He gave her a considering glance. "Okay, thanks."

He gobbled two helpings of chowder in the den while she sat gingerly on the edge of a chair. Lucas built a fire, then took his bowl to the kitchen. Amy's nerves stretched tight when he was gone longer than a minute. Rising from the chair, she walked to the tree and stared at it, anticipation zipping through her. She heard his footsteps behind her, but didn't turn. She felt the warmth of his body when he stopped inches from her.

"You're nervous, aren't you?"

"Not really," she said, turning to face him.

"You have reason to be."

Her stomach dipped. "Why?"

"Because I'm gonna get you."

She gulped and tried to hide it by tossing her head. "In order for you to get me, I have to choose to be gotten."

"And are you?" he asked in a velvet voice that slid through her like rum.

She took a deep breath.

He pulled his hand from his back and lifted her homemade kissing ball above her head. Amy knew she was sunk.

He lowered his mouth to hers. "Gotcha," he muttered against her lips, and kissed her. Scooping her up in his arms, he carried her to the rug in front of the fireplace. "I want to see the firelight on your hair and skin."

He made her feel beautiful when she knew she wasn't beautiful. "I'm not pretty," she said.

"You're the bomb," he told her. "And I'm not stopping until you say it."

"Say what?"

"You're the bomb."

"You're the bomb," she said. "But you already knew that."

He groaned and slid his hands under her silk T-shirt. "I'm not stopping until you say the following words: *I am the bomb.*"

She gaped at him. "I don't know about that."

"You will soon enough," he promised, and pulled her T-shirt over her head. He didn't pause a beat before he unfastened her bra and slid his hands down to her stretch pants.

Amy had stopped breathing two minutes ago…her head was spinning. She wanted him to slow down and hurry up at the same time. He lowered his mouth to hers and dipped his tongue inside as he pushed both her leggings and panties down her legs. The combination of his warm hands on her body and his lips luring and seducing made her shiver.

"Cold?" he asked, pulling her against him.

She shook her head.

"Tell me what you like," he urged her, moving his lips down her throat.

Her heart rate jumped into overdrive. "Everything," she said breathlessly as his mouth slid to her breast. "Everything you do."

He met her gaze, and her secret wish that he could want her, even love her, seemed possible. In his arms, everything wonderful was possible. Following her heart, she unfastened his buttons with unsteady fingers. He took her mouth in an erotic kiss that distracted her.

"Don't stop," he muttered against her mouth, and she lowered her hands to his jeans and unbuttoned them. The whir of the zipper as she pulled it down kicked up the anticipation permeating the air between them.

He was going to take her. What he didn't know was that *she* also planned to take *him*. She slid her hand beneath his briefs and caressed his hard masculinity.

His breath came out in a hiss. "Careful."

"Why?" she asked, helping him push his jeans from his body.

"It's been a while, and it's going to be hard for me to go slow." She touched him again, and he shook his head. "Not yet," he insisted, and gently pushed her back on the floor. His mouth trailed a blazing path over her tight nipples and lower, while his fingers sought and found her hot spot.

Shocked at the power of the pleasure coursing through her, she arched upward, her body clamoring for more.

"You feel so good," he murmured, fondling her, turning her to liquid. "I can't wait to feel you wrapped around me," he said, plunging his finger inside her.

Amy shuddered and felt the waves of sensation take her over the edge. Gasping, she clung to the hard muscles of his shoulders. Just when she was ready to come down, he lowered his mouth and kissed her intimately. His wonderful, wicked tongue brought her to one climax, then another.

Twitching from the outrageous pleasure, she begged him to pause. "Stop," she managed to say. "Just for a minute. I can't—"

He moved up her body, his eyes nearly black with desire. "I love the sounds you make."

Amy reveled in the sensation of his delicious chest hair against her sensitized nipples. She slid her hands over his powerful back, down to his hard buttocks.

He kissed her again, and she wiggled beneath him, wanting more. Shifting to her side, she lowered her hand to touch his hardness and found the first few drops of honeyed arousal. She spread the sensual lubricant over him, stroking him until he groaned, then she took her own trip down his body, running her tongue over his flat male nipples, pressing open-mouth kisses on his abdomen and lower.

"What are you doing?" he asked, his voice strained with need. "What—"

Amy boldly took him into her mouth and made love to him with her mouth.

He began to swear, and the sound was deliciously seductive to her ears. He turned her upside down so easily. She wanted to weave a fraction of the same magic over him.

"Amy," he said, his voice a combination of earthy huskiness and passion.

She swirled her tongue over him, and he swore again.

"That's it," he said, pulling her up his body and rolling them both over. Grabbing a packet of protection from his discarded jeans, he put it on and parted her thighs.

His eyes were so fierce with passion that she felt a twinge of fear. She needed just a little tenderness. She lifted her hand to his, and he paused. His gaze gentled a hair, and he twined his fingers through hers.

"You look afraid," he said.

"A little," she whispered. "You look like you're going to eat me alive."

He lowered his mouth to hers and gave her a kiss that combined an irresistible combination of compassion and desire. "I am. But I'll do my damnedest to make sure you like it," he said, and thrust inside her.

Her eyes widened at the sensual invasion, and she sucked in a quick breath.

"Problem?" He paused, studying her.

The way he looked at her made her feel as if he weren't just invading her body, but also her mind and heart. "You're big."

"Is that bad?" he asked, and she could feel his need to move permeating her.

"Kiss me again, and it won't be bad."

He took her mouth in an achingly slow sensual kiss, but didn't move a millimeter. His tongue dallied and seduced, his lips nipped at hers, he sucked her tongue into her mouth. Her body began to hum again, and she shifted restlessly beneath his.

As if he read her body like a book, he began to move in a hypnotic rhythm that made her crave more and more of him. Amy moaned and squeezed him intimately.

He groaned. "Those sounds you make," he muttered. "They're driving me—" He broke off, increasing the pumping rhythm.

She looked in his eyes and saw his primitive need mixed with something deeper, more powerful. With each thrust, she felt herself bound to him. She wanted everything with this man.

"You—are—so—beautiful," he said in a rough voice.

In that moment she believed him, and they both went soaring over the edge.

Moments passed before she caught her breath. Lucas moved to his side and she rolled over, curling against him. His naked skin pressed against hers, and with her hand on his chest, she could feel his heart pounding. She was so close, she almost felt as if she could climb inside him. Amy sighed at the emotions overflowing inside her.

"Is that a good sigh or a tired sigh?" he asked.

She pressed her face against his throat. "It's a *you're amazing* sigh."

"I could say the same about you."

Her heart turned over and she couldn't contain her secret smile. "You inspire me."

He slid his arms around her. "I didn't hear you say I am the bomb."

"You are the bomb."

He chuckled. "No. I didn't hear you say these words: *I am the bomb.*"

"Oh, well, you made me feel the bomb."

"Close but no cigar."

She pulled back slightly and met his warm gaze. "Maybe you can try again."

His eyes lit like twin flames. "I can do that," he said.

And he did. They eventually made it upstairs to his bedroom, where they made love until early morning. While she slept, Lucas took care of the animals, then returned. She fixed breakfast, and with a foot of snow calling a halt to most outside activity, they spent the day in an isolated cocoon of conversation and love-making. Amy fell completely under his spell and wanted it to never end.

That night, they danced naked in the firelight, and he made love to her with a fervor that shook her soul. In the dark of the middle of the night, she clung to him. "You make me feel the bomb," she whispered in his ear as he held her tight.

The following morning Amy awakened to the sight of Lucas standing in front of his dresser, staring at the photograph of his former wife. Her heart twisted. During the last two days, she'd tried to push the beautiful woman's image from her mind. She could never compete with the woman's beauty, and Lucas clearly still had deep feelings for her.

Amy wondered if even now he was comparing her with his late wife. A knot formed in her throat. She wanted to wipe Lucas's pain away. She wanted to be the one who helped make him happy.

Drawing her covers with her, she sat up in bed and bit her lip. It was as if he was in another world. Far, far away. The notion hurt, especially after they'd been so close. It had been more than sex, she thought. She hoped she wasn't fooling herself.

"You still miss her," Amy said quietly.

As if she'd invaded a private moment he hadn't wanted to share, he whipped his head around in surprise. His eyes full of conflicting emotions, he met her gaze, then looked away. "This is always a tough time of year."

"I'd like to make it easier for you."

He inhaled, then let out a long breath. "I don't think you can."

Amy felt another stab just behind her ribs. "But I care about you, and these last few days have been amazing. I haven't ever been happier, and you've seemed happy, too."

He shrugged. "I don't know. Let's not make this bigger than it is. We're both adults, and we haven't made any promises or big declarations."

Her heart felt as if it stopped. Her worst fear climbed from her stomach to form a knot in her throat. "The last few days were not just about sex," she said, fighting tears and praying he would say what she needed to hear. "There's more between us than sex."

His silence was damning, and she hated the distance between them. Just hours ago, they'd been as close as two humans could possibly be. "I've got work to do," he said finally, and left her alone in his bed.

Shell-shocked by Lucas's retreat, Amy took a shower to wash his scent off of her. Although she knew Lucas still suffered over the loss of his wife, she couldn't believe he would throw away what he and Amy had found in each other. Mostly hurt but angry, too, she searched for a distraction, something she could do to make herself feel better.

Interrupting Amy's thoughts, Debra called and told her that since the roads had been cleared, Debra's husband, Craig, would be returning Amy's car in a few minutes. Debra prodded Amy for information about why she and Lucas had left the party early, but Amy changed the subject by asking about Debra's pregnancy.

While Amy stewed and waited for her car, she checked through her date book in search of any tentative plans she might have made. The nursing home had canceled Christmas Bingo yesterday due to the snow. Amy made a quick call and learned the residents would be thrilled to reschedule today. She hung up resolved to get back at least a smidgen of her Christmas spirit.

Six hours later, after calling countless games of Christmas Bingo, she left the nursing home with a smile on her face. The residents' laughter and gratitude reminded her of all the good things about the holiday season. She tried not to think about Lucas and how much his retreat had devastated her. Deliberately humming a carol, she noticed the temperature had dropped again, and she nearly fell as she walked toward her car.

"Oops, icy," she muttered to herself, carefully stepping into her little coupe. She sank into her seat, started the engine and turned the heater on high even though the air it blew would take a while to warm up.

Thoughts of Lucas slipped across her mind again, making her heart hurt. For a moment she toyed with the idea of not returning to his house. When she realized she was thinking about him, she turned up the volume on her radio in an attempt to drown out her unhappy thoughts.

Driving down the narrow county road, she calculated that it should take her about an hour to get home. Home. The thought was so seductive, so alluring. So dangerous. Not *her* home, she quickly reminded herself. *Lucas's* home.

Approaching a sharp, steep curve, she pressed down her brake. Her car swerved wildly, sending panic racing through her. Ice. She desperately turned the steering wheel first one way, then the other, to gain control. She mashed on the brakes again, to no avail. As if her car had a will of its own, it raced off the side of the road and smashed into a tree.

A scream of horror vibrated from her toes. The air bag slammed into her, banging her face and chest with its force, knocking the breath out of her.

While Lucas sat in front of the fire with the newspaper, trying not to think about Amy, her cat, Cleo, sat just across from him, staring at him. She regarded him with a disdainful, accusing expression, as if to tell Lucas that he had treated her mistress like a jerk this morning.

If that cat could talk, she would have said, "You are lower than snail spit."

Lucas scowled at Cleo, but she merely turned her head and licked her paw.

The phone rang. He glanced in the direction of the kitchen and considered not answering it. He preferred to brood in silence. Cleo eyed him expectantly. The phone rang again.

Sighing, he rose and picked up the receiver, hoping it was a telephone solicitor so he could hang up abruptly. "Hello," he growled.

"Lucas?" Amy said in a wobbly, high-pitched voice.

His heart contracted. "Amy, what—where—"

"My car hit a patch of ice and ran off the road. I ran into a tree," she said in a breathless rush. "I probably should have dialed 911, but I automatically thought of you."

She sounded disoriented. Alarm rushed through him like a cold shower. "Are you hurt?"

"I, uh, I don't think so," she said vaguely. "I might be sore from the air bag."

His gut knotted. "Amy, where are you?"

She sighed. "I'm beside a field."

Lucas gritted his teeth in frustration. *Everywhere* in Kent was beside a field. "Where did you go this afternoon?"

"Christmas Bingo at the Kent Friendship Manor. There was one little old man who was so sweet. He—"

"Route 7. Keep your cell on and hang on.

I'll be there as fast as I can,'' he said, and grabbed his hat and coat on the way to the door.

His heart pounded against his rib cage as he ran to his truck and turned on the ignition before he closed his door. He had to make sure Amy was okay. He couldn't lose her today. He couldn't. Sucking in a cold, quick breath, he narrowed his eyes as he gunned his truck down his driveway. December 20. Was it destined always to be the worst day of his life? He'd lost his wife on this day years ago. He damn well didn't want anything to happen to Amy today.

The drive seemed interminable. As soon as he turned on Route 7, he flicked on his high beams and continually scanned both sides of the road. He didn't blink for miles. His gut was churning.

Where was she?

Just as he reached for his cell to call her, he spotted her car in a field on the left side. Turning off the road, he saw the deployed bag. The front side of her sedan resembled an accordion. Squinting his eyes, he caught sight of her hunched over in the back seat with the door open.

His stomach clenched again. She was hurt, and he hurt from looking at her. He rushed from his truck to her car and bent down. Her eyes were closed and her arms wrapped around her waist.

"Amy," he said, carefully touching her arm.

She opened her eyes and looked at him, pain shimmering in her gaze. "You're here," she said.

"Yeah," he said, a sliver of relief rolling through him. At least she was conscious. He didn't see any blood, although there could be internal injuries. The thought made him nauseous.

"Thanks for coming. I feel stupid. I must have taken that curve too—" She stopped and winced.

"You're hurt," he said.

"A little, I guess," she said. "I—"

"I'm taking you to the E.R.," he interjected, reaching for her. "Let me help you to the truck."

She winced as he picked her up. "Sorry," he muttered, and settled her into the truck. He spent the entire drive to the E.R. swearing and praying. The intake nurse hustled her into an examination room as soon as they arrived.

Twenty minutes later, Debra walked into the E.R. with her husband in tow. Craig waved at him and wandered to a different area in the waiting room.

"How is she?" Debra asked, reaching out to hug him.

Lucas returned the embrace from his baby sister, who was round with her pregnancy. "I don't know. Nobody has told me anything. She was hurting when I brought her in."

Debra shook her head and gave a murmur of sympathy. "First the fire, now this. She's had a rough time."

He pulled his hat off his head and sighed. "Yeah, and she hasn't let any of it get her down. Even me," he muttered ruefully.

"Even you," Debra echoed with a frown. "What do you mean? What have you done?"

He waved his hand and turned away. He struggled

to separate his feelings about his wife's death and Amy's accident. If he were superstitious, he'd swear he was cursed.

"Well I'm going to ask the nurse about her," Debra said, and marched toward the nurses' station. Lucas watched the nurse take her toward the examination room. He walked closer to his brother-in-law and glanced at the basketball game Craig watched on the television.

"Rough night," Craig said.

Lucas nodded, not taking in anything on the television. Hearing his sister's voice, Lucas turned. Debra walked toward him. "Three broken ribs and the doctor says she'll have some colorful bruises on her face."

He felt a load of weight lifted from his chest. "Good," he said.

"Come over here for a minute," she said, pulling Lucas to the side. "Are you okay?" she asked in a low voice. "You don't look so good."

"I'm okay," he insisted.

She surveyed his face and after a long silent moment, then the light of recognition dawned on her face. "It's the anniversary of Jennifer's death."

He nodded but said nothing.

"Are you over her?"

"I've been over her," he admitted. "I've just had a hard time getting over the fact that I wasn't there to save her."

Debra's gaze gentled. "Superman complex."

"Whatever."

"You've gone and fallen for Amy."

His heart squeezed tight. He wanted to deny it, but he couldn't. "What makes you say that?"

"You came to my party. You haven't been to my parties since Jennifer died." She paused. "So what are you gonna do about it?"

"Nothing," he said without hesitation.

Debra frowned. "Why?"

"Because I have nothing to offer her. She's everything I'm not."

"Opposites attract."

"And eventually drive each other crazy."

"So you've hated having her in your house," she concluded.

"I didn't say that."

"And you're perfectly willing to let her get away?"

He needed to be perfectly willing, but he damn well wasn't.

"It's okay to want someone, Lucas. It's even okay to need someone."

"Not if they die."

"You're going to lead a very empty life if you don't do something. For heaven's sake, Lucas. You saved Amy. Now save yourself."

"What do you mean?"

"Replace your sad memories with happy ones. You've found something worth keeping. I dare you to go into that examination room and tell Amy that you love her."

"This is none of your damn business, Debra."

She was unimpressed. "You only swear at me when I'm right. I'm going home. If you don't want to look after Amy, I'm sure I can find any number of male volunteers."

"Forget the volunteers. I'm taking care of her. Now get your pregnant self home," he told her gruffly.

She gave him a quick kiss on his cheek. "I love you."

"I love you, too."

"See how easy that was," she said, moving toward her husband. "Just three little words."

Lucas watched her waddle out the door, then turned toward the nurses' station. His sister's words echoed in his brain. *You saved her. Now save yourself.* He slowly approached the intake nurse and asked if he could go into Amy's exam room. The woman nodded and escorted him.

Inside the room, he found Amy with a blanket wrapped around her. She was singing a slightly off-key rendition of "Rudolph the Red-nosed Reindeer." He remembered how just a week ago Christmas music had made him feel grumpy and melancholy. Now the sweetness of her voice lifted his heart.

"Hi," he said.

She glanced at him, her face coloring with embarrassment. "Oops. You caught me."

He walked closer to her. "I hear you've got some bum ribs."

She nodded. "I'm all taped up, but no snowball

fights for me for a while. Thanks for coming to get me. I should have called 911, but I thought of you.''

''I'm glad you did,'' he said and paused a moment. He felt as if he were jumping off a cliff. ''I want you to always think of me.''

Her gaze searched his. ''What about this morning?''

''I'll tell you about that another time. Now, I have a confession to make.''

She looked at him warily. ''You don't have to confess anything to me. I think you confessed enough this morning.''

He shook his head, frustrated and nervous. ''This morning was all wrong. I want to tell you that I lied about what I want for Christmas.''

She blinked and studied him with a confused expression. ''Uh, okay.''

He moved directly in front of her and took the biggest step of his life. ''What I really want for Christmas is for you to stay with me,'' he said. ''Always.''

She went perfectly still.

''You've given me back Christmas, Amy. You've given me back my life. I love you. I want you to marry me.''

Her eyes rounded in shock. She opened her mouth, but no sound came out. She lifted her arms, and winced at the movement.

The gesture was enough invitation for Lucas. He gently swept her into his arms and inhaled the sweet scent of her head tucked under his chin. His heart felt so full and alive, he thought it might burst.

"You really love me?" she asked in disbelief.

Her doubt pinched at him. He would make that doubt go away. "Yeah, I really love you."

She glanced at him. "Gosh, I hope I'm not delirious. I hope this is true."

"It is," he promised. "And I'll tell you again tomorrow if you forget."

Her eyes welled with tears. "Oh, Lucas, I tried very hard not to love you, and I failed miserably."

"Thank God," he said, looking into the most precious, beautiful face on earth. "Will you marry me?"

"Yes, yes, yes," she said, and smiled through her tears. "I am the bomb."

Epilogue

Despite the short notice, the little white church in the center of town was packed for Lucas and Amy's wedding on Christmas Day.

Amy still wasn't sure how all the preparations had been accomplished so quickly except for the fact that everyone seemed thrilled that Lucas, the favored town son, was to be married. Debra had even found a beautiful white lace dress for Amy.

The brief ceremony was made even sweeter by a song sung by Amy's students. Every minute Amy felt Lucas's gaze on her. The joy and love in his eyes took her breath.

At the casual reception held at the Community Center, raspberry-sherbet punch and good wishes flowed freely. A local guitar trio even volunteered to play music.

Lucas took her in his arms for the opening number. Her ribs still sore, Amy tried to hide her wince.

"You're hurting," he said, sliding her arms down to his waist to lessen the pain. "We don't have to dance."

"Oh, yes, we do. I'm going to remember this for the rest of my life." She looked up at him and saw an incredible future for herself. "You've given me something I've only dreamed of."

"What's that?"

"A home," she said. "It's more than a house. I belong to a person I love more than anything." She covered his heart with her hand. "I belong with you."

Amy could see the emotion brimming from his eyes. He was nearly overcome, and the knowledge that she could be so necessary to such a strong man humbled her. "And I belong to you," he said, lifting her hand to his lips and making promises that would fill her for a lifetime. "Forever."

* * * * *

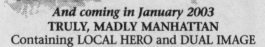
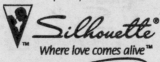

LONE STAR
LSC
COUNTRY CLUB
EST. 1923

Where Texas society reigns
supreme—and appearances
are everything.

On sale...

June 2002
Stroke of Fortune
Christine Rimmer

July 2002
Texas Rose
Marie Ferrarella

August 2002
The Rebel's Return
Beverly Barton

September 2002
Heartbreaker
Laurie Paige

October 2002
Promised to a Sheik
Carla Cassidy

November 2002
The Quiet Seduction
Dixie Browning

December 2002
An Arranged Marriage
Peggy Moreland

January 2003
The Mercenary
Allison Leigh

February 2003
The Last Bachelor
Judy Christenberry

March 2003
Lone Wolf
Sheri WhiteFeather

April 2003
The Marriage Profile
Metsy Hingle

May 2003
Texas...Now and Forever
Merline Lovelace

Only from

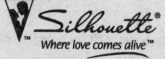

Silhouette®
Where love comes alive™

*Available wherever
Silhouette books are sold.*

Visit us at www.lonestarcountryclub.com   PSLSCCLIST

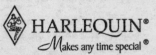

If you enjoyed what you just read,
then we've got an offer you can't resist!

Take 2 bestselling novels FREE!
Plus get a FREE surprise gift!

Award-winning author

BEVERLY BARTON

brings you a brand-new, longer-length book
from her Protectors bestselling series!

ON HER GUARD

As the powerful head of one of the most successful
protection agencies in the world, Ellen Denby believed
she was invincible. Invulnerable. Until she came face-to-
face with the one man who made her remember what
it was to feel. To love. But would her passion for secret
service agent Nikos Pandarus come at too high a price?

Available in November from your favorite retail outlet!

Only from Silhouette Books!

Silhouette®
Where love comes alive™